A FRIEND OF SILENCE

M. LEE PRESCOTT

Published by Quicksand Chronicles
Copyright 2013, Quicksand Chronicles
Cover design by Lees River Studios
ISBN: 978-09855614-4-4

This book is a work of fiction. Names, characters, places, and events are products of the author's imagination or are used fictitiously. Any resemblance to actual people (alive or deceased), locales, or events is entirely coincidental.

For my parents, Louise and Winward.

CHAPTER 1

Dry, cracked lips mouthed a silent scream as the old gardener cradled her lifeless body. Lizzie's ginger curls tangled in the gnarled fingers, silken threads catching on the rough, calloused hands. The dusky light was filtered through dense vines matting the roof of the long-abandoned greenhouse. A shaft of light struck his anguished face. The object of his grief lay in the shadows beneath him.

From his hiding place, Louie had watched uncomprehending, as she drank from the leather-bound flask, Macomber Dore's hiking flask. How it came to be in Lizzie's possession was never discovered. Soon after she set down the flask, Lizzie clutched at her throat, agony twisting the delicate features, hand sweeping clay pots from their shelves as she fell to the earthen floor.

Ferret-like, Louie had skittered from the shadows and rushed to her side. Now, he knelt holding her, shards of crockery cutting into his knees. He felt nothing, lost in a terrible grief from which his broken mind would never recover. He buried his face in the ginger locks, breathing in the scent of rose petals and jasmine. It seemed impossible that he would never again hear Lizzie's laugh. Never hear her musical voice as she read aloud to him. Never feel her warm gaze like an embrace when she smiled at him.

Lizzie was dead, like the sparrows that crashed against the campus' picture windows, their little necks broken. How often had he lifted warm, downy bodies from the hard winter ground, held them as he now held his precious girl? His dearest girl was dead, like his dear mum years ago. On that steamy August night, Mum's unseeing eyes had stared up at him from where she lay, on faded grey linoleum, thrown there by his drunken father.

"She's gone. She's gone," he screamed, in the fading light. Screamed and screamed until someone came running.

CHAPTER 2

Sunlight danced a frantic desperate reel as the shadow moved across the small, cluttered study. Salty breezes followed the intruder's footsteps into the room along with the fecund richness of fallen leaves, the earthy dampness creeping into every corner. Despite the cool wind, the thief wiped a trickle of sweat from his brow, lifting the lid of the glass case with gloved hand.

The knife lay where it always lay, on decaying mauve velveteen long since faded to gray. Like the silver pieces and other scrimshaw laying in the case beside it — letter openers, belt buckles and sperm whale teeth etched in a delicate hand -- the knife looked neglected, forgotten. A gossamer veil of dust draped the antique cherry display case, obscuring the once beloved collection. Mac would have never permitted such untidy housekeeping, but his widow didn't care, or more likely, didn't notice. The thief slipped the knife, sheath and all into the knapsack. As he lowered the lid, the creak of hinges echoed in the silence.

Brilliant choice for a murder weapon, the intruder mused. Not only did the knife have a firm, comfortable grip, but who in their right mind would believe Bess Dore capable of murder? There'd be trouble for her. She'd be questioned, of course, but eventually she'd be cleared with no harm done.

Crossing a sharp ray of afternoon sunlight, the thief squinted, before turning and slipping from the room through French doors that led onto the terrace. Thick shrubbery and grasping tendrils of Boston ivy shielded the terrace from view of the drive and the country road beyond. Acres of fields and woods stretched for miles behind the cottage, thus allowing the intruder to pass unseen.

A rusty bicycle borrowed from the school's bike rack waited propped against a towering elm, its shady canopy casting a deep shadow over small side yard. Her backyard was dotted with hosta and canvas lawn chairs placed helter-skelter. The thief wove in and out around the obstacles, then regained the path leading out to the road. The lane was deserted, not a car to note the stranger's passing.

On the short ride back to campus, the knapsack swished from side to side, its knobby cargo grating and slapping against the cyclist's nylon windbreaker.

"Goodbye, Milt," the stranger whispered aloud, pedaling faster. "After tonight, the world will be a safer place at last."

CHAPTER 3

Carol Richards gazed out her office window spying Louie Predo, one of the school's gardeners as he rounded the classroom building perched atop the Graveley. Louie wasn't permitted to operate the big tractors, but the ancient Graveley and the gardener were of the same vintage and they knew each other well. The sight of the old man on the low, red lawn tractor put Carol in mind of a giant lobster, escaped from the nearby Atlantic. As she watched, Louie stopped at the corner of the building, leaping from the tractor. "What is that silly man up to?" she thought, stepping closer to the window.

Like most of the campus architecture, the two-story classroom building was a simple wood frame design, finished with white clapboards. On each floor, eight-foot windows ran the length of building, their mullioned symmetry shutterless, in keeping with Quaker simplicity. A green skirting of shrubbery — boxwoods, yews and flowering azaleas, all well-established and carefully tended — ringed the building on all four sides.

The gardener began pawing and thrashing his way into the bush. Finally, he withdrew, a green bookbag in his hand. Unzipping it, he peered inside. A long, curling ash had formed on the end of Carol's cigarette, but she didn't notice. Louie's back was turned away, his features unreadable, but fear registered in every inch of the thin, wiry frame as he flung the knapsack back into the shrubbery, jumped onto the tractor and drove away.

"Completely mad," she muttered, turning away. "Never been the same since that poor girl's death."

The year following Lizzie Mederois' suicide, enrollment had plummeted. She had been forced to work especially hard to make the budget stretch. There had been no putting anything by that year.

"Damn," she cried as the tube of ash fell down her sleeve, sprinkling the front of her blouse. New and expensive, the buttery-cream silk picked up the milky strands running through her tweed suit. She wasn't wearing the suit's jacket, since, as usual, the heat in the building was close to ninety. Carol liked things cool, but Milt, her assistant, was always turning up the heat. Insufferable toad, she thought, angrily brushing at her blouse. She simply could not abide the man.

Shrugging thoughts of the gardener and Milt Wickie from her mind, Carol began collecting her things to go home. A thick stack of papers lay waiting to be stuffed into her brown leather attache, papers gathered in stealth. Their removal would help cover her tracks, moving her closer to the retirement she craved. She had only to deal with Milt. Once the little weasel handed over the last few documents, she'd be home free.

It had been so easy — the money and the rest, the school's antiques mysteriously disappearing a few at a time over the years, "into storage." Quakers were so trusting. She visualized the long deacon's table, now the centerpiece of her Cape Cod dining room. It had been taken out for repair during the Coop's renovation years ago and had simply vanished. Once all the modern furnishings arrived, no one seemed to remember or care about the priceless table. Then, there was the rare Goddard highboy, sent out for repairs and, alas, destroyed in a fire at the refinisher's, looked gorgeous in the foyer of her Boston brownstone.

She loved the brownstone, purchased with her cut of the school's last capital campaign. Living in the city would be heaven after Hicksville. It was an expensive address, but she'd earned every penny, deserved every cent. Of course, the art studio expansion had been scaled down a little to keep up with the brownstone's mortgage, but since she kept the books no one was the wiser. Certainly not the little brats who trashed the place. In no time at all, the studio's lovely white walls and soft gray carpets were blotched and stained under their careless tenancy. Carapaldi Construction had rewarded her with a handsome dividend after they received that contract.

Soon, the good life would be hers. No more endless meetings, no more wrangling with the Board, no more being roused in the middle of the night to respond to a foolish prank in the dorm. Now that life beyond Old Harbor Friends was in her grasp, she would not let boorish Milt spoil things. He'd had his chance years ago and he'd blown it, throwing her over for a new conquest. Why, the man had a new tart practically every week. Carol had long since stopped counting. Insatiable, that's what he was. He'd even made a play for goody-goody, Bess Dore, still mourning her dreary clod of a husband, after what, ten years?

Milt had had his chance, but now it was too late. Let him threaten, let him try to stop her and he'd discover just who he was dealing with. Snapping the briefcase shut, she swished out of the office, leaving every light on, the door wide open. "Let the night watchman close up," she muttered. "Let him earn the exorbitant wage we pay him."

Once outside, distant sounds of a tractor reminded her of the gardener and she took a detour on her way across campus, pausing to peer into the boxwood. Search as she might, she could find no trace of the green knapsack. Finally, hands scratched and panty hose snagged, she withdrew, cursing herself for stopping. Brushing off, she headed home to her lonely, gray-walled apartment on the third floor of George Foxe Hall. Sixty-two adolescent girls lived on the floors below her, but she had little to do with them. Her stint of dorm duty had mercifully ended years ago.

As she climbed the stairs, anticipating the gloom waiting in her drafty rooms, she smelled fresh popcorn and cookies baking. The muffled cacophony of voices as girls returned from sports practice faded along with the delicious scents as she reached the third floor landing. Shivering, she slipped key into lock. Turning her back on the warmth below, Carol Richards stepped into a bleak world, her home for the past twenty years.

CHAPTER 4

Ordinarily, Bess enjoyed evening study, the enforced quiet and hushed industry a welcome respite after a hectic day. Tonight was not one of those times. Her empty stomach growled continually, each rumble triggering a chorus of muffled giggles from the students seated nearest her desk. Not the least bit embarrassed, she smiled at Winnie Tavish and Pam Tripp, two of the most persistent gigglers, mouthing the words, "no supper." As she put a finger to her lips, eyes scanning the room pleading for quiet, she caught Betsy Reynolds picking her nose. She averted her gaze immediately, but for an instant they had made eye contact and the shy sophomore flushed crimson, taking cover behind her chemistry book.

The varsity field hockey coach, Bess had missed supper due to a late game. By the time the last day student had been collected and the locker room emptied, she'd had just enough time to grab her things and run across campus to the Commons, the building at the campus' center housing the study hall. Bess lived off-campus so no one ever thought to bring supper to her as they did for resident coaches. Instead, she must wait until eight-thirty when she could go home to fix something for herself.

Later, she would be glad of her empty stomach given her queasiness at the sight of blood, but now, it was an annoyance. Her hunger coupled with a restless unease, made concentration impossible. Finally, she gave up trying to concentrate on the senior portfolios she was grading, pushed them aside and pulled a novel out of her bag. Deathly Whispers, by her favorite mystery writer, Anne Greyson. She flipped to page fifty-seven, hoping the adventures of the indubitable Helen Brown might take her mind off food.

"Excuse me, Mrs. Dore?"

Bespectacled sophomore, Amy Flathers smiled down at her, braces sorely in need of cleaning. As Bess looked up from her book, Amy immediately began to fuss with her clothes, pulling a too-tight sweater down over her plump midriff. The tail of her white blouse, its Peter Pan collar wrinkled and folded inside out on one side, had come untucked from knee length wool skirt and was now bunched under the sweater giving her a somewhat lumpy appearance.

Bess peered over her reading glasses, smiling up at Amy. "Yes?"

"May I go to the restroom?"

"Of course, dear."

As proctors went, Mrs. Dore tended to be lenient, allowing frequent trips to the bathrooms and water fountain, even — heaven forbid — allowing two students to go at the same time. The students knew this, yet rarely took advantage of her largess. The lonely art teacher was one of the most beloved and protected teachers at Old Harbor Friends. Beloved for her kindness and protected because of the sorrow and pain she wore like a mantle over her rounded shoulders.

Bess watched Amy's departure, then returned to her book. Helen, the main character, a teacher and erstwhile amateur sleuth, had just learned of the mysterious death of a colleague and had been asked by her headmistress to quietly look into the matter. Bess enjoyed living vicariously through Helen, a loner like herself, and she sought out each new book in the series as soon as it was published. Deathly Whispers was the fifth book in the Helen Brown series and Bess had yet to tire of the exploits of fearless Helen and her faithful golden retriever, Ruby, who often aided her mistress in solving cases.

The peaceful drowsiness of early evening pervaded the room, the silence as profound as Meeting for Worship embracing them all. At eight-thirty, the silence would break. For the next hour, the building would hum with voices and music as study hall emptied and most students headed next door to the Quaker Coop. The Coop had a snack bar, pool table, ping-pong table and old-fashioned jukebox. Most of the boarders took advantage of this social hour to visit with friends and let off steam. Then, at nine-thirty, Cappy, the manager, flicked the lights and everyone headed back to the dorms for lights out, ten o'clock for underclassmen, eleven o'clock for seniors.

"Excuse me, Mrs. Dore?"

"Yes Amy? Everything alright?"

"No miss, I mean, there's a sign. On the girls' room. It's out of order. I really do need to go and —"

"Yes, I understand," Bess interrupted, wondering why it had taken Amy this long to read an out of order sign. "Well, you'll just have to go upstairs then. You know the way, don't you? The lights are probably out. Mr. Costa made his rounds about a half an hour ago, but the switches are on the left wall, at the bottom of the stairs."

"Yes, miss, but — "

"Is something wrong?"

"Well, it's just. I've never gone upstairs and I don't know exactly where the bathrooms are and I... I'm a little afraid of the dark, you see. 'Specially when it's a strange place."

"Of course, perfectly understandable. Would you like someone to go with you?"

"Oh yes... I mean, yes, that would make me feel so much better if Sarah could come with me."

"I see," Bess said, repressing a smile. "Sarah, do you know your way around upstairs?"

"Yes, Mrs. Dore." Sarah Holcomb was already out of her seat and halfway to the door. As she breezed by, Bess caught a whiff of butterscotch. It looked as if the tall, fair-haired sophomore, one of her best hockey players, had at least two candies crammed into her mouth. No doubt there were more clutched in her fist for Amy.

All these machinations to exchange a couple of sweets, Bess mused, waving them out. "Hurry back you two," she whispered, returning to her book.

She'd read half a page when a commotion at the back of the room interrupted her. Looking up, she spied Arnold Tavil tugging at Patty Whitley's shirt. Patty didn't mind in the slightest, but as proctor, Bess felt compelled to say, "Arnie, please." Nodding sheepishly, he returned to his algebra.

The high-ceiled room, with its huge clerestory windows now shaded against the evening chill, held twenty long, Shaker tables. At regular intervals along the white plaster walls, portraits of former teachers and headmasters gazed solemnly down at the young scholars, admonishing them to diligence. Eight students shared a table, three to a side, one at each end. Tonight only thirteen of the tables were in use.

Satisfied that Arnie had settled back to his math, Bess picked up her book. No sooner had she found her place, when the girls' screams pierced the silence.

CHAPTER 5

Bess took the stairs two at a time, ninety-six students at her heels. They found Amy and Sarah on the landing huddled together trembling violently, a portrait of Elizabeth Keating, daughter of the school's founder impassively staring down at them. Clutching each other, their eyes wild with fright, Amy stammered, "Oh miss, he's covered with blood!"

"Dead," Sarah mumbled, still sucking on the butterscotch.

Bess knelt beside them, the bile already rising in her throat. "Girls, whatever are you talking about?"

"Mr. Wickie, he's, he's in his office." Amy sobbed, collapsing into her arms.

Bess produced a handkerchief from her pocket as she stared in horror at the light coming from the door of the comptroller's office. Turning round, she found ninety-six others in not much better shape than the two in her arms.

"Alright, everyone back to the study hall." Too late. As the throng pushed forward, she cried, "Wait, everyone stop this instant!" Heedless, they pushed past her moving as one, a chorus of screams heralding their arrival at Milt Wickie's door.

"Oh Lord." Bess rose, fighting her way towards the door.

"Gross!"

"Help Mrs. Dore!"

"Aaaah! He's dead!"

"Oh God, help!"

Chiding herself, Bess finally reached Wickie's office, elbowing her charges aside to catch her first glimpse of the dreadful tableau. Milt lay, sprawled to the right of the Chippendale desk, his lifeless form, queerly contorted on the blood-soaked carpet. The cause of death was obvious and Bess gasped in horror as her eyes fell on the object protruding from his chest. It was Mac's scrimshaw blubber knife, there was no mistaking it. To the left of the body, its ornately carved sheath lay covered in blood. Arnie Tavil was just stooping down to lay hold of the sheath when Bess recovered herself. "Arnie, don't touch that! We mustn't touch a thing. Now, everyone out, this instant."

Once the room cleared, she forced herself to look at the body again. Milt's right hand gripped the knife handle close to the hilt as if he'd been trying to pull it out. "Dear God, Milt, I'm so sorry," she whispered, appalled that her knife had been the cause of such suffering. Even if he'd had the strength, he'd never have been able to pull it out. From that angle the knife's deep, serrated edge would have resisted his every tug. Swallowing a sob, she turned away, bumping straight into Teddy Robbins.

"Teddy, please go next door to Miss Richard's office and phone. No, never mind, I'd better do it. Come on everyone. Downstairs. I'll be down, as soon as I telephone the police."

No one moved an inch. Scanning the sea of frightened faces, she realized not one of them was likely to leave her side, as if she, the lone adult, could protect them. Using the tip of her index finger so as not to smudge any fingerprints, she closed Milt's door.

Oh, dear, what would Helen Brown think of her? Cool-headed Helen stampeding up the stairs with a bunch of terrified children in her wake? The idea was preposterous. And, Helen would have used her hankie on the door, not her finger, however, Bess' handkerchief was currently in use, wrung into a tight, tattered rosary by the nearly comatose Amy.

As Bess picked up the phone, it felt as if she'd stepped into one of her mystery novels. This couldn't be happening at Old Harbor Friends, the tiny Quaker school, tucked away in the peaceful, safe countryside. As the muffled sobbing began, all eyes were trained on their teacher, the shivering throng pressed tight together in the stuffy room.

She dialed the school's switchboard, relieved to hear another adult's voice. "Suzie, it's Bess Dore. I need an outside line, immediately. Oh, wait, before you go. There's been a problem. We need security over to the Commons, right away. Please tell them to hurry. Oh, and Suzie? Better call Peter, Mr. Thurbert. Please have him come over as quick as he can. Then, try and ring up Todd Bridgham and some dorm parents, will you? Janie, Kevin, whoever's around. Ask them to come at once."

Ned and Dave, the school's security guards arrived first, followed by the police who walked in with the headmaster, Peter Thurbert. As the men took over, Bess gratefully relinquished her post at the door of Milt's office, herding her charges downstairs to the study hall where they were joined by several dorm parents and resident faculty members.

Bess moved about the room, endeavoring to remain cheerful and reassuring. All the while, her mind raced as she tried to remember when she had last noticed the blubber knife lying in its dusty case.

CHAPTER 6

In tableaux, reminiscent of a dark, Flemish oil painting, a somber group gathered in the study hall awaiting interrogation. Most of the students except for Amy and Sarah had been whisked away by Peggy Barnes, the school psychologist whom Peter Thurbert had summoned via helicopter from a conference she was attending on the Cape. The helicopter, provided by Harold Winthrop, the school's chief benefactor, had deposited the psychologist on the soccer field shortly before eleven; it was now close to midnight.

Amy and Sarah huddled against Bess on a bench dragged in from the hall. "When can we go, Mrs. Dore?" Amy whined.

Any closer and Amy would be on Bess' lap, Sarah pressed against her opposite side. Hemmed in and cross, she patted Amy's hand. "I don't know. We'll just have to wait till the officer comes. He'll probably ask you a few questions, then you can go back to the dorm."

"Oh no," Sarah wailed. "We won't have to walk back alone, will we?"

"Of course not, now hush. Ned or Mr. Costa will take you back and Miss Nettleman's here, too. Dr. Barnes is waiting in the dorm if you want to talk. She's spending the night on campus, I believe. Now, please, dear, try to stay calm, alright?"

Sarah sniffed, slumping down beside her, running her hand up and down the sleeve of Bess' sweater. The old cashmere must be soothing, Bess thought, closing her eyes, remembering the day Mac had given it to her. It had been her birthday. They had been married eight years.

Peter Thurbert pulled up a chair. "Hard to believe, isn't it?" He then maneuvered his chair to face all three of them, his expression full of concern. "I'm sorry you had to find him. Dreadful business."

Bess smiled, but said nothing. Hazel eyes stared back at her, red-rimmed and bloodshot, but otherwise, the headmaster was calmness itself. His role was clear— comfort and support colleagues and students in this time of crisis. He reached out and took her hand, squeezing it gently.

Sixty-three, Peter looked ten years younger. His wiry, brown hair was flecked with gray and a little sparse on top, but aside from a few wrinkles around the eyes, his ruddy face was unlined. An outdoorsman, Peter and his wife, Carrie, usually spent their summer holiday biking in the mountains around Old Harbor and often abroad — Europe, South America and Canada. At six foot-three, he had the lean body of a twenty year old. Bess had always marveled at his seemingly boundless energy. Only in the past year had she noticed him slowing down, as if unseen forces weighed upon him.

Peter had dressed in haste, but still looked natty in Harris tweed jacket and khakis, a long, red muffler thrown round his neck in lieu of a tie. A pipe protruded from his breast pocket, the cloying sweetness of cherry tobacco lingering in the air as he leaned towards her. Peter had been such a comfort after Mac's death, stopping in to see her every evening, offering to help clear out her husband's clothes, running errands, repairing things around the house. He was a good friend whom she would miss when he retired the following June. Peter had hired her and she wondered how a new Head of School would ever fill his shoes. He would be a hard act to follow.

Joan Nettleman stared at Bess and Peter from across the room. Just look at them, she thought. Mr. Chips and his devoted schoolmarm, or Icabod Crane and his plumb, ordinary Katrina. Beneath the disdain, Joan was bitterly jealous of their friendship, any friendship for that matter, and despite her dismissal of Bess as ordinary, she would have killed for her looks. After years of seesaw dieting, Joan had finally given up. Succumbing to an insatiable appetite, she had ballooned to her present gargantuan size in only two short years.

As middle school art teacher and artist, Joan had always been compared to Bess, her counterpart in the upper school. In both arenas, Bess outshone the unmarried, untalented, unfriendly middle school art instructor. In fact, in her quiet, understated way, Bess outshone most of the faculty at Old Harbor Friends.

Joan's dark brown hair, colored to hide the gray, was cropped short, the bangs spiked straight up from her bulbous forehead. Her taste in clothes was what she liked to call "artsy hobo." Tonight, she wore a neon yellow tunic over billowing floral trousers, an altogether frightening ensemble that accentuated rather than diminished her girth. She had been summoned to help comfort the students, but hadn't yet had any takers. As dorm parent, she now waited to escort Amy and Sarah home.

In addition to Joan, Peter, Bess, and the girls, there were three other people in the room. Garrett Rollins, the archivist, slouched across two chairs at the front of the room, feet propped up on the desk. Carol Richards, the business manager and Milt's boss, paced back and forth, sighing repeatedly as she passed Pete Dugan, the police officer standing guard at the door. Since their rooms adjoined Milt's, both Carol and Garrett had been summoned to examine their offices for signs of disturbance or forced entry. Neither had found anything amiss and both had repeatedly requested permission to leave. Garrett appeared to be enjoying the evening's diversion, Carol clearly was not.

"Possession," Garrett murmured, as Carol clicked by for the fiftieth time. Regarding the others superciliously, he felt certain he was the only person who would recognize the scent of Carol's costly, exotic perfume. Nanny, his fiancée, had recently begged for a bottle for her birthday and he'd obliged, setting himself back nearly a week's pay. Absently, he wondered how Carol could afford such extravagance. Even Nanny only used the perfume on special occasions and Garrett wouldn't have called a midnight police summons such an occasion.

Garrett, a historian and writer of biographies and local histories, was the school's unofficial scholar in residence, and he dressed the part in rumpled khakis, brown wool vest and faded blue flannel shirt, his longest sandy hair and goatee completing "the look," as the students called it. In his early forties, he had spent his career at Old Harbor, first as a history teacher, then dean and now archivist, a position made possible by an alum's largess.

"This is ridiculous. How long must we stay cooped up in this room, for goodness sakes? Garrett and I have checked our offices. Nothing's out of place, so what is the point? I ask you, what is the bloody point?"

When these words had no effect on Pete Dugan, she strode up to him, her face inches from his freckles. "Officer, you know perfectly well where I live. Why the bloody hell can't your high and mighty Sergeant what's his name come up to my apartment when he finally decides to show up?"

"Sorry, miss," Dugan mumbled for the tenth time. "Won't be much longer now. He'll be along directly." Carol resumed her strutting at a more frenzied pace than before. Dugan stepped back, perhaps fearing the stiletto heels were coming a little too close for comfort.

Watching Carol from a safe distance, Bess wondered why the business manager had bothered to dress in heels and a silk suit to come out in the middle of the night. She had run into Carol earlier in the day and she had not been wearing the black and white checked suit with flaming red, gossamer-thin blouse and two inch, black patent leather heels she wore now. I'd have remembered that outfit, Bess thought, her head beginning to pound to the rhythm of the relentless clicking heels. Turning back to Peter, she was embarrassed to find he'd been talking to her.

"What do you think, Bess?"

"I'm sorry Peter, I'm afraid I wasn't listening." She blushed, pushing strands of hair from her face. Suddenly quite desperately tired, she longed for the warmth of her bed, piled high with eiderdowns, a pot of herbal tea on her bedside table and an hour to lose herself in her Anne Greyson mystery. Yes, that's what she needed, escapist fiction, to take her away from the insane reality in which she now found herself. "I'm just a little tired, Peter, forgive me, you were saying?"

"Do you suppose they'll question us en masse or one at a time?"

"I haven't any idea. I...." Her voice trailed off, as the door opened and Roger Demaris stepped into the room. Of course, it would be Roger, who else would they send? Why hadn't she thought of it before? The detective's eyes scanned the room, resting briefly on her own before moving on.

"Well, it's about bloody time." Carol stalked up, confronting the short, stocky officer. "Now, see here, you. I insist upon being questioned first. I've got nothing whatsoever to do with this matter and I've had a very long day, not to mention a busy day tomorrow. I have absolutely nothing to contribute to this inquiry, so, if you would just —"

"Take a seat, Miss?"

"Richards, and I will not take a seat."

Demaris regarded her, anger flashing for an instant in the icy blue eyes. "Miss Richards, please take a seat." His voice was calm, soft. "We'll get to you as soon as we can. We've all had busy days, I'm sure, and no one wants to keep you here a minute longer than necessary. I'll be talking with the children first, if you don't mind." As she opened her mouth to speak, he added, "And, we'll be the judge of what you might contribute, thank you. Pete, did you find us a place?"

"Yes sir. Next door in the student center. Janitor's put on the lights. Do you want to go upstairs first?"

"Already seen him, thanks. Now, then, Mrs. Dore, why don't you bring the two girls and follow me. That's right, you can come with them. Come on."

Like he's talking to a two-year-old, Bess thought, rising obediently. As they followed the sergeant out of the study hall, Bess dared not glance in Carol Richards' direction.

Chapter 7

The janitor, Don Costa, had switched on the single row of lights directly over their heads, but beyond this narrow pool of light, the Coop lay shrouded in darkness, its tables and chairs eerie, misshapen goblins surrounding them. Like treed raccoons, the three sat curled up on the sofa, facing the hunter seated four feet away on the edge of a straight-backed chair.

"Okay, girls, 'spose you tell me about Mr. Wickie."

Amy drew in a sharp breath and Bess felt an involuntary shudder pass through the body pressed against her.

As Demaris leaned forward, elbows to knees, Bess wished she, too, sat in a hard chair instead of squashed between two frightened coeds. In this cramped position, she couldn't think straight, couldn't remember when she'd last seen the knife.

"Well, we..." began Amy, looking from the detective to her companions. She still clutched what was left of Bess' handkerchief, now a shredded cord of twisted knots. "I mean... I asked to go to the ladies room, only when I got there it was out of order. The one downstairs near the study hall, I mean."

"From what I understand, that bathroom's been out of commission all week. Didn't you realize this before you asked to use it? You do have study hall every night, don't you?"

Bess smiled, the girls' ruse now exposed. As a coach, she only proctored evening study once or twice a month. As such, she was probably the only one who hadn't known about the out-of-order bathroom.

"Oh, sir, I don't know, I —"

Demaris' eyes warmed. "No need to be upset. No one's in trouble here. Please, go on. What happened next?"

"Well, Mrs. Dore suggested I go upstairs. She let Sarah come, too, on account of the darkness. I don't like the dark." Amy paused, waiting for the detective's understanding nod. Demaris did not disappoint her.

"We were on our way up, on the way to the lav, I mean, when we noticed a strange light coming from under Mr. Wickie's door."

"Strange in what way?"

"Real spooky," Sarah chimed in. "Like something out of a horror movie."

"His computer monitor was on," Bess added dryly, unwilling to allow the tale to venture too far into the supernatural. "Then what?"

He looks tired, Bess thought, watching her one time lover. And, he's let himself go since Mary left. She tried to recall how long it'd been since she'd heard about the divorce, at least five years. However, even with the slight paunch he had developed in recent years, she had to admit he was a good-looking man. Her same age, 42, Roger Demaris' thick mane of curly, black hair hadn't a trace of gray and his clear blue eyes sparkled with intensity.

"Well," Amy continued. "We thought we'd better peek in and see if everything was alright, you know?"

"No, Amy, we went in to see about the computer, remember?" Sarah broke in.

"Well, that, too," Amy replied, petulantly. "Anyway," she drawled, glaring at Sarah. "We opened the door, switched on the light and there he was, lying on the floor all covered in blood. The knife! Ooh, it was sticking out of him. Yuk, it was gross."

"That's for sure," Sarah piped in, unable to contain herself.

"Then what?" He glanced at Dugan, as he had several times during the interview to make sure his assistant was taking notes. It seemed a nervous habit rather than a necessity. Dugan's pen hadn't stopped moving since Amy'd begun speaking.

"Well, we screamed, of course. Who wouldn't?"

"Of course," he replied, solemnly. "Did you go further into the room? Rearrange things, touch the body, anything like that?"

"Oh no," they both replied in unison.

"Think hard, girls. It's very important that we know exactly how the room looked when you entered it. Don't worry, you won't get into trouble."

"No, we didn't go any further or —"

"Wait, Amy. We did pick something up, 'member? It was that little purple cord."

"Cord?"

"Yeah, that's right," Amy agreed. "It was right near the door on the rug. I picked it up and put it on the little table near the door."

"Pete?" Dugan disappeared and he turned back to them. "Anything else?"

"No, we stepped right out and waited on the stairs for Mrs. Dore and the others."

"Others?"

"Yes." Bess blushed. "There was quite a stampede, entirely my fault, I'm afraid. I'm so sorry. When we found the girls on the landing several students went upstairs ahead of me. Three or four of them were already in the room when I got there. I don't believe they disturbed anything, but —"

"Yes, I'm sure," he cut her off, sarcasm evident in his tone. She half expected him to roll his eyes, but he simply said, "Names?" pulling a small notebook from his breast pocket.

"I'm sorry?"

"Of the early birds."

"Oh, of course. Well, let's see, there was Ronnie Cottrell, Kyle Blish, Steve Vallencourt, and I think Ali Berstein, too. Yes, I'm quite sure that's all."

"Nothing funny or out of place in the office, then?"

"I've never been in Mr. Wickie's office," Amy replied, assuming the question had been directed at her.

"Me neither," Sarah concurred. "Looked fine to me, except for the... you know, Mr. Wickie himself."

"Yes, well, thank you, girls." He motioned to Dugan, who had returned with the purple cord, which he handed to his superior. "This the cord?" Both Amy and Sarah nodded, their eyes as big as saucers. "Well, ladies, that's it then. Officer Dugan here will see that you get back to your dormitory all safe and sound. Pete, see if you can locate the dorm parents before you leave 'em."

"All taken care of," Dugan replied, opening the door. "Miss Nettleman's waiting next door. Want me to send Eddie up to take over here?" he asked, holding up his notebook.

"I'll be fine. Got my pad right here." Dugan opened his mouth as if to protest, but Demaris cut him off. "And, here," he added, tearing the page from his notebook. "These five boys apparently reached Wickie's office before Mrs. Dore. See if you can round 'em up and get a statement from each of them, okay?"

"Couldn't it wait till morning? It's almost midnight," Bess asked, but Demaris ignored her.

"See what you can do, okay?"

CHAPTER 8

As the door shut behind the others, he stared down at the cord, lying like a coiled serpent in his hand. After several minutes he spoke, "So, how are you?" The blue eyes held the same disconcerting mix of warmth, wariness and resentment. Bess felt cornered.

She managed a crooked smile. "I've been better."

"Want some coffee or something?"

"No, thanks. What I'd really like is to go home."

"I know, I won't keep you long. Want to tell me about it? About this?" he asked, holding up the cord. "Belongs to you, doesn't it?" Seeing her surprise, he added, "I know you, remember? Or I used to anyway."

"It's from the knife. It was tied to the sheath. The knife... my knife," she burst out, her voice shrill and trembling, much louder than she'd intended. "I mean it was Mac's knife, from his scrimshaw collection. Oh, God, Roger, why didn't I donate the whole lot to the Marine Museum when they asked for it last year?"

"Same reason I keep Mary's fuckin' knick knacks around... 'cause you can't let go. Pathetic, huh? Mary doesn't give a shit about all that crap anymore, but here I am hangin' onto it."

"I was sorry to hear about you and Mary."

He shrugged. "Ancient history. I remember that knife, you know? Recognized it the minute I saw it."

"Oh, Roger, I don't know how it got there. I don't even remember when I last saw it. I never look in that case, I never touch the things or even dust them. I should have gotten rid of it all years ago."

"In your den, right?"

She nodded, amazed that he remembered. It had been ten years since he'd been in the cottage. After Mac's funeral. And, to the best of her knowledge that had been the first and only time he had been there.

"How could this have happened?"

"I was hopin' you could tell me. What's the story on this Wickie? Popular guy, was he?"

"Hardly. He's, well, he was, excuse me, kind of a jerk. I'm sorry, but he was. Always minding everyone else's business, very officious and full of himself."

"Liked him, huh?"

Giving him a wry smile, she said, "In truth, I barely knew him. I've probably only been up to his office two or three times in all my years here and one of those times was tonight." Silently, he regarded her, scratching his chin. He needed a shave. She knew he was waiting for her to continue, but she wasn't quite sure of what to say. "I know he annoyed a lot of people, but —"

"How so?"

"I'm sorry," she stammered, blushing. "I don't understand what you mean."

"How'd he annoy people?"

"Well, he had a roving eye. Had many women "friends" over the years and some of those romances ended badly. Naturally, there were hurt feelings."

"Whose?"

"Well, Joan for one. The heavy woman downstairs."

"Heavy? Ha, that's an understatement. That one makes Mama Cass look like Twiggy."

"Joan's had a tough life and Milt didn't help. She was crazy about him. Told everyone they were getting married. Then, he just up and left her for someone else. It was awful. I don't even remember who his next conquest was. He's had so many different girlfriends over the years one loses count."

"Wonder what the ladies saw in him? What did Romeo do here anyway?"

"He was the Comptroller, that's his official title, I believe. More accurately, he was the Assistant Business Manager, although I don't know how much assisting he did. Carol doesn't like him. They don't, didn't get along. She's downstairs, too."

"The witch in heels? Probably down there makin' mincemeat outta poor ole Pete."

"It is almost midnight, you know."

"Tough shit. We all gotta stay up and she can damn well cool her heels a few minutes longer. You got any ideas 'bout who'd want to kill our Lothario?"

"Sorry, but I don't."

"Well, guess I gotta let you go. Though I'd much rather talk to you than the whip woman."

Managing a tired smile, she started to rise, relieved to be headed home at last. As she gained her feet, the room began to spin and her vision clouded. Afraid of falling, she leaned forward, grabbing hold of his chair back to steady herself.

"Whoa." He slipped his arm around her waist, nearly pulling her into his lap. "You okay?"

"I'm fine, just hungry. I haven't eaten since breakfast and I'm a little light-headed, that's all."

"Sit down and I'll —"

"No, I'm fine, Roger, really." Extracting herself from his embrace, she added, "I'll go right home and have something to eat and I'll be fine."

"Sure?"

"Positive."

"Bess, I —"

"Goodnight." She turned away.

"I'm right behind you," he whispered, as she reached the door. "Down to collect my next victim." He reached across opening the door, his arm brushing against hers. Bess feared she would cry if she lingered a second longer. Almost running down the corridor, she grabbed her things from the study hall and fled the building. As the fire doors clanged shut behind her, she heard Roger's voice saying, "Mr. Thurbert, I'll take you now."

She didn't wait to hear Carol Richard's cry of protest or the two men's murmured conversation as they strolled back down to the Coop. Instead, she sprinted to her car and drove off, for the first time in her life failing to heed the campus' five mile per hour speed limit.

CHAPTER 9

Home at last. A bowl of creamy carrot soup and whole wheat toast slathered with jam on a tray, Bess retreated to her study. The study, her favorite room in the house, had been Mac's room.   Filled with his things — Audubon bird prints, beautifully carved decoys, books, scrimshaw and silver tools and papers, stacks and stacks of papers in files, on the bookshelves, in boxes in the closet — everything was as it had been during his lifetime. As if the room, like she herself, existed simply to wait for his return. Friends often begged her to get rid of some of it, but she still wasn't ready. It had been ten years, but she couldn't seem to let go.

Ordinarily, a warm refuge with its fieldstone fireplace and paneled walls, tonight the room seemed alive with a quiet, pulsating menace. She'd checked the case immediately upon her return, finding as expected a dark, curving arc, starkly delineated in the original mauve color, unbleached like the cloth surrounding it. After checking the case, she double-bolted the French doors and then walked through the entire house checking every door and window. She never locked the cottage, had never had reason until now.   After assuring herself that everything was secure, she made a fire, warmed the soup and now sat, thinking about Roger Demaris and her life before Mac.

Bess and Roger had been classmates since the second grade. Roger's family had been dirt poor, his father an intermittent presence in a chaotic household that included seven brothers and sisters. Rose Demaris had done the best she could, working two jobs to feed her children, insisting that they remain in school. From a young age, Roger, the eldest, worked after school and summers, paper routes, local saw mills, construction and even occasionally fishing, although he hated the water. The Guilfords, Bess' family, represented all that he despised — the wealth, the country club memberships, extravagant travels to all corners of the globe.

Both good students, they had taken many of the same classes, but although they were friends and often collaborators at school, they remained virtual strangers outside its walls. During their teens, the strain of their differences became even more pronounced, exacerbated by the insecurities and upheavals of adolescence.

Much as he despised her lifestyle, however, Roger Demaris could not despise her. From a very young age, he loved Bess Guilford with a passion no amount of disdain could bury. The summer after graduation they fell into a desperate, albeit brief love affair that lasted until Roger broke it off a week before Bess left off for college. A shy teenager, Bess blossomed into womanhood during the affair and his rejection shattered her.

Freshman year at Middlebury had been bleak indeed, but the following summer she met Macomber Dore and her life changed forever. Mac helped heal her wounded heart, opening up new worlds to the timid, lonely girl, worlds that stretched far beyond Old Harbor.

Occasionally she ran into Roger, but they seldom exchanged more than the requisite pleasantries before parting company. Without the mutual pursuits of school, they had little in common leaving them with nothing to say to one another. In truth, Bess avoided him, unwilling to subject herself to his criticism. Although she had given most of her inheritance to charities upon her marriage, keeping just enough to buy the cottage and a little to put aside for their retirement, that wouldn't have mattered to Roger. He would have found fault with some other aspect of her new, happy life.

Part of her would always love the complicated, angry friend of her youth, but Bess no longer had the strength to fight her way past the tough exterior Roger had erected to protect himself. Mac had been so easy to love, his simple grace, his embracing warmth and his absolute integrity drew people to him as completely as Roger's bitterness drove them away. Bitterness had no doubt destroyed his marriage, Bess mused. Mary Demaris was a good, kind woman who had appeared to care deeply for her husband, however, in only three short years something had driven her away. Now, Roger was alone again, as he'd been for most of his life.

"Oh, Mac," she whispered, tears welling up in her tired eyes as she reached for a framed black and white photograph of her husband taken during their last trip together before his illness. At her urging, they'd spent four weeks on Prince Edward Island and the photo she now held had been taken on the beach during one of their last days. An idyllic, summer day, they'd spent it roaming the cragged, rocky shoreline, eating their picnic perched high on the cliffs, the surf pounding beneath them, lying on a blanket their bodies entwined as they drank up the sun's warmth.

A wary, half-smile always lingered at the corners of Mac's soft, brown eyes and the camera had captured it. No one would ever have called her husband handsome. His features were too sharp, too angular, his nose too long and his body, even when healthy, was rail thin, almost gangly. An agile, quick man if circumstances required it, Mac had never been an athlete. Rather he'd been a creature of nature, most at home when he was hiking the fields and shoreline, traipsing through his beloved woods.

Running her fingers over the glass, Bess longed to reach into the picture, to smooth back the wispy, blond strands that fell across his face, the soft, fine hair that had been ravaged, then completely lost during his last months of treatment. "I miss you, my darling," she whispered. "What I wouldn't give for two minutes in your arms."

CHAPTER 10

A faint rustling, punctuated by occasional coughs and sneezes distracted her thoughts at Wednesday's Meeting for Worship. Sitting amongst her restive students, Bess shivered in her thin cotton jacket. Why hadn't they turned on the heat? In austere silence, they sat on plain, white benches, thin fabric cushions threadbare and lumpy. Bess gazed out twelve-foot windows into the grey autumn sky, framed by craggy leafless branches of elm and oak trees. She often used Meeting for Worship to relive her ten years of marriage, grasping every memory, teasing each recollection from the recesses of her mind.

Jack Ransom, a tenth grader, sat beside her, elbowing Win Chace to his right. Shifting slightly, Bess caught the scent of aftershave as she turned to give him a pleading look. Grinning, Jack settled down, allowing her to return to her memories.

She was thinking about their first summer together when Mac had taken a job on the ground's crew of Old Harbor Friends. Raised a Quaker, he had grown up in a Friend's community outside of Philadelphia. Like Roger, Mac had little time for the rich and what he perceived to be their wasteful, meaningless lives. However, unlike her childhood friend, Mac had never held Bess' origins against her, never teased or criticized.

Where Roger's temper flared at the slightest provocation, Mac was even-tempered, calm. They had spent hours together that summer, discussing literature, art and history, walking the beach, exploring the woods, talking into the wee hours as they swung on the Guilford's creaky porch glider. Before each returned to college in the fall — Mac to Haverford and Bess to Middlebury — their friendship had deepened into love, love that grew stronger and deeper with the separation.

Two days after Bess graduated, they married. They spent their first year of married life in Middlebury pursuing graduate studies. For several more years, they remained in Vermont completing graduate work and teaching at a small, cooperative school. Through Friends' connections, they learned of two openings at Old Harbor Friends, one for an upper school art teacher, the other for an instructor of Chemistry and advanced Biology, and jumped at the chance to return.

In those days, teachers were required to live on campus as dorm parents the first five years of their employment, but Bess and Mac had purchased the cottage right away. In the early years, they used it only during vacations, summers and occasional weekends. They spent countless happy hours painting, restoring and furnishing their new home. Situated as it was, a quarter of a mile from campus, it was easy to slip away for a few hours when they were off-duty.

She remembered one particular afternoon during their first summer as homeowners. They had spent the morning building bookshelves in the den and stopped at midday for a picnic on their newly-laid fieldstone terrace. Sitting in the sun on old canvas cushions, each covered from head to toe in sawdust and grime, they had laughed, talked ate tuna fish sandwiches and lukewarm sun tea, lukewarm because the freezer was broken and there was no ice. If she closed her eyes, she could almost feel his touch, feel his gentle fingers brushing errant strands of hair from her face, see him leaning forward to kiss her.

"Good morning." Outstretched hand and her friend's voice called Bess back to the present. Meeting for Worship had ended. "Off roamin' the woods with Mac again?" The tall, red-haired woman whispered, squeezing her hand, kind eyes regarding her.

Bess blushed, looking up to meet Jane Fellows' eyes. "Good morning to you. How are you?"

"Okay, but I've just about had it with my sophomores."

"I know what you mean. That class is tough, but they'll grow up soon, don't you think? I can't believe it's been almost a week since I've seen you."

"It's all this murder business," Jane continued in a whisper as they exited the Meeting House. "How many more times do we have to be grilled by that dreadful Sergeant Demaris. I don't believe he's discovered a thing despite all his scowling and prowling, do you? And look at all the classes we've sacrificed to be at his beck and call. What do you think's going on?"

"I haven't any idea." Bess nodded to several students as they made their way down the tree-shaded walkway. She felt guilty for not rising to Roger's defense. Instead she kept silent, her feelings for the brooding friend of her youth too complicated to explain away in a few words. And, Jane would never rest until she had every detail.

Two years younger than Bess and never married, Jane had been teaching biology at the school for fifteen years. Although she owned a tiny beach house, she still lived in the dorm claiming "the kids would miss me too much," retreating to her cabana during the summer months. The two women had been friends from the time of Jane's arrival from Indiana and they had grown only closer as the years went by. Jane had been with her day and night during the terrible months after Mac's death. However, close as they were, Bess had somehow never quite gotten around to telling her friend about Roger.

"Oh, look, it's Mrs. Extreme Exerciser," Jane whispered, directing Bess' attention towards upper campus as Carrie Thurbert, Peter's wife jogged by. As they watched, she slowed her gait, untangling a jacket from round her waist and slipping it on as she reached the bicycle rack alongside the admissions building, unlocked an expensive looking racing bike and pushed off towards the front gates.

"Sh." Bess elbowed her friend, looking over her shoulder to see if anyone had heard.

"She's training for a triathlon, did you know? That's all she talks about at the gym, and how hard it is to get time at the Y pool in Marshfield. If she and

Peter were staying, she'd probably have cajoled him into installing a lap pool at the Head's House."

"Come to think of it, as the Head's wife, why does she never come to Meeting for Worship? That should be one of her duties, don't you think?"

Bess shrugged. "Can we please change the subject?"

"Did Sergeant Grumpy bother you again after that first night?"

Bess rolled her eyes, wondering if she should reintroduce the topic of Carrie Thurbert's exercise regime. "No, he just called to let me know about the fingerprints. I told you that, didn't I? The knife had been wiped clean."

"Did they give it back?"

"No, I doubt I'll ever see that horrid thing again and I won't be a bit sorry. I wish I'd given it and the whole lot to the museum when they asked for it."

"Oh Bess, I've upset you. Let's forget the whole mess, shall we? Go to Perry's tonight for supper, what do you say? Or, better yet, come to my place. I'll whip up some exotic culinary delight, we'll drink lots of wine and not mention a word about this whole disgusting business."

"I don't know about the wine on a school night," Bess laughed, "But, I'd love to come for dinner. What can I bring?"

"Nothing. I'll see you around six-thirty. Ta-ta!" With that, Jane was off and running. Bess watched her friend, the other's red ponytail bobbing as she loped across the green towards the science building. Then turning away, she headed for her studio on the second floor of the Arts Building. Her first period of the day was free, but she usually tried to be in the studio in case her advisees or other students wanted to drop in.

CHAPTER 11

As Bess crossed the largest of the school's parking lots, she spied Louie Predo, the gardener, rolling a wheelbarrow full of tools and equipment out of the Maintenance Barn. Louie had been at Old Harbor Friends his entire life. His father had served as head of maintenance until his death a quarter a century earlier. During his father's tenure, the family had lived in the village of Old Harbor, but now Louie alone and unmarried, had been granted living quarters on campus, a drafty second floor apartment above the Maintenance Barn that he shared with Billy Blackburn, head groundskeeper. "Hi Lou," she called, strolling over to meet him.

"Hello yourself, Mrs. D. How you?"

"I'm getting along, thanks Lou."

"Mr. Mac 'twas a nice man."

"Yes, he was," she replied, repeating her lines in the familiar script played out almost every time they met.

"I miss Lizzie, too, Mrs. D."

"I know. I do, too. She was a sweet girl. You take care now, okay? I'll bring your supper tomorrow, alright?"

"Oh, don't trouble yerself none."

"I enjoy it, Lou, you know that. See ya."

Neither Louie or Billy did much cooking, Bess wasn't sure Louie even remembered how. At least two nights each week, she brought them supper, either dropping it at the maintenance in the mornings or sometimes delivering at dinnertime and sharing it with them. Lizzie Mederois had been gone twelve years. Louie had never been the same.

"Bess, hi!"

A voice called from behind her and Bess turned to spy Todd Bridgham, Head of Upper School, loping towards her. Todd had been Head of Upper School for three years and Bess didn't much care for him. Most days, he flew around campus, barely stopping to say hello. The rest of the time he seemed to be constantly traveling, off to a never-ending array of conferences and professional development workshops. When not traveling or flying around the campus, he sequestered himself in a grand, newly refurbished office except when presiding over biweekly faculty meetings. Since Kevin LeBlanc clerked these meetings, Todd's presence was superfluous at best. Todd had particularly raised Bess' ire with his habit of calling the art program "one of our little extras." More than once, Bess had wondered what possessed Peter Thurbert, usually a careful recruiter, to bring Todd to Old Harbor Friends. She stopped walking, waiting for Todd to reach her.

"Bess!" He gasped for air, face beet red from running, liquid blue eyes scanning the campus as he paused to catch his breath. Slightly overweight, with a balding pate, Todd was a few years her senior, but looked much older. Dressed in his usual sport coat and khakis, he looked more rumpled than usual and took a minute to smooth back his few strands of top hair and straighten his tie before speaking. "Thanks for waiting. How are you?"

"Fine." Bess regarded him curiously, unaccustomed to such friendliness.

"Terrible business, Milt's death."

"Yes."

"Yes, well, I see from your expression that you're baffled as to why I've flagged you down. Fair enough. Well, it's this—" As he spoke he looked down at the ground, over her head, past her to the art studio behind her, anywhere but directly at her. Todd rarely made eye contact. "Sheila's having a party. What I mean to say is, Sheila and I are having a dinner party. She's furious at me for forgetting to ask you last week, but, with Milt's death and all it completely slipped my mind. She's, we've been trying to have small faculty groups over every other weekend instead of those huge gatherings of past years. This Saturday's crew is mostly English department, and a few artsy types. Joanie's coming, of course. Sheila'd never give a party without Joanie." According to campus gossip, Joan Nettleton was one of Sheila's new "best friends."

"So, Bess, I'm in a huge bind. I'll be in the doghouse for months if you don't say yes. Please, say you'll come."

"I don't know, Todd." Caught off-guard without a ready excuse, her mind raced. What a load of rubbish, forgetting to invite her. Clearly she was either a replacement for someone who had regretted at the last minute, or there was an ulterior motive for him wanting her there. Either way, she had no wish to become a convenient substitute to round out Sheila's table.

"Please Bess, don't punish Sheila and the rest of the guests 'cause I'm an absentminded jerk. It would mean a lot to us for you to be there, particularly at this very trying time. The Thurberts'll be there and Kevin. Please, if you don't come Sheila'll have my head."

Completely nonplussed, Bess was appalled to hear herself saying, "Well, yes, alright, thank you."

The pudgy, dimpled face was completely transformed, the expression of abject pleading replaced by a mask of alarming, almost surrealistic glee. "You're a perfect love, Bess. Thanks a million. Gotta run, see you Saturday, then? Seven okay?" Not waiting for her reply he said, "Great. I'll pick you up?"

"No, that's okay. I may even walk if it's a nice night."

"Great. Count on me for a lift home if you do. Gotta go." She watched him trot off, furious at herself for accepting. Suddenly, he turned, calling back over his shoulder, "Oh, almost forgot. You'll have an interesting dinner companion. Never met him, but he's 'sposed to be a great guy. Name's Winthrop, Harry Jr. If he's anything like his old man, you'll be in stitches all night."

"Todd, wait!"

"See you then. Gotta go. Really late."

What a fool, I am, she thought. Why didn't I just say 'no?' Well, she muttered climbing the back steps to the studio, I won't go, it's as simple as that. I'll think up an excuse and cancel and that's that.

CHAPTER 12

If she squinted, her surroundings blurred and Jane Fellow's living room became one rosy hue, the softness of its pastel colors like a warm embrace for her battered spirit. For the first time since Milt's demise, Bess felt safe sipping her wine as her friend chattered away on the sofa beside her. All legs beneath a flowing mauve tunic, its cowl neck the same gray as her leggings, Jane's auburn hair fell loosely over her shoulders, shining in the soft light. The saffron and cinnamon smells of Jane's dinner simmering on the stove surrounded them.

"So? What do you think? We haven't had a chance to talk all week. Think someone here at school killed him? Or, do you believe that ridiculous story Peter's circulating about it being a robbery? As if a robber would bother to sneak into your house, grab Mac's knife, then toddle back to school and whack old Milt? What a load of rubbish. Besides, what robber with half a brain would think there was anything worth stealing in Milt's office? The whole thing is preposterous."

"I don't think Peter really believes that." Bess stiffened, defensive already. What had happened to Jane's vow not to mention the whole disgusting business? While Jane never disguised her dislike for the headmaster or his wife, she never gave Bess a reason for her strong antipathy. Most times, she dismissed him with a snide remark and a shrug, referring to him and most male teachers as "good old boys." Bess suspected there was more to it than her friend let on, but never pressed her assuming that Jane would tell her in good time.

"He'd have to put up a good front, so as not to scare the students or their parents. Can't very well go around publicizing the fact that there may be a murderer loose on the campus. If he wants to keep any students that is. By the way, you're remarkably calm about all this. We have a murderer in our midst. We have to face it."

"I know." Her voice betrayed her annoyance, despite efforts to control it. She had endured countless conversations like this one all week, everyone on the edge of hysteria, all of them dangling at the precipice with no one to pull them back. "The police will find the person soon, I'm sure of it. Then we can all breathe easier."

"If you believe that, I've got a dandy tract of swamp land to sell you. The way we've all been instructed to clam-up, that poor detective'll be lucky if he ever uncovers a clue. Now, we're to be subjected to Boy Wonder, Junior Detective? What a joke!"

"What are you talking about?"

"Golden Boy Winthrop. Supposed to be the next Peter Wimsey from what I hear. At least that's what he fancies himself to be. Sleuth extraordinaire, international P.I. and what have you. Why, I wouldn't be surprised if he comes complete with a valet or sidekick named Mr. Lugg."

"Jane, who are you talking about? Not Mr. Winthrop?"

"No, no, not Harry Senior, you ninny, his son, Harry Junior. He's been summoned by Lord Parmenter to head up the internal investigation, the one we'll all be encouraged to cooperate with. The Board's asked him to conduct a discreet poke-around, dredge up all our dark, ugly secrets and report every gory detail to their illustrious chair."

"You're not serious."

"I kid you not, my poor, dear uninformed, Bessie. You really should get on the gossip hotline. I have it straight from the mare's mouth. Carrie Thurbert was full of it at aerobics yesterday. God, I detest that woman. She told Susan LeBlanc and me that in spite of Peter's objections, the Board had voted unanimously to hire a private investigator, in case it turned out to be an inside job. Wouldn't that be a surprise?"

Jane reached over refilling her wine glass, green eyes sparkling with mischief. "I'm sure the police are frustrated as hell right now, what with our orders to close ranks. Apparently old Harry convinced Cornie Parmenter that young Harry's the man for the job. Perhaps a little cash changed hands, always does when Winthrop's involved. Rumor has it the old man wants his son home again and what better way to lure him back? So, I guess we're his guinea pigs so he can practice sleuthing."

"Oh, Lord," Bess groaned, nearly spilling her wine. "And, I'm meant to be his 'dinner companion' Saturday night. At the Bridghams, no less!"

"What? When did you get so chummy with Todd and Sheila?"

"Very funny. Todd accosted me this afternoon and I couldn't think up an excuse fast enough, but I will. What a detestable toad Todd is. Probably cooked the whole evening up so this Harry could get a look at the prime suspect. Well, I won't give him the satisfaction."

"Oh, no, you don't, Bess Dore. Don't you dare back out. I want to hear every juicy detail. And, don't go blaming the whole thing on Todd, he's an ass, no question, but this doesn't sound like his work."

"Then who?"

"Sounds more like our illustrious head's doing, matching people up, getting just the right group together. I mean, once he resigned himself to the inevitability of junior snoop's arrival, I'll bet he put on his headmaster's hat and orchestrated this entire affair."

The bitterness in her friend's voice made Bess shudder. "Jane, why do you hate him so much?" she asked, bracing herself for a tongue lashing.

"I don't hate him. I just think it's time for a change, that's all. He's been around too long."

"Jane, this is me you're talking to, remember? What's wrong?"

"I think I smell the bread, don't want it to burn. Better check on it." The pocket of her tunic caught the edge of the coffee table as Jane stood, untangling herself and disappearing into the kitchen.

Bowls of cioppino, brimming with lobster, mussels, clams and chunks of delicate white fish, before them, they talked more amiably, Peter Thurbert forgotten. Jane's homemade bread saturated with garlic butter and herbs, complimented the soup perfectly. Small, tossed salads, made with the last remnants of Jane's garden, dressed with a light vinaigrette and sprinkled with Gorgonzola rounded out their repast.

"Heaven," Bess pronounced after her first bite. "Pure heaven."

"Thanks," Jane said, mouth full of bread. "And, your sinful butterscotch sauce over the Haagen Daas should finish this off perfectly. What more could one ask for?"

Later, over coffee, they returned to their earlier conversation. Bess asked, "Jane, what exactly do you know about Harry Winthrop? I don't ever remember seeing him at school."

"Never been here. According to Carrie he's only been to Old Harbor once for a very brief stay not long after his father moved into the Hall. That was long before Harry Senior became involved with us. Harry the younger's been abroad for years apparently, quite the world traveler according to Carrie who met him a couple of years ago in St. Tropez. She and Peter were at some regatta. I'm sure the school footed the bill for that little jaunt. He probably pretended he was chatting up potential donors."

"That's right, they were. I remember when they took that trip."

"Disgusting." Jane spit out the word.

Startled, Bess took too big a swallow of hot coffee, burning her throat. "About Mr. Winthrop?"

"Carrie says he's a hunk, but who can trust her. Her taste in men is highly suspect."

Suddenly weary of the subject of Harry Winthrop and her friend's repeated jabs at Peter Thurbert, Bess asked how Jane's sophomore class was doing and the evening passed pleasantly as they discussed the current collaboration between the biology and English classes for tenth graders. An attempt had been made to integrate the two curricula and sophomores were reading nature essays and expository texts in English classes directly related to their studies in biology. In biology they were writing more in their labs and on research projects. Bess' art classes had recently been drawn tangentially into the integrated curriculum when her sophomores sketched insects, small mammals and other creatures related to their studies, using specimens from the biology lab and their field collections.

CHAPTER 13

Only later, as Bess prepared for bed, did her thoughts return to Harry Winthrop and the dreadful prospect of the Bridgham's dinner. She knew she would never come up with an excuse that the relentless Todd would accept, and now Jane had practically dared her to go. She had to admit that she was curious about Harry Winthrop. While she had seen his father, the elder Winthrop walking in the village and occasionally on campus for a ceremony or building dedication, she knew little about the school's generous benefactor. People claimed he was bedridden now.

Rumor had it that the Winthrops, originally from Boston, had always summered in Maine. Why had Harry Senior broken tradition and come to Old Harbor? The five hundred acre estate bordered the school grounds to the north and west. Upon his death, all five hundred acres would go to the school.

Not long after moving into the white Victorian on the bluffs, Harry Winthrop, the elder had made his mark on all civic matters in the village of Old Harbor, donating considerable sums to village organizations, making instant friends of his fellow residents whether they knew him personally or not. Once he'd gotten the town in order, he strode into Peter Thurbert's office, plunked down a check for two million dollars and said, "Your school's got a fine reputation, son. Do some good with this and there'll be more." Doffing his hat, the eccentric Mr. Winthrop had then strolled out without waiting for so much as a thank you.

A large portion of the initial bequest had gone to scholarships, enabling Old Harbor Friends to support a diverse and vibrant student body, almost two thirds of whom received some sort of financial assistance through the Harold Winthrop Trust. A portion of the original gift had also gone into refurbishing the science labs. A second gift built the Thurbert Field House. Mr. Winthrop had insisted it be named for the headmaster, despite Peter's objections. He then proceeded to finance extensive grounds work resulting in six new playing fields, four tennis courts and a pool complex, completed with matching funds from the capital campaign. The most recent bequest had been the monies used to add onto the classroom building with funds sufficient enough to renovate the art studios, adding new windows, restoring a fireplace to working order and adding twenty potter's wheels and two kilns.

In the beginning, Winthrop's motives had been questioned by the school community. Why would a recluse like Harold Winthrop give millions to a school that not one of his family had attended? During the early years of his residency, speculation abounded concerning the motives behind Mr. Winthrop's largess. As time went by, people came to accept his kindness, holding their breath in silent gratitude, while awaiting the next miracle wrought by the Winthrop millions. Winthrop's generosity had contributed to substantial boosts in faculty salaries. Old Harbor teachers were the highest paid of all New England independent schools. That fact alone curbed loose tongues and quieted cynical speculation.

New faculty members often wondered aloud about the mysterious Mr. Winthrop, but like everyone else, they soon came to regard him as the father of Old Harbor Friends, as central to the school's rituals and traditions as Meeting for Worship or community service. Without a shred of proof upon which to base her assumptions, Bess suspected that Harry Winthrop gave to Old Harbor Friends because of a wish to belong. Not just the "thanks a lot" kind of belonging that one earned after a large gift to the annual fund, but the deep, abiding sense of inclusion in the heart of the school community. Even though a recluse, perhaps Harry Winthrop yearned to be revered and loved as family?

CHAPTER 14

"Where in the hell do these people get off? Jesus. friggin' Christ!"

Demaris slammed down the phone, face crimson, eyes watering. Pete Dugan sat across the room, waiting for the furor to subside. He knew his boss well. The controlled patience with which Demaris had listened to the largely one way conversation forebode the worst.

"Is there a problem, boss?" Pete asked, wanting to help, while having no wish to have the rage directed in his direction.

"That was Cornelius "Fuckin'" Parmenter, Chairman of the Board. He was calling to 'keep me abreast of the investigation'. Do you believe this shit? And that's not the friggin' worst of it. They've hired some rich dip-shit, old man Winthrop's son. According to Cornie, he's the next Sam Spade. Claims he's the man for the job. Like I'm 'sposed to roll over, play dead and kiss his ass for helpin' me out. Here we've been bustin' our butts all week on this friggin' case, tryin' to pry information outta these people. Worse than pullin' teeth and now, as if things ain't bad enough, we gotta deal with Junior P.I. Do you believe this shit? God, I hate this job."

"I wouldn't worry too much. This clown'll probably poke around, get bored, and then we'll be back in business. Who knows, maybe they'll open up once this guy shakes the bushes."

"Come on, Pete. It's me you're talkin' to here. Fat, friggin' chance. They're only bringin' this joker in so they can keep everything 'hush, hush'. You know,

I've got a good mind to go public with what we've got so far. Serve the bastards right. All the mommies and daddies'd be packin' their precious darlings so fast it'd make your head spin."

"Might mean your job," Dugan mumbled, bracing himself for the tirade sure to follow.

"Almost be worth it," Demaris muttered, the fight knocked out of him.

Watching him, Pete wondered how much of his boss' ire was the case and how much rose from concern for his old girlfriend, Bess Dore. Fiercely protective of his superior, Pete hadn't missed the longing in Demaris' eyes when he looked at her. When she walked into the room, his boss had looked ready to swoon, but for the life of him Dugan couldn't understand why. She was pretty, in a plain sort of way, but Rodge could do better. Little Betsy down at the Bayside, for instance. She was a knockout and she'd give him a good time besides. What the hell did he want with a mousy, little schoolmarm? Dore's one virtue, from what Dugan could see, was her height— she was shorter than Rodge and it wasn't easy for the five foot, five inch detective to find a woman he could look straight in the eye. His ex, Mary had been a good four inches taller.

Dugan knew the history of the relationship— at least some of it. He had been with Demaris sixteen years, had gone with him to Macomber Dore's funeral and afterwards to the Dore's home so his boss could pay his respects to the widow. One glimpse of the two of them together told him all he needed to know. It was clear to Pete that Demaris, engaged to be married at the time, was still in love with Bess Dore. After that, Dugan had made it his business to find out all he could about the Widow Dore. Over the years, he had listened to many second and third hand accounts of her brief, ill-fated romance with his boss. While Demaris had never discussed his high school sweetheart with his deputy, Dugan felt that he, too, had lived through the years of torment after saying goodbye to Bess Guilford.

Like many a loyal subordinate, Dugan forgave his boss' faults, while remaining highly critical of others' shortcomings. Mary Demaris had been the friggin' bitch of the century. They were both better off without her. During their five years of marriage she'd made Rodge's life hell, every minute of it. Good riddance to Mary, he thought with finality, and as soon as we wrap up this case, good riddance to Bess Dore, too.

As if reading his assistant's mind, Demaris said, "Ring up the school, will ya Pete. See if you can get Mrs. Dore for me."

"Somethin' special ya want me to ask her?"

"Just get her, will you? I'll ask the questions. I'm goin' for coffee be right back."

Wounded, Dugan nonetheless did as he was told. When Demaris returned, he was holding the receiver. "Hold on, Mrs. Dore, here he is."

Grabbing the phone, Demaris thrust Pete's coffee across the desk, turning to face the wall. His expression might be hidden, Dugan thought, but it didn't matter, the raging bull of a few minutes earlier was now a lamb, his voice soft and soothing, "Hi, sorry to disturb you. Did I get you out of class? We need to talk. Is there a good time today or tomorrow? Four? Great. Where can we? Fine, see you then."

Setting the receiver down, more gently this time, he eyed Dugan, "Don't say it, Pete. Don't say a friggin' word. I know what you're thinkin' and it's bullshit, so just forget it, okay?" Dugan shrugged. "We're meetin' about the case, period, end of story. Now let's get back to work. What'd you guys find out yesterday?"

"She dated him you know."

"Who?"

"Your Mrs. Dore."

"She's not my Mrs. Dore, and what the fuck're you talkin' about?"

"Mike's been askin' around, the cleaning staff, maintenance people. Talked to a woman that cleans Dore's house. Saw 'em together, her and Wickie, goin' out on dates. A couple of times, she said."

"How the hell does this woman know they were goin' on a date. He might've been pickin' her up for a meeting or something. We don't know what the —"

"He kissed her, Rodge. Lady said so. Plus, we got a couple of other people say Dore did have a brief fling with him a while back.   Maybe she's a scorned lover for all we know."

"Bullshit." Demaris stared straight ahead. In the sudden stillness inside the office, the muffled rustling of the squad room intensified to a roar. Finally, he said, "Well, that's one more thing Mrs. Dore and I will have to talk about, isn't it? Let's see the woman's statement and anything else you got."

CHAPTER 15

Bess placed the receiver back in its cradle and wandered back to her studio. Amy Flathers caught up with her, "Mrs. Dore? I know you're in class now, but can I talk to you later?"

"Of course Amy, I'm free after school. Will that work for you?"

"That'd be great. Can I meet you here?"

"That's would be fine. See you then." Bess peeked in on her drawing class, pleased to find her students carrying on beautifully without her. A senior elective, the class was drawing from life this week, the model a village woman in her early twenties. She was their first model to pose in the nude, but after some tittering and unease on the first day, the class had settled into their drawing, enjoying the challenge of sketching the body in its stark, purest form.

Bess stepped inside, closing the door behind her and began circling the room, offering encouragement, direction and criticism. As she passed from easel to easel, she felt her oppressed spirits begin to lift. Amidst the warm camaraderie of her students, a fire blazing in the newly-restored hearth, Milt Wickie and his sordid, miserable life seemed to slip away. She put thoughts of the case aside, immersing herself in her interactions with students. This afternoon, Roger would probe deeper and she would have to answer his questions. Now, she could relax, in the light-filled studio, the smell of mineral spirits mingled with wood smoke filling the room, the air thick with clay dust and laughter.

Class ended, students trickled out as Bess gathered her things, preparing for the faculty meeting, which had inexplicably been scheduled during lunch. Usually, meetings were Wednesdays, after school, but Peter had emailed that morning, calling them together. A knock startled her and she looked up to find Will McGuire, Chair of the English Department in the doorway.

"Will, hi. What brings you to this side of campus?" She couldn't recall ever seeing the tall, slender English teacher in the arts building.

Not exactly handsome, Will had a craggy, well-lived in appearance, balding, tan and fit. He was dressed in khakis and a soft green sweater, a tweed jacket thrown over one shoulder, brown canvas briefcase over the other. "Can I walk a lady to lunch?" He gave her a crooked smile, dark eyes warm.

About her age, Mac and Will had been close friends, but she hadn't seen much of him the past few years. A confirmed bachelor, there had been speculation over the years that Will was homosexual, though he dated women from time to time, including several faculty members. He had asked Bess out several times the year after Mac died, but she always declined.

"Of course, why not?" She smiled, grabbing her bags and following him out.

As they made their way from arts center to the faculty dining room located on the second floor of the Commons, he said, "So, what do you think about all this?"

"Do you mean Milt's death?"

"Milt's death, Junior Private Eye soon to be in our midst, police all over the place. Surreal, isn't it?"

"Unsettling, that's for sure."

"Not that anyone's sorry about Milt."

His sharp tone startled her. "His family must be devastated and I'm sure Susan is very upset."

"Surely you jest? Susan, upset about that bastard? After all he did to her?"

"Oh, I didn't know. Were they having—"

"Wait up you two!" Joan Nettleman called from behind them. Bess wondered if she had followed them out of the arts building and for how long she'd been within earshot.

"What's the latest? Do tell?"

Bess turned to spy Joan, hair wild, face beet red, dressed in a flowing caftan and matching slacks, in an alarming shade of orange. The effect was not flattering. Her companion shook his head, not even attempting to hide his disdain. He gave Bess a sidelong glance, rolling his eyes. She ignored him. "Hi, Joan. We didn't see you."

"Course you didn't in the middle of your cozy tete a tete."

Bess wondered why she bothered to be cordial to Joan since all she ever got in return was insults and sarcasm. "We were talking about Milt's death. Do you know anything about the service for him?"

Like troops falling into formation, Kevin LeBlanc fell in step beside them as they entered the Commons. In his mid-thirties, Kevin looked about 15, his pale skin dotted with freckles, brown curly hair tousled and sorely in need of a trim. He had always reminded Bess of Beaver Cleaver. It seemed incongruous, when he looked too young for the prom, that Kevin had been married and divorced, his former wife, Milt Wickie's girlfriend and lover. "Family's taking him back to Ohio for a funeral," he said, "But I imagine Peter will arrange a memorial here sometime this week. Maybe that's what this meeting's about."

"Like you'd know," Will said, eyes flashing fire in Kevin's direction.

As Bess wondered what she'd walked into, Joan muscled between her and Will, ignoring Kevin completely. "You wait, this is gonna be all about cooperating with Harry the super sleuth, who is rumored to be arriving this afternoon."

"If you'll excuse me, Bess, I have to talk to Todd before this starts." With that, Will hustled away to collar the upper school head at the buffet table. Joan quickly found someone more important and bustled off, leaving her standing with Kevin.

"Kevin? Is everything okay?"

He shrugged. "Everyone's on edge right now. Who knows what's eating him. Better get in the line, don't you think?"

She nodded, turning to use the ladies room before lunch. As she washed her hands, Juanita Hays, the Spanish pushed open the door. A striking woman, long, thick black hair braided halfway down her back, coal black eyes and flawless skin, her wardrobe was exotic, like she was, multi-colored, vibrant. Today, she wore a patchwork tunic in bright shades of red and gold, long black skirt and high heeled black boots. "Hey, Bess, how goes it?"

"Fine, thanks, and you?"

"I'd be careful with those two, if I were you."

"Excuse me?" This was turning into a most baffling day.

"Will and Kevin. They're at each other's throats right now. I'd steer clear."

"What's wrong?"

"Not sure, but I heard it was a woman."

"Any idea who?"

"A few, but I better not spread gossip."

"Of course." At that moment, Peter's secretary, Annie, who took faculty meeting minutes entered the bathroom. Bess nodded to Annie and Juanita, deciding it was time to get lunch, sit down and collect her thoughts.

As was customary in many Friends schools, the headmaster was not the Clerk of Faculty Meeting, even if he or she led a large portion of the meeting. At Old Harbor Friends, the clerkship rotated yearly and this year's Clerk was Jane Fellows. Once most people were seated with their plates, she opened the meeting, requesting people move into silence. Plates set aside, the room quieted for 10 minutes after which, Jane made several quick announcements, then called upon Peter, seated beside her, to continue with the agenda he had set for them.

Setting his plate on the sideboard, Peter removed his reading glasses, eyes scanning the room. "Thank you, everyone, for coming together in such a hasty, impromptu fashion. I am deeply grateful to one and all. A few of us could not make it, so please, do let everyone know the sum and substance of what we discuss.

"First, let me say how proud I am of all faculty and staff for the way people have pulled together after poor Milt's death. It is times like these when I am so enormously grateful to be at Old Harbor and when I realize how much I will miss you all.

"I brought us together for two reasons. One is to briefly discuss the impending arrival of Harry Winthrop, who will be quietly assisting us in the investigation of Milt's death. The other is next Tuesday's community forum and Milt's memorial service. Perhaps we should discuss these latter two first?

"Garrett, who could not join us today, and Will have agreed to facilitate this month's forum. Thank you, Will. Most of the Overseers will be there as well."

Bess turned at that moment to find Kevin LeBlanc alternately shaking his head and glaring at Will McGuire, who clearly would not have been his choice for facilitator. The facilitators' roles alternated each month, but clearly forum contributions next week would include the subject of murder. Whoever began and oversaw the discussion could maintain reasonable dialogue or incite chaos. Bess thought Will would be fine, but Garrett Rollins? What an odd choice.

Before she could take a survey of the room, her attention was diverted by Joan's outburst. "Garrett Rollins? Why in the world did you ask him? Most of the students haven't a clue who he is and he's a… well, let's just say he's not the most sensitive person in the world."

Pot calling the kettle black, Bess thought, turning with her colleagues to hear Peter's response.

"Actually, Joan, it was the Board's idea."

"Well, of course it was. He was Darrell's roommate at Amherst, for God sake. That doesn't mean we have to go along."

Darrell Rosen, an Overseer and outspoken critic of many school policies and the headmaster in particular, was a good friend and former classmate of Garrett. It was this relationship, in fact, that had no doubt landed Garrett the enviable, well-paid part-time job as archivist. "Peter, look, I know Darrell's been a thorn in your side, but do you have to roll over and play dead every time he opens his mouth?"

Watching Peter's face drain of color, Bess cried, "Joan!"

At this juncture, Jane, as Clerk, took charge. "Joan, I believe we will allow Peter to complete his report and then we will open the floor. Please wait until I call for questions and discussion."

Joan harrumphed, then fell silent, turning her attention to the huge plate of food she had in front of her.

Sitting taller, Peter took 30 seconds to collect himself, straightening papers in front of him. "As I was saying, Cornie Parmenter, as Board Chair, brought word from all the Overseers that they wanted Garrett to co-facilitate with a faculty member of my choosing and I asked Will who has generously agreed. The Forum will be held from 1-2 in the Field House. Obviously, those classes will not be held tomorrow. Those of you with morning classes, particularly those right before lunch, please remind students to head over to the Field House by 12:50.

"I have spoken briefly with Harry Winthrop and he plans to attend as does Sergeant Demaris from the police." He held up his hand. "Now before there's an outcry about that, remember—the Forum is not Meeting for Worship and there is not the sanctity of the meeting nor is there an expectation of confidentiality."

As a number of people stirred, Jane also raised her hand, perhaps sensing an outcry was coming. "We will have a time for discussion shortly."

Peter sighed and continued. "I have asked Garrett and Will to provide some framing questions. If you have ideas for them, please call or email, preferably by this evening."

"The Memorial for Milt will be next Wednesday at 3 PM. I do not anticipate many students, but they, of course are welcome. This is by no means required for anyone, but wanted you to be aware. Milt's family will not attend. Jean Davol has agreed to clerk." He referred to Jean Davol, an Overseer and one of three birthright Quakers on the Board.

"Finally, let me say that I am encouraged by the arrival of Mr. Winthrop, the younger. Contrary to the rumors that have been flying around, he does, indeed, have some experience with private investigating and seems to have a good head on his shoulders. When we were abroad last year, Carrie and I met him and were very impressed."

At the mention of Carrie Thurbert, Bess saw her dear friend, Jane stiffen. Jane had never liked Carrie, but would never give a reason for her obvious, undisguised antipathy.

"I would ask everyone to be forthcoming and welcoming to Harry while not spreading gossip. There have been any number of wild rumors swirling around the past few days. And, there always are the odd bits of unsubstantiated gossip on a campus like this, but I would ask everyone to operate from a place of decorum, honesty and factual revelations. I say this all with utmost appreciation for the difficult conversations that may be ahead for many of us as the police and Mr. Winthrop endeavor to learn what happened to poor Milt." With those words, he turned to Jane who called for questions.

A few people asked for protocol for the Forum or what they should say to students about the memorial, but the rumblings seemed to have subsided in regards to the Forum facilitation. There were few comments about the amateur sleuth descending upon them, but even those were tepid at best. By that time, most had finished lunch and appeared eager to get back to prepare for their two o'clock classes.

Bess walked out with Jane and Kitty Bigalow. Kitty taught physics and sometimes assisted Bess with coaching duties. Her husband was minister at the village congregational church. At least a decade older than his 45-year old wife, Rich Bigalow was Kitty's second husband. Between them, their blended family numbered six children ranging in age from 14 to 20. About Bess' height, Kitty was a strawberry blonde, attractive and stylish, her curvaceous figure accentuated in the pencil skirts and tight cashmere sweaters she favored. Today, she was dressed in a creamy cashmere turtleneck over blue and green tweed skirt and low heels, a scarf in teals and blues, tied jauntily round her neck.

"So, ladies," Kitty whispered, poking her companions. "What'dya think? Carrie says our sleuth is gorgeous. Are you two ready to rock?"

Jane rolled her eyes, giving Bess a look. "Really, Kitty, for a minister's wife, you are completely inappropriate."

"Oh, phooey, a girl can dream, can't she? Bess, what about you? What have you heard about Mr. Adonis?"

"I couldn't care less, Kitty, and hope my interactions with him will be short, sweet or completely unnecessary."

"Don't count on it, you being chief suspect and all."

Three students called to Bess, mercifully sparing her the need to answer Kitty. Meeting over. Back to class.

CHAPTER 16

Like the frenetic dance of a strobe, light filtered through the canopy of sycamores distorted oticular functions. Its effect on his body, restless unease and a wish to crawl into his skin and zip up tight. The Mercedes' speedometer climbed to ninety, but Harry pressed on, heedless of the danger. Driven by unseen demons, he hurdled down the winding road, not quite successful in outracing the pain. He had traveled halfway around the world, but his heart still ached with loss. His soul ravaged by grief, wandered the earth in search of peace. Would he finally find it here, at home?

To meet him, one would never guess Harry Winthrop was anything but the cheerful, easy-going soul he appeared to be. Always up for a good time, always ready to step in and help. However, there was darkness lurking beneath the cheery façade.

Inquisitive by nature, his investigating work of the past few years had not only provided distraction and respite from the pain, and it had been fun, a welcome change from teaching and the endless years of study. When Cornie Parmenter called, asking him to come to Old Harbor Friends, he'd jumped at the chance. Now, he was having second thoughts. At least, he could spend time with the old man.

Father and son were good friends and the separation had been hard on both of them. Although Harry wrote several times a week and called every Sunday at noon without fail, they were still worlds apart without the companionship of daily routine and the long talks by the fire in the evenings they both enjoyed. It would be good to see his father, even if coming home proved wrenching, the sorrow brought on just walking through the front door, catching sight of the familiar things.

The white Victorian perched on the bluffs was new, no painful memories lurking in its corners, however, every stick of furniture had come from the Beacon Hill house. The carved love seat covered in midnight blue velvet, had been his mother's favorite hiding place for Easter eggs. Colorful baskets in hand, Harry and his siblings had run to it, tiny fingers probing the carved recesses, extracting the eggs tucked between curlicues and polished bunches of mahogany grapes. His mother's harp, Jonathan's piano, Rachel's paintings and sculptures, they were everywhere. There was no escape. Why had his father kept it all?

After the accident, Harry had begged his father to get rid of things or at least put them away, but the old man wouldn't hear of it. Escaping to the obscurity of Old Harbor, he had sold both family homes, the Beacon Hill brownstone and the rambling beach house in Bar Harbor, but Harry Senior had been unable to part with the personal furnishings that framed his family's history.

"We're all that's left of the Winthrops, my boy. Who will remember if we don't? And, how are we to remember without all this?"

How indeed, Harry thought, screeching to a stop as several dozen Holsteins crossed the road, their bursting udders nearly scraping the ground as they trundled towards relief, waiting over the hill in the milking barn. The pungent scent of manure filled his nostrils as Harry glanced across the fields, a weathered rust-colored barn in the distance. The sight put him in mind of a barn in the Scottish highlands where he had slept, milked the cows for his supper and romanced the comely Jenny MacFarland. "Ah, my bonny Jen, where are ye now?" he said aloud, as the last of the black and white cows trundled through the gate, their master turning to doff his hat, before following his animals. With a wave, Harry drove on, his spirits temporarily lifted by the bucolic scene and the happy memories it had evoked.

Old Harbor, the quaint seaside village his father had grown to love so dearly over the last eight years, was unfamiliar territory to Harry. He had visited it once, for less than a week, soon after his father had moved in, but had noticed little and met no one. That had been less than a month after Stella's death and he'd been wrapped in grief, speaking to no one, eating little, hardly noticing the passage of time, his own body still healing from the accident he had caused. From Old Harbor, he'd gone to a Sanatorium in Switzerland, arranged by his father's physician. After almost a year, he had reentered life somehow, returned to his work.

The only people he knew in Old Harbor, aside from his father's household staff, were the Thurberts, whom he'd met several years earlier in St. Tropez. Harry's recollections of the headmaster and his wife were of two anxious souls, always looking over their shoulders, neither comfortable together nor conversing with him, a stranger. After dining together, the couple had seemed in a great hurry to be off and he did not see them again. Troubled, had been Harry's assessment, troubled and running away from something or someone.

Reaching his destination, he turned off the road, following the winding, tree-lined drive through the fields until the Mercedes began its climb to the top of the bluffs. The house came into view, its delicate gingerbread shone like gilded lace in the golden light of late afternoon and Harry breathed in the sea air, letting out a whoop. Tooting the horn, he brought the car to a stop opposite the front door. Home. He had missed it after all.

CHAPTER 17

Jane Fellows spent a restless night. The tension of the past week had driven her to distraction and the guilt, coupled with the need to confide in someone, made it impossible for her to sleep. It would have been so easy to tell Bess, her dearest friend, at dinner the other evening. Bess had known something was wrong, had given her the opening, but still Jane had kept silent. How could she tell her dirty little secret to Bess. Pure, chaste, loving Bess who still mourned her saint of a husband? Jane couldn't face the reproach in her friend's soft, kind eyes. Besides, Peter and Bess were friends. Oh, Lord, what will she think of me?

To make matters worse, Peter hadn't come to see her, hadn't spoken to her in passing, hadn't even called since Milt's death. She knew about the blackmail, Peter had told her about it months ago, but what did it matter now? To her knowledge, Milt, nosy, weasly little Milt was the only person aware of her relationship with Peter Thurbert. The only person who knew she and the headmaster had been having an affair for nearly eight years. Why hadn't she told Bess? She was going crazy! The thought of that glowering detective questioning her about their weekly trysts at the Capri Motel ten miles up the coast sent shivers up her spine.

Looking back on the beginnings of their relationship, Jane liked to think her motives had been pure. Befriending the lonely, troubled head whose cold, unfeeling spouse had lost interest in him or his dreams. "Carrie doesn't listen like you," he had whispered in the heady days when they'd first fallen in love. And, it had been love, hadn't it, not just close friendship with sex? Or was she one side of a tired, well-worn cliché? If anyone had told her before the affair began that she would fall so hopelessly in love, would care so deeply about his every thought, his inner turmoil, she would have called them crazy.

Why hadn't she broken it off? He would never leave Carrie like he promised repeatedly during the early years. Then, their lovemaking had been desperate and frenzied, stolen kisses in the hallway, whispered words of love, weekend rendezvous at her beach house. Now, like so many long relationships, the sex had become predictable and ordinary, a part of their weekly routine like attendance at church or grocery shopping, no more. The passion was gone.

It had been Peter who decided that the beach house was too risky, too close to school. He might be spotted coming or going by a student or teacher walking the beach. The Capri Motel had been his solution and eventually, their undoing. It turned out that one of Milt's girlfriends worked the night desk and Milt had spotted the lovers one night leaving the motel as he was checking in. Rather than confronting Jane, Wickie had gone straight to the person to whom his knowledge of the affair would hurt the most. As headmaster, Peter Thurbert was expected to be above reproach yet here he was in the middle of a sordid, "motel affair" with one of his teachers.

First, it had only been money that Milt wanted, then special privileges, better benefits. Finally, not satisfied with bleeding his boss dry, Wickie demanded the headmaster's resignation. At first, Peter had resisted, but when it became clear that Milt could and would not be put off, Peter had announced his intention to retire, effective at the close of the current school year. In his twisted, tortured mind, the conniving comptroller had designs on the position himself, although how he ever expected to succeed in his candidacy was beyond Peter's or Jane's comprehension. A search committee was hard at work screening applicants, whittling down the pool to about a dozen candidates who would be visiting the school within the next month or two and while Peter had not yet been privy to the committee's short list, he felt sure that Milt Wickie's name was not on it. Unless, of course, Milt had been blackmailing all members of the search committee, too.

It was no secret that Carrie Thurbert was disappointed in her husband's decision. Unaware of the real reason behind Peter's sudden wish for early retirement, she bitched and moaned to anyone who would listen about her impending, "premature exile." A social climber, Carrie had looked forward to at least five more years living in the baronial splendor of the Head's House, before retiring to the obscurity of their modest condominium in Bristol Bay, twenty miles south of Old Harbor. "I'm just not ready to go old," she was fond of saying, to anyone in earshot. The expression nauseated Jane.

CHAPTER 18

"That's enough Pete." Demaris shoved the sheaf of papers, notes and statements (transcribed and color coded by Lottie, his secretary) into his well-worn L.L.Bean briefcase, a gift from Mary their first Christmas together. When it was new he'd hated it, the bright, kelly green canvas a stark contrast to his usual attire — khakis, grey sweats and faded denims. They'd been in love then, however, so every day he carried the accursed bag to work so as not to hurt her feelings. Now, eight years later, its colors faded and the straps frayed, it suited him. Unlike his marriage, the bag was still in one piece.

"I'll be out at the school all afternoon. Tell Lottie she can get me there if she needs me. She's out on one of her five hour lunch breaks."

"Want me to come along?"

"Nope." Demaris eyed his assistant over reading glasses perched at the edge of his nose. The look he gave Dugan was far from cordial. It said, "watch out" loud and clear. "I already told you — I want you over at the bank, checking the school's accounts. And, for Chrissakes, quit lookin' at me like I'm a fuckin' charity case. The woman's ancient history, period, end of story."

"Why is it I don't believe you?"

"Fuck you, Dugan, now get outta here. And I'm goin' straight home after I finish with Mrs. Dore," he yelled as Pete walked out of the office. "So you won't be able to study my face for signs of despair or suicidal tendencies."

"What's with him?" Kate Blake, the desk sergeant asked as Dugan passed by the desk.

"Don't ask," Pete muttered, slamming the door on his way out.

Driving through town, Demaris ran through the previous week. He and his men had conducted hours of interviews and what did they have? Zip. Now this rich Bozo'd waltz in and trample over what little evidence they had, confusing people, getting in the way. Then again, maybe they'll all spill their guts, 'fess up and the Junior P.I.'d make the killer. Then they could wrap up the friggin' case and get the hell outta there, everyone looking down their friggin' noses at him and his men.

Before his meeting with Bess, he had an appointment with Susan LeBlanc, Milt's paramour at the time of his death. Since moving out of the dorm and her marriage, Mrs. LeBlanc lived in a rented condo at the beach and she'd been one tough lady to pin down. They'd made numerous attempts to reach her at home, at the gym where she taught aerobics classes and at her arts and crafts shop in town, but all efforts had thus far been unsuccessful.

After a week of "oh, you just missed her", or "sorry, this is her day off" and Mrs. LeBlanc's silky voice on answering machines inviting them to leave a message, Demaris had had enough. He dispatched a man to the condo to lay in wait till he spotted her. Once he'd collared the elusive Mrs. LeBlanc, the officer had politely requested, then insisted, that she call the station, even offering to dial the number himself. After all the trouble she'd taken to avoid interrogation, Demaris decided this was one interview he should handle himself.

Eating a quick lunch at Ellie's Diner, he hopped back in the jeep and headed out to Atlantic Avenue. "Ask Susan, why don't you?" had been Carol Richards' suggestion on the night of Milt's death when Demaris had asked who she thought might have killed the comptroller.

Demaris shuddered recalling the interview with the indignant business manager. Carol Richards had declined his request to take a seat, instead pacing back and forth, her red heels clicking on the linoleum floor of the Coop, a stiletto-heeled army marching through his head, keeping perfect step with his rapidly escalating migraine.

"Could you please have a seat, Ms. Richards," he had pleaded in his gentlest voice.

"No, I could not!" Her scream added insult to injury and his head had nearly exploded.

Attempting to ignore the pain and the growing nausea that invariably accompanied it, he'd begun, the slow, patient peeling back of the layers, inching along the arduous road towards the truth. He knew that this first interrogation would barely scratch the surface. No way this lady was spillin' her guts tonight in her state of indignation, but he had to begin somewhere. "So, tell me about your colleague."

"If you're referring to Milt, he was not my colleague. Colleague to me implies that the person is someone with whom you collaborate. I'd sooner have collaborated with a cocker spaniel than that moron! No, my dear, Sergeant Demaris, Milt Wickie was my assistant, not my collaborator. I told him what to do and he did it."

"Is that the usual function of a comptroller?" he asked, knowing full well it was not.

"I don't know, nor do I give a shit what the usual function of a comptroller is. I organized my office to suit my needs."

"Don't you mean the school's needs?" Demaris made a mental note to check the school accounts as well as Ms. Richards bank statements.

"Give me a break, will you? It's late and I've had an incredibly long day so, if there's nothing else, I'd like to go to bed."

"We'd all like to be in bed," he had said, smiling through clenched teeth. "Just a few more questions then my assistant will walk you home."

"And, another thing. Why the hell did I have to be last? I arrived before most of those people and I—"

"Ms. Richards, if you'd let me ask the questions, we'll all get to bed sometime soon."

As she swished by for the hundredth time he wondered if she'd taken a bath in perfume. Click, click, click, his stomach had rolled over. "So what exactly did Mr. Wickie do for you?"

"Accounts receivable, accounts payable. All that was Milt's responsibility, and believe me, that was all he could handle."

"How 'bout the budget, long range plans for the school's needs? I know there's been a lot of building these past seven years what with Mr. Winthrop's hefty gifts and all."

"All mine. I wouldn't have dreamed of allowing that imbecile to touch the budget! He could barely handle the few jobs he had. He used to be in charge of all faculty and staff compensation, making out the checks, arranging for deductions, and so forth but, he got things so screwed up that I had to step in and take that away from him."

"What kind of screw-ups we talkin' about?"

"You name it, Milt screwed it up. Paychecks misprinted, the dates all wrong, benefits neglected, overcharges, under payments — what he did to our pension funds would make your hair curl — social security was breathing down our necks for months. The man was hopeless."

"Why'd you keep him then?"

She hesitated just a second, but long enough. Demaris sat back, waiting for the lie.

"Peter loves him. Peter Thurbert, our headmaster. God knows why, but he does. So I've been saddled with Milt, my own personal albatross."

"Can you give me an account of your whereabouts this afternoon and evening?"

"This is absurd. If you think for one minute that I'm going to stand around and listen to this, you're sadly mistaken. Why I—"

"Ms. Richards," he had whispered, seeing her now through a seething red lens of pain. "It was your choice to stand, there's a chair right there, now let's cut the crap, shall we? It's a routine question, we ask everyone the same thing, so you're not getting any special treatment. You have two choices. You can either tell me what you've been up to the past few hours or you can come along to the station and do your "clicking heels act" in one of the cells."

"Why, of all the nerve! You —"

"Okay, that's it. Pete, take her away."

Before Dugan could step out of the shadows, Carol Richards began a rambling, but detailed account of her afternoon and evening's activities. Straight home from the office, saw no one on the way, hadn't seen or talked to Milt since before lunch, hadn't gone out, had a quiet supper in front of television. "And," she added, finally. "I received no calls until the one from Suzie instructing me to hurry over here."

"Suzie?"

"Suzie Millman, the switchboard operator."

As he'd watched Dugan escort the business manager out of the building, Demaris thought to himself, "With her for a boss, old Milt's better off dead." His subsequent meetings with Carol Richards during the past week had done nothing to dispel this initial impression. The woman was a bitch.

CHAPTER 19

On Atlantic Avenue now, he slowed down reading the house numbers. Number eighteen, Susan LeBlanc's house was an enormous turn-of-the-century summer "cottage", now converted into three upscale condominiums with spectacular ocean views. He swung the jeep into the circular clam shell drive and parked. The house's weathered shingles blended perfectly with the surroundings, the muted colors of marsh grasses and dunes and the sparkling blue of the ocean beyond. A row of straight-backed rockers, freshly painted dark green to match the cottage's trim, invited guests to linger on the wide, open porches circling the house on three sides. Maybe I ought to change professions, Demaris mused, making his way up the flagstone walk, I had no idea aerobics and arts and crafts paid so well.

He stood on the porch ringing and knocking for at least five minutes before she finally appeared. "Oh, hi," came a sultry drawl from the other side of the screen door. "Come on back."

Demaris followed through the house, his hostess a wisp of a shadow in the dim light as his eyes struggled to readjust after the bright sun outdoors. They passed through a sleek, European style kitchen, all chrome and black marble and stepped out into a plant-filled solarium. Only then did she turn to face him. "Iced tea?"

"Sure, great," he mumbled, startled at the apparition in front of him, so different from what he'd expected. Doesn't look like Milt's type, he mused as she busied herself with the glasses. Conservative, natty little Milt alongside, who did she

remind him of? Of course, he thought, marveling at the resemblance. Morticia.
Dressed from head to toe in black, black suede Mary Janes, black leggings, silky
black tunic top and her hair, straight and very long streaked with white, she bore
a remarkable resemblance to the Charles Addams character.

As she sliced lemons and poured the tea, he gazed around. The room was
done in sage green and corals, over stuffed couches and chairs, a wicker rocker, its
cushions covered in pale floral chintz, sisal rug and several huge urns filled with
pampas grass. The dunes and marsh grasses outside were an integral part of the
room's decor, a restful summer retreat, out of the wind and weather. At one end of
the room, there was a glass-topped, wrought iron table with two matching chairs
finished in the same verdigris finish as the statuary scattered around the room.
Picking up one of the chairs, he turned to his hostess, "May I?"

"Of course." She batted thick, industrial-grade eyelashes. "But, it's much
more comfortable over here." She patted the cushion beside her, stretching catlike
across the sofa.

Well, well, he thought, wondering where he would fit if he decided to take her
up on the offer. At least she was friendlier than the others. That was something.
"Thanks, but this'll be fine. Now then, Mrs. LeBlanc."

"Oh, please, call me Susan. All my friends do."

"Susan, how long have you and Mr. Wickie been seeing each other?"

"Long enough," she purred. More eyelash batting.

"What's that supposed to mean?"

Sitting up, clearly annoyed at his sharp tone, she snapped, "Long enough for
me to decide to ditch my husband and move out permanently."

"How long would that have been exactly?"

"Well, let's see, I started seeing Milt about a year ago. It, we started. Let's
just say we 'found each other' a year ago September."

"How did that come about?"

"Is it really necessary for you to know that? I mean, what relevance does it
have to this?"

"You're right, sorry," he said, putting on his best display of contrition. "Please go on."

"I moved out, of our apartment in the dorm last summer."

"Your decision or did your husband give you the boot?"

"What a delicate way of putting it, detective. I'm only sorry my answer can't be as colorful. Kevin did not 'give me the boot.' I left. It was very hard. Kevin is, well, anyway, we'd been married for nine years. We had, what I mean is, we, we, it was good in the beginning and then, it wasn't." She shuddered, looking away, losing her composure for just an instant. He couldn't tell if her distress was genuine, but if not, he decided she was a pretty good actress.

"Anyway," she continued, shrugging thin, pointed shoulders, "I just couldn't take dorm life any longer. Truth is, I used Milt as an excuse. I wanted out, Kevin didn't. And, Milt and I had fun. We weren't starry-eyed lovers or anything, but it was a gas. He made me laugh and that's something Kevin hadn't managed to do for a long time. Believe me, I went into the relationship with my eyes open. I knew Milt, knew his reputation with women. It was all a big game with him, racking up points on his sexual scoreboard. The man wasn't capable of sustaining a long term relationship, no way. I had no illusions. I knew he didn't love me, wasn't capable of it but, hell, we had a good time and the sex was great. Should've been, for God sakes," she snorted, "He'd certainly had enough practice!"

"You met here, did you?"

"After I moved out."

"How 'bout before? When you were still living on campus?"

"Is this how you get your jollies, sergeant, probing into people's love lives? What possible relevance can this have to Milt's death?"

"Let me worry about that. For now, everything is relevant", he said, quietly.

"Fine, whatever you say." She leaned towards him. The front of her tunic was unbuttoned almost to her waist and she was not wearing a bra. Taking his eyes from hers for an instant, he glanced down at a surprisingly muscular chest and firm, rounded breasts.   Aerobics, he decided, looking up, expecting to find smug, satisfaction in her eyes.   He was not disappointed.

"We met at various spots.   Milt's office, the woods, motels around the area, once in his apartment, but he was petrified the boarders had seen me going in so we never tried that again.   In the early days, we'd have each other anywhere, closets, hallways, men's rooms, you name it.   Then as time went by, passions cooled and we became more discreet, if you know what I mean.   More boring, let's face it."

Keeping his eyes above her neck, he asked, "So?   What now?"

"I'll get over it.   I don't need a man around to give meaning to my life."

"What about this place?   Can you afford it without Milt's help?"

"Oh, my God, where have you been getting your information?   You think I'm a kept woman?   You think poor, pathetic Milt was footing the bill for all this?   Oh, that is rich."   She laughed, a genuine guttural laugh that Demaris found rather appealing.   When she smiled, she looked younger, prettier.   "If you think Milt paid one cent to keep me, my dear Detective Demaris, you've been grossly misinformed.   Why that cheap sonofabitch rarely bought me dinner, never mind helpin' out with the rent.

"No honey, this is all mine.   My money, or my parents, at least.   They're deceased.   I was an only child and they were well-off.   I've got plenty, believe me. That's another reason Kevin and I split.   We could've bought this or rented it together to use on weekends and summers, but no, he couldn't tear himself away from the kids.   He had to be in that God forsaken dorm all the time.   Christ, I hated that place."

"Think you're in Milt's will?"

"Surely you jest?   Milt probably left everything to the school or maybe one of his old girlfriends."

"Why is that, do you think?"

"Well, he knew I didn't need it, for one thing."

"Who would these girlfriends be exactly?"

"I wouldn't even know where to begin, there were so many. The man was a lech. He put the make on every woman on campus and most in town at one time or other."

"So who played along?"

"Off the top of my head? Well, let's see, there was Joanie, you know, the art teacher."

"Nettleman?"

"Poor Joanie, what he ever saw in her, I'll never know."

"Was he still seeing Ms. Nettleman?"

"You're kidding, right? Have you seen her? The woman's the size of a pregnant hippo and Milt liked 'em skinny, or at least small enough to get his lecherous arms around. No, that affair was at least five years ago. Joan was actually kinda cute back then. But, when Milt broke it off, she went berserk, ate everything in sight. She was devastated, pestered him constantly, me, too. Always calling, writing letters. A tiresome, pathetic woman. Have you spoken to her yet? I'm sure she still holds a grudge."

Ignoring the question, he went on, "How 'bout other women?"

Mischief danced in the violet eyes. "Well, he made a brief attempt to seduce the grieving widow, prim and proper Mrs. Dore. Long before my time, of course. He always thought I didn't know, but I have my sources. I make it my business to know things like that, if you know what I mean? I like to know who I'm dealing with. Can't be too careful nowadays, with AIDS and all."

"And, who might those sources be?"

"Now, that'd be telling, wouldn't it Roger?" She leaned forward again.

"What do you know about Mrs. Dore?"

"You're interested in her, aren't you?" She smiled, pleased at the reaction she'd gotten. The poker face wasn't infallible after all.

"Mrs. LeBlanc, I'm interested in anyone with a connection to this case and the victim. This is a murder investigation, not a garden party. Now, if you would please answer the question."

"No need to get testy. From what I hear old Milt wasn't too successful with Bess. Goodness knows he tried, but she was into heavy mourning, still is, from what I hear. They may've gone out a few times, but whatever they had was short-lived, like most of Milt's liaisons."

"How long ago was this?"

"Six, maybe seven years ago. Pre-Joanie."

"How 'bout more recently?"

"Well, there's Kitty Bigalow. Physics, Upper School. That was a couple of years ago. Kitty was a true conquest for Milt, a real feather in his cap. Married with six kids, husband's a minister. It was only a brief fling as far as I know and then Milt dumped her. She went crying back to hubby, he forgave her and they kissed and made up."

"What about the past year?"

Anger flashed, turning her violet eyes darker, but she quickly harnessed it, a Cheshire cat smile masking the fury. "I've kept him very busy the past year. He barely had time to come up for air."

Bullshit, Demaris thought. Old Milt was screwing around and Ms. Just-Out-For-A-Good-Time didn't like it. Unfortunately, if there was someone else, he wasn't going to hear about it from Susan LeBlanc. "So, at the time of his death he was seeing you exclusively?"

"Asked and answered."

"So where were you, last week, the afternoon and evening of Milt's death?"

"You can't be serious. My dear detective, why do you think I'm wearing black? I'm in mourning. He may have been a louse, but he was my louse. I was devastated by Milt's death. Besides, do I look like a murderer?"

Like a cat poised and ready to pounce on a mouse, he thought. "Look, Mrs. LeBlanc, I'm not unsympathetic, but it's routine. We ask everyone the same question."

"That's crap and you know it! Bet you didn't ask your precious Bess Dore that question? Oh, yes, detective, I've got my sources in town, too. I know all about your high school romance."

Refusing to take the bait, he pressed on, "As a matter of fact, we didn't need to ask Mrs. Dore that particular question. Her whereabouts were accounted for."

"How convenient for both of you."

"Look Mrs. Le Blanc, could we get back to the matter at hand? Where exactly were you the afternoon and evening of Mr. Wilkie's death?"

"I was at the gym teaching all afternoon, till nine. Then I came straight home. Alone."

"Anyone vouch for all that?"

"My students, but I'd rather they weren't bothered. They're intense, busy people." She smiled, reminding him of Cruella DeVille from the Disney film he had recently watched with his nephew.

"Your gym is?"

"Harbor Gym." She rose, as he did.

"Don't get up, I'll see myself out."

"Oh, no trouble at all." She rested her hand on his arm. "I'll walk you out."

"Mrs. LeBlanc, more than likely, I'll be back."

"How lovely. I'll look forward to it." As they strolled through the house, she brushed against him repeatedly. "I'm always at your disposal," she purred as they reached the door.

"Better have a chat with your students, let 'em know we're coming in. We'll need to talk to them either way. We'll try to be brief."

"How gallant of you." She waved as he made his way to the jeep, not at all sorry to see the back of her.

Old Milt had his hands full with that one, he mused pulling out of the driveway. I wouldn't want to be around when she found out he was cheating on her either.

CHAPTER 20

Bess sat across from Amy Flathers. The ninth grader was perched bird-like on a tall stool made for Bess by a former student in woodshop. Instead of tapering, the legs went straight down, making it a precarious perch.

"So, what's up, Amy?"

"It's about Mr. Wickie." Amy stared down at her hands and Bess followed her gaze, half-expecting to see her shredded handkerchief still writhing in Amy's grasp.

"It was an awful experience, I know. Still not sleeping?"

"No, it's not that. That's not why I wanted to talk to you. You see, Mr. Bridgham is my advisor, but he's hard to find and I don't. Well, I thought it'd be easier to talk to you, Mrs. Dore." Tears welled in the brown eyes as the stool pitched forward and Bess reached out, grabbing her, both of them crashing to the floor in a tangle of arms and legs. Helping Amy up, Bess suggested they adjourn to the couch in her office. Once settled, she patted Amy's hand. "What is it, dear?"

"It's Mr. Wickie. He tried to, last year, right after I got here. I was so homesick and I'd went to the orchard almost every afternoon to cry. So the other girls wouldn't see me. When they caught me crying, they made fun and called me a baby. Mr. Wickie found me there one day and he was so kind. He took me into town to the diner and we drank hot chocolate and I told him about home. He didn't laugh at me and he listened, like he was interested, like he really cared. Then —" She stopped, swallowing hard.

"One day just before dinner, he asked me to go for a drive. By then, I was feeling better. I'd been home for a weekend and it was only a week till Thanksgiving vacation. Plus, I'd made some friends and I wasn't so bummed.

"He stopped me on my way back to the dorm, after field hockey practice. I said, thanks, but I didn't think I could go. He looked a little hurt and then I felt bad. Not bad enough to go, 'cause Sarah and I had plans, but anyway, I needed to get back and I said so. He said he understood, but would I just come and sit in the car for a minute and talk to him. I didn't want to, but I figured he'd been so nice and all that I owed him at least a few minutes.

"I got in and he told me to shut the door 'cause it was cold. I did and he —" She fought for control her whole body trembling as the tears welled in her eyes again. "He had one of those automatic locks, you know? Where you push a button and lock all the doors. I was surprised when he did that and I turned to ask him why and he just started grabbing at me. It was awful." Amy buried her face in her hands and Bess put her arms around her.

"He grabbed at me and ripped my shirt open. I started screaming, but he wasn't saying anything, not a sound, just breathing hard and grabbing at me, putting his face on my chest, kissing me there. I kicked and scratched, but he was strong and he started to get on top of me. He put his hand over my mouth so I couldn't scream. I couldn't breathe. Then, I just closed my eyes and thought about home, hoping he'd let me go when he was done and that's when it happened."

"What?" she asked, afraid to hear what Amy would say next. "Someone smashed his back window, some of the glass even sprinkled on us. The car's alarm went off. It made an awful noise. Then, he unlocked the door and shoved me out. Almost ran me over he drove away so fast."

"Did you see who'd smashed the window?"

"No. I looked around, but there was no one there. I heard voices on the far side of the parking lot, but I ran. I was so ashamed and I didn't want anyone to see me with my blouse all ripped."

"Did you tell anyone about this?"

"Only Sarah. She's the one that told me I should talk to you."

"Amy, you need to tell the police. Sergeant Demaris will want to know about this."

"No, then my parents will find out."

"That's alright, you did nothing wrong. They'll want to know, to comfort you and the police, too. Did Mr. Wickie ever bother you again?"

"No, never. He never even looked at me again, never said hello or anything. Oh God, Mrs. Dore," she wailed, "What if they think I killed him?"

"Amy, don't worry. I can assure you, they'll think no such thing. Now, come on, I'll walk you over to class, okay?" Offering the Kleenex box one more time, Bess helped Amy to compose herself before they left the studio together. "Don't worry," she said, depositing Amy at the door of her history class. "Sergeant Demaris doesn't bite. He'll be grateful for this information, I guarantee it."

Chapter 21

Bess walked Amy out and spied Billy Blackburn crossing the campus green with a shovel and rake. She waved and he stopped, allowing her to reach him. "Hi, Billy. Finally, a nice day."

"Yup." He gave her a shy smile, setting down the shovel and resting his elbow on the rounded wooden handle. "Thanks for dinner last night. With everything going on, it was kind of you to remember."

"Probably needed salt," she said, thinking about the chicken and rice casserole and whether she had made it too bland.

"Nope, was perfect. We loved it. Can probably get another meal out of it, too."

"Billy, what do you think about all this? About Milt's death? Did you or Lou see or hear anything that night?"

He shook his head. "We were watching the basketball game, Celtics. Lou's getting hard of hearing so he had the television cranked up to top volume."

She smiled, wondering how much Lou followed anything on television, basketball or otherwise. "Well, I won't keep you. I'm thinking meatloaf next week. Would that be okay?"

"One of our favorites!" He waved the rake, setting off in the opposite direction as Bess made her way across campus to the front entrance of the classroom building where she had arranged to meet Roger Demaris.

When she reached the entryway, Roger was nowhere in sight so she sat on one of the benches that flanked the doorway, pulled out her Anne Greyson mystery, hoping Helen's intrepid sleuthing might pull her away from the present. If only Helen were here, she mused. She'd get to the bottom of things. Bess smiled, opening the book.

Students passed in and out and a few faculty members, but for the most part, she read uninterrupted, except by the occasional nod or hello as someone passed. That is until Ramona Stark, the athletic director, approached. "Bess, hi, I've been looking for you."

Closing her book, she looked up. "Hi, Ramona. I've been meaning to call you about field hockey."

Ramona had been director for two years, bringing organization to what had been a very disorganized, haphazard sports program under the old director. Just over five feet, a sprinter in high school and college, she had retained the lean, sinewy look into adulthood. Bess wasn't sure, but guessed Ramona to be in her late thirties. One could never tell with people like Ramona who had probably been "old souls" since their toddler days. Her long, auburn hair was tied in a haphazard ponytail and she wore an Old Harbor warm-up suit and what appeared to be brand new running shoes. Not exactly pretty, Ramona was a handsome woman. Never married, and, to Bess' knowledge, seldom dated. She waved her hand in dismissal. "No problem. Meredith told me you guys have switched for a couple of weeks, right?"

"Seemed easier, if that's okay. And she needs coverage in January, for volleyball, while she's away. Not my sport, but I can probably hold down the fort."

"No, no, that's okay. I didn't want you for that. I just wondered what you'd heard about the murder and all."

Surprised, Bess studied her colleague, wondering what had prompted this burst of friendship. "Oh? Probably not any more than you do."

"But, you were there. Did you see anybody? Hear anything? I mean, before the kids found him?"

"No, nothing."

"What about other faculty or people in the building? You must have seen someone?" Ramona's eyes sparkled as she gestured and Bess wondered again what was going on.

"No, I didn't see a soul. Do you know something, Ramona? If you do, you should tell the police."

"Me, no, why?" Hands on hips, Ramona looked left and right, before her eyes met Bess' again. "Just curious, that's all. We never hear anything over at the gym, till weeks after the rest of the campus. Kids have been abuzz, of course, but what do they know?"

"Well, hopefully with the police and Mr. Winthrop looking into things, someone will get to the truth."

"What about him? Have you met him yet?"

"No, but I expect we'll all have the pleasure over the next few days."

"Got that right. I'm having dinner with Sam Spade at Todd and Sheila's tomorrow."

"Me, too."

"Well, at least there'll be one normal person there. Listen, gotta go. See you at the Bridghams if not before." Ramona jogged off and Bess returned to her book, relieved to return to Helen's comforting companionship and orderly investigation.

CHAPTER 22

"Damn," Demaris muttered. The clock on the dash read ten minutes after four. He was late. A stickler for punctuality, he cursed himself for dawdling with Susan LeBlanc. Of all appointments to be late for, he sighed, heading up Orchard Hill. As he reached the crest of the hill, the headmaster's home came into view to his right.

In sharp contrast to the stark simplicity of the rest of the campus building, the Thurberts' home was a large, rambling farmhouse in the gothic style. A three story tower facing east looked out over the fields and orchards to the ocean beyond and large walls of glass on its east and south sides provided the Head of School with vistas that encompassed practically every inch of school property. The house, built by a whaling captain at the turn of the century, had originally stood across the road on the old Westgate estate. When the Westgates died off, the property was sold, but no one wanted the "old dinosaur" and the house had been bought and moved across the street to its current spot in the 1930's so that the headmaster at the time, Jacob Rollings, could move his family out of the dorm and into their own home.

Demaris gave the house nary a glance as he drove through the front gates, nearing colliding with a cyclist exiting the campus. "Watch where you're going!" Joan Nettleman called, setting feet down, struggling not to fall over.

Now that's something you don't see every day, Demaris mused, stopping to make his apology. "So sorry, Ms. Nettleman, didn't see you." How did I miss? "You okay?"

"No, I am not okay! You nearly killed me."

"Would you like a ride? I can throw the bike in my car and —"

"No, I would not. I'm out for a bike ride, so if you don't mind, I'll continue." With that, she regained her seat and miraculously rode off with surprising agility.

Smiling, Roger watched her disappear around a bend in the road before getting back in his car. He parked in the small visitor's lot adjacent to the administrator's building, so late now that he wondered if she would still be around.

She's just another suspect, he told himself, hopping out of the car, breaking into a run. That's what he'd told Pete, but who was he kidding? His whole body went into meltdown every time he looked at her. Even after twenty-five years, Bess still had that effect on him.

Rounding the corner of the classroom building, he collided head-on with the groundskeeper, the man and his rake crashing to the ground in a heap along with the policeman. His victim let out a whoop, at the same time flailing out with both hands and feet. The rough, calloused hands scratched and clawed. "Keep away! Keep away! I'm safe! I'm safe!"

"Jesus Christ, man, I'm sorry." Demaris helped him to his feet.

"Get away! Get away! I'm safe! I'm safe!"

"Course you are, 'course you are. Look, I'm really sorry." He recognized his victim. It was the man they called Crazy Louie. At the moment he seemed to be living up to the name. "It's okay, really. I'm a policeman, see?" He held his wallet out, badge inches from Louie's face. "I won't hurt you, honest. That was stupid of me. All my fault, not lookin' where I was goin'. Don't blame you for bein' pissed off."

"I saw her, I saw her. Must stop her, must stop her. Not again, not again!"

"Saw who? What do you have to stop? What don't you want to happen again? Is it something to do with Mr. Wickie's death?"

"Don't pay him any mind." The voice from behind startled him. Demaris turned to find a tall, dark haired young man smiling at him. At least a head taller, in his late twenties early thirties, he reminded Demaris of his brother Michael. The same broad shoulders, dark curly hair and deeply tanned face, already etched like sand-carved canyon walls from long hours in the wind and sun. Despite the chill of the afternoon, he was dressed in an Old Harbor Friends tee shirt, an azure cobra tattoo slithering down his muscular right arm. Done by a real pro, Demaris, mused, admiring the tattoo. The man's denim work pants, permanently stained with grass, grease and oil, were ripped in several places and Demaris wondered absently why the school didn't spring for a couple of uniforms. From the look of things, both men needed 'em. Maybe it wasn't the Quaker way.

"Billy Blackburn," the other said, extending his hand. "I'm head groundskeeper. Me and Louie are partners, ain't we Lou?"

"Partners," the other man mumbled, nodding his head. "Partners, me and Bill."

"So, what's he mean by that? When he says he saw her?"

"I saw — " Louie started, but the other cut him off.

"No tellin'. Might be talkin' 'bout his ole lady, died a while back. Or, might just as easily be talkin' 'bout somethin' he saw on T.V. It's pretty hard to tell with Louie, ain't that right, Lou?" No response, lost in thought Louie was miles away.

"Could he have seen somethin' last week do you think? The day Wickie was killed? Did one of my men question him?"

"I think they did, but I wouldn't guess he made a lot of sense. Hard to drag much outta Lou."

Intrigued, Demaris watched Billy Blackburn, wondering about his background. One minute the man sounded crude and unschooled, throwing in the 'ain'ts and garbling up his grammar, the next minute, refined, educated. The detective knew a little bit about this kind of inconsistency since his own speech, a carefully cultivated mix of vulgarity and colloquialisms, had taken a long time to perfect. Sometimes, when he was tired or anxious, he blew his cover and slipped back into proper usage. Was this the case with Billy Blackburn?

"Don't know him, I'm safe."

"He's a little shook up right now. Maybe you could talk to him later?"

"Sure, I gotta get going anyway. Listen Lou, I'm sorry, man, catch you later, okay?"

"Okay." The old gardener turned back to his raking.

"See you around," he called back over his shoulder. He jogged along the side of the building, this time slowing as he reached the front entrance.

CHAPTER 23

"Roger, I'm here." She rose out of the shadows where she had been sitting on one of the white, wooden benches that flanked the entryway. Her slight frame looked lost in an old, mustard-colored canvas jacket, several sizes too big. Mac's, he decided, gazing down at the slender wrists at sea in the cuffs of the jacket's wide, gaping sleeves.

"Bess, I'm sorry. I was late to begin with, then I had a collision with Joan Nettleman on a bicycle, no less."

She smiled. "It's a cycling campus. Lots of us ride to and from work or for pleasure. The village really does need to put in a bike path."

"I'll take that up with the Selectmen. Really, I am sorry. After I practically killed Ms. Nettleman, I ran into the gardener. Scared him, I think."

"Louie, yes, I saw you." She smiled, gathering the coat around her as she walked towards him.

So incredibly soft and beautiful, he thought, his chest constricting. "Is it too late? Do you have to be somewhere?"

"I'm at your disposal. My studio's empty, do you want to talk in there?"

"I'd rather be outside, if you don't mind. Can we just take a walk or something?"

In answer, she started walking along the path leading to the apple orchards that stretched for ten acres to the easternmost boundaries of the campus property. Old Harbor Friends was still a working farm and all students, day and boarders, were given daily chores. Besides the orchards there were livestock to care for, fifty dairy cows, several dozen chickens, eight pigs, various and sundry goats.

Supervised by the farm's overseer, the students fed the animals, milked the cows, slopped the pigs, made cheese and butter, cleaned stalls and coops, gathered eggs and pitched in to help at slaughtering time. In the spring months, students planted over five acres of vegetables, herbs and flowers. The summer session students harvested and replanted, helping to run the school's roadside stand. All the school's extra produce, eggs and dairy products were sold at the farm stand or at the village's Farmers Market. A self-sustaining operation, the farm provided valuable work experience for the students as well as a little extra money for school trips, travel abroad programs and scholarships.

"So you still doin' your glass work?"

"Not really," she replied, surprised at his question. "I've been painting, water-colors mostly. It's been fun and something I haven't done since college. I've had a few commissions, but the stained glass windows were something Mac and I did together."

"You were the artist. My God, Bess, you have incredible talent."

"I grew tired of it, that's all." End of subject. In the orchard now, and she sat down on one of the stone benches. The polished granite seats were placed strategically along the crest of the hill inviting people to sit and enjoy the view. "So? What did you want to see me about?"

"Bess, I need your help." There, he'd said it. It wasn't so hard. "These people won't talk to me."

"Who?"

"All of 'em. The Richards woman, the teachers, Thurbert. They answer in monosyllables, then clam up like oysters in heat."

She smiled, her gaze mischievous. "I never knew that about oysters."

"Kidding aside, everyone on this campus seems to have taken a course in the fine art of dead air and I need you to loosen 'em up."

"What makes you think they'll talk to me?"

"Of course they'll talk to you. They know you and more importantly, they trust you."

"They won't trust me long if I start asking a lot of pointed questions. And, someone like Carol Richards? Why, I barely know her. We've both been at the school for a good many years, but she'd go crazy if I started asking probing questions."

"Well, then leave her to me. You seem to be pretty tight with Thurbert though."

"Tight? I don't know about that. Peter's a good friend but I don't know how I could help there. What is it that you think he's not telling you?"

"Damned if I know. That's why I'm askin' you. The guy won't say a thing to me except Milt did his job. What the hell's that 'sposed to mean?"

"I don't know, but that sounds like Peter. We all know Milt was no saint, but Peter always tries to see the best in people. He wasn't raised a Friend, a Quaker, I mean. He's Old Harbor Friends' first non-Quaker Head, but he does believe in the Quaker principles and practice. He really believes in the divine light in each person and he looks for it. He finds it, too. That's one of his greatest strengths."

Saint Peter, Demaris thought. "What about you? Do you see the divine light, too?"

"I try."

"Mac converted ya, huh?"

"Yes, I suppose he did. It wasn't difficult."

"So, how difficult is it for you to see the divine light in Carol Richards?"

"As I said, I don't know her well."

"Come on, Bess. The lady's a first class bitch, excuse my language. What about Wickie? What was he really like?"

"On the surface, friendly and self-effacing. Underneath, he struck me as rather superficial and mean-spirited, but again, I didn't know him well. He seemed to do his job and beyond that I couldn't —"

"You dated him, Bess."

Startled by the change in his tone rather than the words themselves, she stared at him, trying to read his expression. "Excuse me?"

"Susan LeBlanc and others say you dated the guy."

"Well, they're wrong."

"Okay, then why do you 'spose they're sayin' it?"

"How would I know? And, more to the point, how would Susan or anyone else for that matter know what I was doing? What kind of gossip have you been listening to? You're a fool if you think —"

"Hold on now."

"Hold on, nothing." She stood up, hands on hips. "I did not date, nor did I have an affair with Milt, though clearly you're implying that I did. If you think I'm going to sit here while you go on —"

"Truce, please. I'm sorry." He grabbed hold of both her wrists, forcing her to sit down. "All I want you to do is tell me about it. Give me your version, so that we can clear this up, okay?"

"It has nothing whatsoever to do with his death so I don't see why you or anyone else is interested. It happened years ago."

"Humor me."

"Oh, for goodness sakes," she sputtered, nonplused by the unexpected warmth of his gaze. "It was about five years ago, maybe six. Milt and I worked on a committee together, Buildings and Grounds. We were planning the new wing of the classroom building among other things. I'd had some architectural training in college and Milt had some drafting experience also, so we were asked to work together on preliminary sketches so that when the architect came in, the committee would have a clearer sense of what we wanted.

"The school had always used Bill Foxe, an alum, as their architect. He worked free of charge you see, but, unfortunately, Bill died about seven years ago and they'd been forced to hire a new architect. We aren't all that comfortable with change, here at OHF, I'm afraid. The prospect of this young upstart from Boston coming in and running things had the Board members on our committee very unsettled. The upstart turned out great, by the way, and has subsequently worked on a number of other projects. His name's Philip Erskine.

"Anyway, close proximity seems to be all Milt needs with a woman. It soon became clear he was interested in me and our planning sessions when the two of us were working alone became increasingly uncomfortable."

"How so?"

"You know, the usual things, suggestive glances, roving hands grazing my back, brushing against my leg, patting my knee. Hands lingering longer than was appropriate, that sort of thing. Then there were the comments. Subtle at first, you know, suggestive. I assume it was his idea of light flirtation. Then, he became more blatant, mentioning parts of his anatomy."

She blushed crimson, turning away, but Demaris caught a hint of a smile. "Parts of his anatomy that he assured me had been very pleasing to other women in the past. It was quite pathetic, really. If I hadn't been so annoyed, I'd have felt sorry for the man, but as it was, well, it was just a colossal annoyance when we were working hard, trying to get things done. I tried to ignore it, but Milt was not put off easily. Finally I spoke directly. I told him I'd go to Peter Thurbert or one of the Board members on our committee if he didn't stop.

"He just laughed and asked me what I was talking about, like I'd imagined the whole thing. He also had the nerve to say since I'd brought up the subject that perhaps I would indeed like to go out with him. After that I lost all patience and said that if the harassment didn't stop immediately, I'd finish the plans myself, take full credit and inform the Board the reasons for why it had been necessary for me to work alone.

"That stopped him, but I made certain never to be caught alone with him unless we were working in a public place like the library or student center.

"Then, one evening, we'd been working late, four members of the committee and Milt and myself. Everyone cleared out while I was still gathering my things, everyone except Milt, that is. It was after ten and the Coop was closed so we were alone in the building. The meeting had been in Milt's office. I was hurrying, hoping to avoid another unpleasant scene. Then, Milt insisted on walking me to my car.

"I know, I could have, should have said, 'no,' but I allowed him to accompany me. As we walked toward the parking lot, he grabbed hold of me and began dragging me towards the bushes near the classroom building. At that time, that particular section of the campus was poorly lit and I struggled in almost total darkness. Finally, I screamed and pulled away, pushing him down. He wasn't very strong. I ran to my car then —"

She paused, remembering her recent conversation with Amy, making a connection.

"Then?"

"Sorry," she said. "I just, it's just. Remind me when I finish to tell you about Amy Flathers. Anyway, I jumped into my car and drove away, but as I went past the stop where I'd left Milt on the ground someone else stood in the shadows."

"Any idea who?"

"No, none."

"Man or woman?"

"I couldn't be sure. I sensed rather than saw the person. Anyway, Milt never bothered me again. In fact, from then on he acted as if we were strangers. Our work together was nearly completed, thank goodness, and what little remained could be done in committee so I never had to be alone with him again. The funny thing is, I don't think it would have mattered. What I mean is, I don't believe he would have bothered me even if we had been left alone. After that night it was almost as if he were afraid of me. Then again, perhaps he was busy chasing someone else."

"Did you ever tell anyone about all this?"

"No, never. I know, I should have, not only for my own self, but to protect others. It was wrong of me not to tell." She was thinking of Amy, but how many others had Milt preyed upon?

"Bess, I'm sorry I have to ask you this, but your cleaning lady remembers Milt kissing you. What's that all about?"

"I have no idea. Milt picked me up a couple of times for meetings, but that's all. There was certainly no kissing involved. Let me tell you something about Ruby though. Since the day Mac died, she's been trying to marry me off. First to her brothers, then to a constant parade of cousins and friends. She's tried to fix me up with every eligible bachelor under sixty-five within a thirty mile radius of Old Harbor.

"Ruby loved Milt. She practically threw herself at him whenever he came to the house. He did have a certain, perverse charm. Not to me, but to many others. But, if Ruby saw Milt kiss me, she was hallucinating. She has coke-bottle glasses, you know, for distance. Did she say whether or not she was wearing them when she observed this kiss?"

"So what about these other women?"

"I couldn't say. I try not to listen to rumors."

Bullshit, he thought. "You must've heard about someone?"

"Well, there was poor Joan, the whole campus knew about her. Then, there were stories about Kitty Bigalow. And, of course Susan. She and Milt have been involved for a while, I believe."

"Others?"

"Not that I know of, but there have been rumors over the years about Milt and almost every female on this campus which brings me to something I think you ought to know. It's about Amy Flathers."

"One of the girls that found Wickie?"

"Yes, it would seem so. Perhaps I shouldn't betray a confidence, but I did tell Amy to speak to you so she'll probably be contacting you or perhaps I could bring her to your office?"

"Bess, let's have it."

"Well, it's just, she seems to have had a very similar incidence to mine involving Milt. Not the harassment, but he apparently attacked her, too." She quickly related Amy's story. "And, there was someone there, just like with me, only this time he actually appears to have rescued Amy by causing the disturbance."

"Could've helped you too," he said speaking more to himself than to her. "Could've held Wickie down so you could get away. Who'dya think this mysterious knight in shining armor is? A security guard? She shook her head. "Yea, probably would've identified himself. The old gardener, maybe?" She shrugged.

"Got any ideas of who might want Milt dead or who knew about your knife?"

"Believe me, I've thought of nothing else since Milt was found. Almost everyone at school has been to the cottage at one time or another. I've hosted meetings, picnics for students, faculty gatherings, lots of things. We've, I've been here for most of my adult life as you know."

Reaching out to touch her arm, his voice suddenly hoarse, he said, "It's been a long time since Mac died. It's none of my business, but aren't you getting tired of being alone?"

"You're right." She turned, staring out at the ocean across the fields, in the distance. "It is none of your business."

"Look, I'm sorry. I didn't mean to upset you."

"I've got to get back." She rose, refusing to meet his gaze.

"Sure, I understand. I'll walk you to your car." Why the hell had he brought up Mac? They'd been almost friendly. The frightened doe look had just begun to fade from her soft, hazel eyes and now because of his stupid remark she was stalking off, fighting back tears, shoulders bent, her dead husband's jacket wrapped around her like a life jacket. You asshole, he thought, wracking his brain for something to say to bring her back.

"What have you heard about this Harry Winthrop character anyway?"

She stopped, turning to regard him suspiciously.

"Do they think I can't handle the job?" He had her attention now. "I'm too stupid so they gotta bring in some rich Bozo from God knows where."

Anger forgotten, she threw up her hands. "Isn't it unbelievable? Just because he's the son of you know who, we're all supposed to bare our souls to this nitwit playing detective. It's beyond ridiculous."

"My sentiments exactly." He laughed, relieved to see her anger directed at someone other than himself. In the growing twilight, her face, flushed with color, eyes blazing, he thought she had never looked lovelier. "So what's it all about, do you think?"

"I haven't the foggiest, but, you want to know the worse of it? I have to have dinner with him Saturday. I shouldn't go to the stupid party, but I'm hopeless at thinking up excuses and Todd would never let me wriggle out now."

"Todd?"

"Todd Bridgham, head of Upper school. Have you met him?"

"Ah, yes, a pompous little pr —, jerk."

"Yes, well, I'll be dining with the pompous little jerk. I'm sure the only reason I was invited was to give Junior Sherlock a chance to look me over, me being a prime suspect and all."

"Uh-oh."

"You've got that right." She had reached her car and she was searching for her keys.

"Try your right coat pocket," he said.

"How did you?" she said, looking up as she extracted the keys.

"Heard 'em jingling earlier." He lied. Actually, he had felt them poke his side when they had brushed together walking side by side. Sensitive was he to every touch, every breath in her presence, that he had felt the keys like the point of a knife, through the thick canvas of Mac's jacket.

"Well, good-bye." She slipped into the car and he shut the door behind her.

"Bess, be in touch, if you hear anything, okay? Peter Thurbert told me you're on a bunch of committees." She nodded, surprised at the change in his voice, ignoring the softness in the steely blue eyes. "You come into contact with lots of people, the murder's a hot topic, just see what you can find out, okay? I'd really appreciate it."

"All school meetings are confidential."

"You know what I mean. I'm not interested in any deep, dark secrets, but I'd sure as hell like to hear anything about that business office, Milt or his boss, anything, okay?"

"I'll try, but I wouldn't count on much."

He grinned. "Thanks, and listen." His hand gripped her car door, eyes serious as he gazed down at her. "Be careful. If the guy can break in once, he can do it again."

"What a cheerful thought."

"I mean it, Bess, take care. Lock all your doors and windows and don't —"

"Bye Roger," she called, waving as she backed out.

As he walked back to the jeep, parked in the next lot, Demaris felt almost happy, a rare sensation for him. There was no way he and Bess would ever get together again, he knew that, but being around her lifted his spirits. Even after twenty years, the regret pressed, a dead weight between his shoulder blades. Yet somehow, in the growing darkness of the warm autumn night, it seemed as if his burden had grown a little lighter.

CHAPTER 24

Bess trudged through sheets of rain, muttering to herself. "Oh, no thank you, Todd. I don't need a ride. I'd love the walk. Just love walking in the rain." Stupid, stupid, stupid woman!

The night was black as pitch, thick clouds obscuring moon and stars. A faint mist when she had started out, Bess had traveled a quarter of the distance between her cottage and the Bridghams when the deluge began. In one hand, she held fast to a bag holding her shoes, in the other, a large, black umbrella with several broken spokes. She wore knee high Wellington boots, wide brimmed, Nor'easter hat, and Mac's oilskin duster, which reached her ankles. Between the two garments, she was relatively well-protected.

As she pushed onward, she thought about her recent conversation with Roger. As always, he wanted too much of her. Beyond help with the investigation, he wanted something she could not give. Not now, not ever. Their conversation had touched so many nerves, awakening memories best left buried.

The Bridghams lived in one of the six faculty houses that bordered the campus. Theirs was a little past the base of Orchard Road, the farthest from Bess' home, of course. A quarter mile to go, she reached the crest of the Orchard Road hill, the wind in her face, rain stinging her cheeks. As she descended the hill, she spied an enormous puddle, spanning the road that already appeared to be at least six inches deep in places. How had that happened so fast?

As she inched her way along the edge of the puddle, holding the duster above her knees, a car appeared over the rise. She turned just as the dark blue Mercedes sports coupe splashed into the center of the puddle sending a cascade of water over her. While still dry underneath, her outer garments were completely drenched, cold, muddy water running in torrents down the front and back of oilskin.

"Imbecile!" she screamed at the car, already disappearing in the mists ahead.

Five minutes later, she stood on the Bridgham's front stoop, looking like a bedraggled canary, caught in a hurricane. Trying vainly to collect herself, Bess rang the doorbell. Immediately, it was opened by Sheila Bridgham in gold lame vest, black pencil skirt, and six inch heels, her reddish, blonde hair teased to the ceiling. "Why, Bess, here you are. You made it. Hooray, come in." Sheila reached out to grab Bess' coat sleeve, then thinking better of it, simply stepped aside and gestured her into the warm foyer.

The house smelled delicious. The scent of yellow roses in a vase in the foyer mingled with sage, garlic and other spices wafting out of the kitchen, the guests' perfumes and colognes completing the mélange of scents that felt comforting after her rainy trek.

"Why, if it isn't young Miz Dore. Quite the adventuress, aren't we?" Cornie Parmenter, Chair of the Board of Overseers, helped her out of her coat, clearly regretting his gallantry once he laid hold of the sodden oilskin. "My heaven, my dear—traipsing about in weather like this, what?"

Once again, Bess chided herself for accepting Todd's invitation. "Hello, Cornie. Good to see you, thank you." She straightened and smoothed her skirt, a soft pastel blue tweed that she had paired with a matching blue cashmere sweater.

Cornie took her arm, ushering her into the living room. "How you holding up this semester?"

You mean how is the owner of the murder weapon holding up, she thought. "Fine, thanks. My students are exceptional, as always, and the field hockey season has been going well so far." Nodding his head, Cornie was already scanning the room, searching for someone more important. "Cornie, would you excuse me? I believe a trip to the powder room is in order."

Not waiting for his reply, Bess scurried toward the kitchen, intending to scoot into the powder room in the hallway.

"Bess, thank goodness, a friendly face." She nearly collided with Peter Thurbert who bent to kiss her cheek and give her a quick hug.

"Hello, Peter. What are you talking about? These are your people. You're in your element. Unlike myself, whose invitation clearly came because I am the wretched owner of the murder weapon and still considered a prime suspect."

"Nonsense, my dear. It is an unusual group Todd has assembled, though. Always glad to see faculty, of course, but." He paused, lowering his voice to a whisper. "I've seen enough of Cornie Parmenter to last two lifetimes. I swear the man is trying his darndest to make my final year hell."

"Why would anyone want to —oh, Jean, hello, how are you?" Bess greeted Jean Davol, vice chair of the Board as she stepped out of the powder room.

Jean smiled, looking from one to the other. "Sorry you two. Didn't mean to interrupt. Talking shop?"

"Not a bit of it," Peter said, stepped forward to hug her. "Jean, so good to see you." His demeanor changed completely, as he moved into headmaster mode. "Did you just arrive? Is Bill with you?" Bess watched as her friend's ease gave way to stiff formality, his natural warmth now obsequious attention. In her opinion, this kind of behavior was unnecessary with Jean, but then, she did not inhabit Peter's shoes.

"Came in just after Bess," Jean said, reaching over to squeeze her hand. "And, I headed right for the spot all us girls go, don't we, Bess?"

Bess nodded, returning Jean's greeting. "Exactly where I'm headed, if you two will please excuse me."

'Of course, but I'd love to find a few minutes to chat. If not tonight, then sometime soon? It's about Religious Life next week. I have some ideas I'd love to run by you."

"Anytime, Jean, of course, at your convenience." With that, Bess left them, slipping into the powder room.

A birthright Quaker and longtime board member, Jean was chair of the school's Religious Life Committee on which Bess served as secretary. Jean often sought her opinions and ideas over what Jean called "working dinners" at the Davols' home. Jean and Bill Davol had always impressed Bess as sensible, down-to-earth people, ones that did not need to be fallen over. Peter was right, she thought, washing her hands, then endeavoring vainly to smooth her bedraggled hair, it was an unusual group. Was Todd Bridgham on the short list for headmaster and this dinner was his way to impress Cornie, Jean and other board members? Bess hoped not.

CHAPTER 25

A short time later, glass of Pinot Grigio in hand, Bess found herself stuck in a tiresome conversation with Joan Nettleman. The middle school art teacher had sought her out, wielding her considerable girth through the crowded room to reach Bess' side, where, for some inexplicable reason, she seemed intent on remaining. As she stood in the corner of the living room, half-listening to Joan's incessant chatter, most of it snide remarks about the other guests, Bess caught her first glimpse of Harry Winthrop.

There were sixteen guests in the party, clustered in small groups in the living room and Todd was making the rounds, introducing Harry to each cluster. Like Bess, Cornie had come alone, his wife, Muriel, already ensconced in St. Croix for the winter. Junaita Hays had also come solo as had Joan and Will McGuire.

Kevin LeBlanc arrived shortly after Bess with Ramona Stark. The two had always been very close friends, and Bess wondered if their friendship had blossomed into something more now that Susan was out of the picture. Rounding out the party were Jean and Bill Davol and Darrell and Bianca Rosen.

Darrell, an alum and board member, was one of the school's most outspoken critics. Armed with a seemingly endless supply of misinformation, Rosen saw himself as a lone crusader, working to bring Old Harbor Friends up to the standards of top tier prep schools. He wasted hours of board meeting time railing about fallen standards and lack of academic rigor. Eight years earlier, when the extremely affluent Rosen had been asked to join the Board, Harry Winthrop Senior had not yet moved to Old Harbor. Now, with Winthrop's millions behind them, many people wished Darrell would disappear, taking his Botoxed, liposuctioned wife and three obnoxious children with him. Darrell and Bianca were two of Todd and Sheila's current "best friends," according to Joan.

"Look at her," Joan whispered, gesturing at Bianca Rosen who was, as usual, overdressed in black and gold sheath and matching jacket. She and Sheila had apparently coordinated colors, Bess thought, wishing Joan would stop. "If she has anymore plastic surgery, her face will disappear. Looks like a fish, or maybe a wedge of cheese."

"Joan, hush," Bess said, endeavoring in vain to step away. As Todd and his guest of honor neared their corner, Bess picked up snatches of their conversation as Joan chattered on. Harry Winthrop greeted Cornie, who he had clearly met before, and above Joan's prattle, she heard Cornie bellow. "Hal, my boy, great to see you again. What's it been? Two, three years? What a life you've been leading, what? The envy of all of us stay-at-homes, I can tell you. Your old man keeps me up on your escapades, what? Me and the missus live vicariously, doncha know? What a life, what a life. Oh, to be young again."

Cornie was interrupted by Jean Davol, who uncharacteristically stepped in, eager to introduce herself. As Harry turned to greet the vice-chair, he caught Bess' eye and she blushed, averting her gaze. When she dared to look again, he was hanging on Jean's every word, the picture of rapt attention.

Joan elbowed her. "What a hunk."

"Is he?" Bess replied, feigning an indifference she did not feel. One look from the tall, ruggedly handsome stranger with his tousled brown hair and brilliant blue eyes, made her go weak at the knees. She gripped a chair to steady herself.

"You'd have to be blind not to think so. God, what I wouldn't give to be eighty pounds lighter."

"Joan, really! And, stop poking me. My arm's turning black and blue." Bess turned away from Todd and his star attraction to listen to Juanita, standing in a group beside them, who was describing an upcoming exhibition of Latin America art that she and her husband, Alvaro, a teacher at Bay College twenty miles north of Old Harbor, had helped bring to the village gallery.

As Bess and Joan listened to Juanita, they found themselves suddenly shoved aside by Carrie Thurbert, in her headlong rush to greet Harry Winthrop. "Why, of all the nerve," Joan said, loudly enough for Carrie to hear, though it mattered not a whit. Carrie was one of those people who only saw and heard those who she deemed the crème de le crème.

The wraith thin headmaster's wife was, like Bianca Rosen and their hostess, overdressed for this "informal dinner party" in pale green sheath, pearls and cream colored flats, a silk shawl in swirling pastel florals skimming her shoulders. Carrie's ash blonde hair, straight and shoulder length, was held back in a wide headband that matched her dress.

Juanita, large boned and heavy set, a good six inches taller than Carrie, could, along with Joan, have held her ground, but had graciously stepped aside, allowing the Thurberts to pass. "How does Peter stand it?" Juanita whispered, as they watched Carrie's advance, dragging Peter along in her wake.

"Come on, Peter. I want to speak to him now!" Peter glanced over at Bess and she smiled sympathetically. Formidable, that's what Carrie was, her pinched face, the result of "minor plastic surgery" and thousands of hours of aerobics, a mask of ruthless determination.

"And, here are the Thurberts," Todd announced, stepping aside. "You met before, I believe?"

"Caroline Thurbert, Mr. Winthrop. So nice to see you again." Carrie leaned forward, giving their guest air kisses on both cheeks.

"Of course," Harry said, stepping back to shake Peter's hand. "How are you both?" He had a pleasant voice, full of depth and resonance, Bess mused. Not the wise cracking, smarmy voice of the boy detective she had conjured up in her imagination.

At that moment, attention was diverted by Sheila's voice, screaming for Todd.

"Harry, old boy. It appears that I'm wanted in the kitchen. You're on your own. Didn't quite make the rounds, but maybe Peter can help? Thanks, old man." Sheila screamed again, and Todd's face turned crimson. If Sheila was auditioning for the part of headmaster's wife, this outburst had not furthered her candidacy. "Duty calls, excuse me, folks."

Sensing the vacuum, Carrie leapt in, taking Harry's arm. "Shall we pop over to the buffet for some nibblies, Harry dear?"

Aghast at the sight of the hunk heading in the opposite direction, Joan moved with astonishing speed, ambushing the pair and blocking Carrie's path to the buffet table. "Joan Nettleman, middle school art, Mr. Winthrop. Hello. And, this," she added, laying hold of Bess' forearm and dragging her from behind her, "Is Bess Dore, my counterpart in Upper School."

Juanita stepped forward, introducing herself as Harry shook each of their hands in turn, Carrie fuming beside him. As he shook Bess' hand, his grip was strong, hand surprisingly rough for a dilettante.

As she returned his grasp, Bess felt her knees buckling as she fought for control. "Lord Peter has arrived," she blurted, her tone and sarcasm startling those around her. "And, I'll just bet he drives a dark, blue Mercedes."

Blue eyes regarded her, curious, watchful, as if they stood in the room alone. "Why, yes. How did you know?"

"Just a wild guess. Now, if you'll excuse me."

"I'm sorry, we, I have broken into your conversation. I'll just—"

"No need," Bess called, waving over her shoulder as she walked away. "Carry on without me. Out of wine."

Mouth agape, Joan watched her colleague cross the room. "What's gotten into her?"

"Just shy, I expect," Peter said, kindly. He had been standing patiently beside Carrie throughout their exchange and wondered himself about Bess' uncharacteristic rudeness.

"Oh, Harry," Carrie drawled, attempting to draw his attention back to herself and away from the insufferable, boring Bess Dore. "We're all so frightfully glad you've come to take over the case from that macabre detective, what's his name? Why he's a perfect ghoul."

Harry watched Bess retreat, already intrigued by the Widow Dore, of whom he had already been briefed. Her shoulder length, light brown hair, windblown and unadorned, was probably just the way her husband had liked it. Still, she was far from the dowdy schoolmarm he had expected. She may be a little old fashioned in dress, but Bess Dore was lovely, all soft curves instead of bony, sharp angles like many of the women he dated.

Harry already knew quite a lot about Bess. Knew she still grieved for a husband ten years gone. Knew that she had dated the murder victim. Knew that she loved to hike and was an avid reader of mysteries. Definitely not a murderess, he decided, watching her run off like a scared rabbit.

CHAPTER 26

After refilling her wine glass, Bess had decided to hover around the dining room sideboard, far away from Harry Winthrop. "What's up, Bess?" Kevin LeBlanc reached across her, grabbing a stuffed mushroom, popping it into his mouth.

"Taking a breather." She, too, grabbed a mushroom, her third. Stuffed with pesto, cheese and garlic, they melted in the mouth.

"From what? I'm surprised you aren't over there with the rest of the hens, salivating over Mr. Wonderful. Even Ramona's smitten."

Laughing, she set down her glass. "I've already had the pleasure. How are you, Kevin?"

"Okay. Been better." He pointed towards the kitchen, Todd and Sheila's voice clearly audible. "Sounds like the chefs are at odds. Shall we?" They moved across the room, farther from the kitchen door. "Haven't seen you much since this whole Milt thing, you holding up okay?"

"I'm fine. I just wish the police would catch whoever did it and things could return to normal."

"Whatever that is. Gonna take a while. My kids," he said, referring to the students in his dorm. "Are scared to death. Won't cross the campus at night, even to the Coop, without me. And, they hang around my room till all hours. They'd sleep on the floor if I let 'em. Like I have some magical power to protect them."

"I know what you mean, but it's only natural, don't you think? For most, their first brush with death, never mind a murder. I felt so helpless the night we found him. Responsible, yet powerless."

"I'm seeing Ramona," he said, abruptly. "Have been for over a month."

'That's good news. I'm glad for you, Kevin. For both of you."

"We've" he began, but was interrupted by more screams from the kitchen.

"I don't care who the hell hears me! Thanks to you, we don't have enough fillets! You told me fourteen and now there are sixteen. I'm not a miracle worker, Todd. I can't conjure up two more steaks from thin air!"

"Kevin, sorry, would you excuse me?" Bess said, heading for the kitchen and pushing open the door. "Sorry to intrude," she said, confronting the battling spouses, both in matching white aprons embroidered with "His" and "Hers". Squared off at opposite ends of a long, marble topped island littered with bowls, open bottles, boxes, pans and wrappers, they looked ready to kill. "Sheila, I think I can help. About the meat, I mean. You may not have remembered that I'm a vegetarian, so you see —"

"As am I," he said, the already familiar voice speaking from behind her. As Harry Winthrop stepped fully into the kitchen, his arm brushed hers and for an instant, Bess thought he meant to take her hand. "So, all is well. With two less carnivores, the beef crisis has been averted. Am I right?"

"Well, yes," Sheila stammered. "That's very kind of you both. Of course, Todd and I were prepared to abstain."

"No!" Bess and Harry said in unison.

"I haven't eaten red meat since high school," she said.

Todd stepped forward, spatula in hand. "Harry, my man, I couldn't possibly ask you, as guest of honor to—"

Harry raised his hand. "Haven't touched meat since India. Couldn't stomach now, even if forced. Really."

Setting down the spatula, Todd removed his apron with a flourish. "Well, in that case, dinner is served. Shall we?" As he ushered them into the dining room, he called to the other guests, then moved to clear platters from the sideboard.

"Well, Ms. Dore," he said, as they followed their host from the kitchen. "At least, we have one thing in common. That's a start, anyway."

CHAPTER 27

Sandwiched between Peter Thurbert and Bill Davol, Harry Winthrop a safe distance away, at Sheila's left elbow, Bess actually enjoyed her dinner. Her companions kept up the conversation, including her as they discussed village politics and the school's participation in an upcoming cultural festival. Aside from the occasional toast — to the chefs and a welcome to Harry — the diners conversed with their immediate neighbors throughout the meal, sparing her any further discourse with Mr. Winthrop.

Sheila and Todd began the meal with a delicately seasoned cream of leek soup followed by smoked bluefish pate served with toasted rounds of Todd's homemade French bread. After the fish, came the controversial filet of beef served with a sherried mushroom sauce accompanied by wild rice, gratin of cauliflower and fresh snow peas. Bess and her fellow vegetarian were served heaping portions of the rice and vegetables.

Carrie Thurbert to his right and Sheila on his left and Cornie across the table, Bess noticed that Harry had little chance to taste, much less savor the Bridgham's repast. From the moment he sat down he was bombarded with questions about his travels, his plans in regards to future residency in Old Harbor and his impressions of the school after a five minute drive through the campus. Only as dessert appeared, crème de caramel with almond-infused whipped cream, did his fellow diners grant him a brief respite.

"Sheila, you've outdone yourself. Best meal I've had in years." Cornie proclaimed as their hostess, served the custards, Todd trailing behind with silver coffee pot.

Sheila beamed. "Why thank you, Cornie. That's high praise coming from a gourmand like you. And, let's not forget this was a joint effort. Todd's responsible for the beef, the bread and the bluefish, the three b's, shall we say? And, you can thank Darrell for the excellent wines."

"You don't say? Well, now, aren't we fortunate, what? Harry, my boy — no one has a wine cellar like Rosen here. I'll bet with the circles you run in you've seen some wine cellars. Even so, better have old Darrell give you a tour. His cellar rivals any I've seen, doncha know?"

"Anytime," Darrell replied, looking less than enthusiastic.

Joan leaned forward, steering the conversation onto the topic everyone had thus far avoided. "So, Mr. Winthrop, what are your plans for the investigation? How long are you planning on staying in Old Harbor?"

Silence. All eyes turned to the newcomer. "Not sure, to answer your first question and probably a few months to answer the second."

"More than a few months if we can convince him, what? This is a hard guy to pin down, folks. Always yachting off here or there on some new project or what have you, but we've got him now, don't we, my boy?"

Ignoring Cornie, Joan persisted. "Where will you be staying, Mr. Winthrop?"

"With my father. And please call me Harry. Mr. Winthrop sounds like a character from a gothic mystery."

"Oh, I hate mystery novels," Joan said, clearly basking in the light of his attention and determined to keep it. "All that complicated mumbo-jumbo. I can never guess the murderer, I'm just a hopeless sleuth."

Harry wanted to ask what she meant by mumbo-jumbo, but lost the chance as she prattled on. "Bess loves mysteries. She simply devours them, don't you, dear? Every time I see her she's got her nose stuck in a mystery novel. Why she's a real expert, aren't you, Bess? Maybe she could help with the investigation?"

"Joan, don't be ridiculous," Bess interrupted. The whole table was listening now.

"Who're you reading these days?" Bill Davol asked. "Only askin' 'cause I'm an addict myself. Always looking for new writers, new series, what have you. I do like following a character's development over a series of books, don't you?"

"Yes, I do. Lately I've been reading Elizabeth George's series, do you know her? My favorite author right now is Anne Greyson, but perhaps she appeals more to women. A woman writing about a female sleuth, I mean. I also enjoy Marcia Mueller, Grafton and Paretsky and a Cape Cod writer, Sally Gunning, but Anne Greyson's books have a feminine perspective that I really appreciate." She had wanted to say more, but had glanced down the table to find Harry Winthrop grinning broadly. Now, he was laughing at her choice of reading material! She lapsed into silence, unwilling to give him further cause for smirking.

"Well, I'll try her," Bill said, unaware of Bess' discomfort. "Really like those young gals, myself, Grafton and all. Then, there's always good, old Mrs. Pollifax. Thanks for the tip. I'll give your Ms. Greyson a try."

All through the meal, Bess had surreptitiously studied Harry Winthrop marveling at the ease with which he conversed with his hostess and the others, wondering at the same time what Mac would have thought of this amateur detective thrust in their midst. Bess often judged situations and people according to what she imagined Mac might have felt or thought. A stupid habit, and one which Mac would have strongly disapproved of, she couldn't seem to change this almost involuntary response to life particularly when she felt threatened or vulnerable. Now, the accursed habit seemed to be working against her. Much as she hated to admit it, something told her that Mac would have liked Harry Winthrop. Maybe not his lifestyle, but he would have liked the man.

Like every other woman in the room, she found him intriguing. She had to admit, he was attractive, the mischievous light dancing in his deep, blue eyes only making him more so. But detective? Ridiculous, the school hiring this rich, middle-aged adolescent to play detective. Just the sort of nonsense Cornie would dream up. Be that as it may, Harry Winthrop had certainly won over this crowd.

He had all the women, excluding herself, of course, eating out of his hand and the men seemed at ease and comfortable around him. Perhaps he was the right person to pry the secrets out of them after all.

As they sipped their coffee, Jean Davol took the floor. "I'm not sure if your father's told you, but, Peter has done extraordinary things for the school. You can't imagine. Why, before he arrived OHF was a warehouse for spoiled, rich boys whose parents wanted to be rid of them, the sooner the better. Standards were, well... Let's just say there were no standards to speak of. The school really went downhill in the fifties and early sixties, I'm afraid. Enrollment was steady, but —"

"Dreadful business," Cornie interrupted. "We needed a leader by golly, and we got one. Peter's brought us into the modern age, what? Has turned Old Harbor into a top flight prep school."

"Enough, you two," Peter said, clearly basking in the praise, which had been largely absent the past year. "If the school's stronger today, it was a team effort. We have an outstanding faculty and a hard-working, dedicated Board of Overseers. That has made all the difference."

"True," Todd said. "But, you deserve most of the credit, Peter and I know the faculty would agree."

Not Jane Fellows, Bess thought. "They're right, Peter. Yours and Carrie's legacy will stand the school in good stead for many generations to come." Where did that ridiculous phrase come from, she thought, cringing. Stand in good stead? She sounded just like a prissy schoolmarm!

"How strong's the Quaker connection?" Harry asked, looking directly at her. She was even lovelier when blushing.

Kevin LeBlanc rescued her. "Very. That's been one of Peter's greatest contributions. As the school's spiritual leader, shall we say. Our Quaker roots had been seriously weakened under previous administrators. Bess could tell you more about that. She's been here longer than anyone at this table, I believe. Anyway, OHF had severed relations with New England Yearly Meeting. Left the fold so to speak. Peter not only reestablished the relationship with Yearly Meeting, but he also reached to other Friends schools all over the country."

"Quakerism has always intrigued me."

He sounds like he's talking about a new hobby he'd like to take up, she thought. I was wrong, Mac would have hated him.

"As a religion and a way of life," he continued. "I've attended meetings in different parts of the world and I always come away with such profound respect for Friends' spiritualism and reflective wisdom. Were you raised a Quaker, Peter?"

"No, Carrie and I are Baptists. We attend St. Martins in the village as well as weekly Meeting for Worship, but I like you, have a deep respect for Friends'd principles and values, especially as relates to the education of young people. As you may know, the Society of Friends' contributions to education are enormous, as you no doubt are aware, and our affiliation with Yearly Meeting enriches and supports our lives here at OHF in countless ways."

"How many Quakers in the school?"

"Roughly a third of the faculty. Bess and Joan are both Friends for instance, and we have forty-seven Quakers in our student body, out of three hundred and fourteen."

"And, don't forget the Board," Jean added. "A third of us must be Quakers according to our charter."

"So were you born a Quaker, Mrs. Dore?"

"No, it was my husband's faith. I joined the Meeting soon after we met." She lowered her eyes, retreating from the intensity of his gaze. "Joan was though, weren't you?"

Before Joan could reply, he went on. "What about other personnel?" From the gleam in his eye, Bess knew immediately where the question was headed. "The Business Office follows Quaker business procedures, does it?"

"Hardly," Joan snorted, eager to rejoin the conversation. Suddenly, remembering the three board members at the table, she turned beet red. "What I mean is —"

Cornie cleared his throat. "Perhaps that's a topic better left for a private conversation, Harry, but I will grant you, someone wasn't none too Quakerly in regards to old Milt's last minutes on this earth."

Harry chose to ignore the uncomfortable silence surrounding him. "No idea who yet?"

Cornie shook his head, waving his hand, nearly slapping Juanita who sat beside him. "No, and we're not likely to. With that bumbling ass of a policeman in charge — excuse my French, ladies — we'll never get to the bottom of this. By Jesus, that man leaves me cold. That's why we called you in, my boy. Couldn't leave the school's future in the hands of that incompetent constable another day."

"He's not a constable." Bess said, her voice more strident than she'd intended. "And, he's far from incompetent."

"Now Bess, honey. You know what I mean. I know he's an old school chum of yours and all, but he's gettin' nowhere with this case, and, he's harrassin' folks needlessly to boot. Why, it's just, well, it's just not acceptable."

She wanted to scream 'do not call me honey' and defend Roger's slow, meticulous investigative methods, but she restrained herself, knowing if she spoke, she would regret it. Instead, she rose with her hostess saying, "Sheila, can I help?"

The lady doth protest too much, Harry thought, watching the scarlet blush fade from Bess' cheeks as she circled the table clearing the dessert plates. Quite lovely, he decided, and graceful, too.

CHAPTER 28

After more coffee and cognac, the first guests rose to leave. Since it was still pouring outside, Bess reluctantly decided to accept Todd's offer of a ride home. Cornie and the Davols made their hasty farewells as well as did the crew that lived on campus, Kevin, Joan, Juanita, Will and Ramona. The Thurberts were on their way out the door when Bess began searching for her coat.

Engrossed in conversation with Darrell and Bianca in the front hall, Todd had forgotten all about her. After the important guests had departed, Sheila had retreated with a wave to the kitchen where the sounds of splashing water and clanging pans heralded the evening's end.

"Can I give you a lift?" His voice from behind startled her.

"Oh, no, thank you, Mr. Winthrop." She turned to face him. I've observed your driving and I'd rather reach home alive, thank you just the same. "Todd's taking me."

"That might prove —"

"Care for a nightcap?" Todd interrupted, closing the door behind the Rosens.

"Thanks, but I think I'll pass," Harry said, running fingers through his hair. The expression in his eyes suddenly distant. The affable facade had vanished and he appeared distracted, anxious to be gone. "It's been a long couple of days and jet lag and too many hours on the road are finally catching up with me."

"I'd like to get home, too," Bess said. "It's been a lovely party Todd, but I'm done in. I'm ready, whenever you are too."

"Oh shit, Bess, your ride. I'm sorry, I completely forgot about you needing a lift. Right after I talked to you this afternoon, Sheila sent me on an errand, but when I went to start the car, nothing. Damn thing's been in the shop more than out the past two months. Anyway, the long and short of it is, we're carless. Garage came and towed it away so. Winthrop, it's right on your way, could you possibly?"

"I've already offered." He smiled gazing down at her. "Shall we?"

"Oh, I couldn't, thank you, but I'll just walk, really. It was very foolish of me not to drive in the first place. I'll be fine, the air'll do me good." She felt trapped, aware that she was babbling yet unable to stop herself, the prospect of a long walk in soggy overcoat and freezing rain almost too much to bear.

"Don't be an ass, Bess," Todd said. "It's coming down in buckets. You'd probably drown before you got halfway home. What can you be thinking? Winthrop here isn't gonna bite you. Besides, you'll like tootling around in that car."

"Todd, I'll be fine. I'm perfectly capable of walking and besides —"

"Besides what?"

"Nothing."

"Oh, for goodness sake, go ahead. Harry's a great sport and the car's a gas. All kinds of gadgets and stuff." Wondering when Todd had found the time to tootle around in Harry's car, she heard him saying, "Took it out myself, on Sheila's errand. Winthrop here arrived early and handed me the keys. Damned decent of him, wasn't it?" Todd went on, talking away as if Harry weren't standing beside him. "Must've passed you on the road come to think of it. Did I? Was so dark, I must've missed you."

And, suddenly she was laughing. Laughing till tears ran down her cheeks. Laughing without being able to stop — at herself and her foolish insistence on tromping back in the rain, at Todd's incessant, ridiculous chatter, at all her stupid assumptions about the man standing beside her, at the whole stressful evening now mercifully at an end. "Thank you Todd, and Sheila, too," she called towards the kitchen.

"It was a great dinner and now, I believe I will accept Mr. Winthrop's offer of a ride."

"Harry, please," he said, as they headed out the door.

"One step at a time," she said, tripping down the front steps, dizzy from too much wine, cognac and her sudden attack of giddiness.

"Steady now," he said, gripping her elbow.

As they made their way down the front walk to his car, he whispered, "You can relax now, Mrs. Dore. The party's over."

CHAPTER 29

Try as she might, Bess could remember nothing about the drive home from the Bridghams. From dessert onward, the remainder of the evening was a complete blur. Unaccustomed to drinking, she had somehow downed five glasses of wine — white, red and champagne with dessert. Then, there were the two generous snifters of cognac, gulped as she sat between Harry Winthrop and Darrell Rosen with no escape. Forced to listen as Darrell ranted and raved about the absence of Chinese in the Upper School, she felt as if her head would explode.

As she struggled to recall what had happened during the five-minute drive home, she flipped the pillow to find a cool spot for her burning face. She had fuzzy recollections of babbling on, although she couldn't remember about what. Somewhere through the fog she heard Harry Winthrop's bemused "good night Mrs. D.," as if he were mocking her, but she couldn't recall whether she had said anything in return. Did I even thank him?

Why hadn't she picked up her dark glasses on her recent trip downstairs? The glare of the sun streaming in the window was tortuous.

An hour earlier, she had inched her way down to the kitchen to get the paper, toast a bagel and fix a pot of tea and she was now back in bed, exhausted and unable to eat more than a bite of bagel. Huddled under an eiderdown, paper unread beside her, she closed her eyes, hoping a little nap might revive her.

No sooner had she shut her eyes than the phone rang sending spasms of pain to her head. Her heart pounded unnaturally as she reached a shaky hand towards the receiver. "Hello," she whispered.

"Mrs. D.? That you?"

She groaned.

"She lives!"

"Who's calling, please?" she asked, knowing full well who it was.

"Harry, Harry Winthrop, remember me? Just calling to see how you're feeling."

Closing her eyes, she could almost see his grinning face. He knew perfectly well how she was feeling. "Fine, thank you."

"Glad to hear it. When I left you last night you were a little —"

"I was very tired last night, Mr. Winthrop. It's been a very stressful week!"

"Understand completely, I've felt better myself. Wine and cognac, mixed with jet lag makes for a pretty lethal combination."

He was lying. She'd watched him for most of the night and he had hardly a drop of alcohol. He would politely accept proffered drinks, then set them down with little more than a sip. "Mr. Winthrop. Was there a reason for this call, because if there isn't I —"

"Oh, yes, indeed, sorry. I was wondering if you'd have dinner with me tonight. Early, of course, I know it's a school night."

"I'm sorry, but I have a load of papers to grade."

"Look, I'm not asking for ten course repast. We can go for burgers and milkshakes. Chocolate milkshakes are a sure cure for a hangover, by the way."

"I do not have a hangover!" Her foolish shouting brought the pain in her head to new crescendos. "And, furthermore, I —"

"I'm sorry, I was out of line. But please say you'll come. We can go wherever you like. Your choice. Strictly business. I'm anxious to get started with the investigation. Parmenter's putting the pressure on and I figured you were the logical person with whom to start. All roads lead to Mrs. Dore, or something like that."

He was right, of course. He should speak to her first, before making the rounds. Perhaps if he heard her version at the outset, he'd have a sensible lens through which to filter all the wild rumors flying around. He'd probably already heard a few. And, an interview in a neutral place, off the campus was probably a wise idea.

She knew she should decline, but instead heard herself saying, "There's a small restaurant in Windy Cove, about eight miles down the coast. Mostly seafood and fairly quiet. I think it's open on Sunday nights. I could call and check?"

"Sounds perfect. What time should I pick you up?"

"Six would be great."

"Six it is then. Thanks, Mrs. D., I'll look forward to it."

"See you then."

She set down the phone gently and reached for her aspirin bottle.

CHAPTER 30

As they took their seats by the window at Ahab's, he asked, "What should I know about Old Harbor Friends?"

In the twilight, the coastline stretched its rocky fingers northward, the Old Harbor lighthouse at the school's northernmost point of land sending an undulating beacon of light hovering over the evening tide.

The ride to Ahab's had been strained, both of them attempting to keep conversation alive with innocuous subjects of which neither had the slightest interest. Bess had finally given up, leaning into the soft leather seat. Half a bottle of aspirin had subdued her headache, but she felt queasy and light-headed, not at all herself. Ordinarily a shy, reserved person, in her present state of diminished capacity, she seemed to alternate between timidity and uncontrollable giddiness, a disconcerting mix that left her unsure of what she might say or do next. She always found silence best in unfamiliar waters.

Seated now, he had gotten right down to business. "Tell me about the school, please."

As she wondered where to begin, the waitress, "Doreen", emblazoned across her ample chest interrupted, "Can I bring you folks somethin' from the bar?"

Bess opened her mouth, intending to order a ginger ale as Harry said, "Two Bloody Marys, on the weak side, please. With celery, if you have it, Doreen."

"Sure, honey."

Before Bess could lodge a protest, Doreen disappeared, clearly already in love.

"Hair of the dog, Mrs. D. Trust me, it's just what we need. You do trust me, don't you?" He had a wonderful smile. His eyes sparkled with warmth, not a hint of sarcasm.

To her surprise, Bess nodded. She did trust him, but why?

"Good, then fill me in."

"What exactly do you want to know? I'm sure you got an earful last night."

"Anything. What's it like to work in a Quaker school? I'd like to get a feel for the place before I start giving people the third degree."

"It's a wonderful place, recent events notwithstanding. A good place to be a student, I'd guess. At least, I hope students feel that way. You'll have to ask them. They'll enjoy talking to you."

"How 'bout the faculty?"

She smiled, wondering whether she should be candid or coy. "With a few exceptions, it's a collaborative, friendly group. People are always willing to help, to share ideas and so forth. There are about seventy of us, I believe. Most are creative, innovative, open-minded and —"

"Liberal?"

"Yes, I guess you could say we're a very liberal-minded group for the most part. It's our openness, and the continuing interest in growing personally and professionally, that makes Old harbor Friends such a stimulating place to work."

"Sounds too good to be true."

She shrugged. "Yes, I guess it is, in many ways, but then that's only my opinion. You'll have to ask the others. In general, it doesn't seem to me that people are simply going through the motions, you know? Most of us love our jobs, and consider teaching a calling. We don't have a lot of burn-out."

"You're lucky."

"Yes."

"Is that that the Quaker influence, do you think?"

"Perhaps. Friends do value excellence in education and there's also the emphasis on service. To the community, to the school and the farm and all. There's a real sense of giving back, not just taking. That's as much an expectation of the faculty as it is the kids. Peter's had a lot to do with fostering the present climate. He's been a wonderful leader and truly committed to Friends education."

"How long have you been at the school?"

"Twenty years."

"Your first job, right out of college?"

"No, my husband and I worked abroad for a year, before settling in Old Harbor. I'm a bit older than you, I believe," she went on, wondering why she felt it necessary to furnish this unsolicited information. "I'm forty-two."

"Not by much." He gave her a quizzical look, winking at Doreen, who set the drinks down with a flourish. "I'm an old thirty-nine," he added.

"Need a few more minutes to consult your menus, folks?" It was clear that the only "folk" Doreen had eyes for was Harry who winked, waving his hand and she dutifully disappeared.

"And your husband?"

Harry had already heard a great deal about Macomber Dore, by all accounts one of the finest teachers in the school's history. Not only did he know when the legendary Dore had died, he had also been told again and again how his widow visited the small cemetery at the south end of the orchards every Wednesday morning before classes and on Sundays rain or shine, laying fresh flowers on his grave. How she kept his study exactly as it had been when he lived and he knew, from firsthand experience, that she kept at least ten photographs of him in her bedroom. No matter where one sat or lay in that room, Macomber Dore stared back.

"He died ten years ago." She lowered her eyes, but not soon enough.

"I'm sorry, Bess. I didn't mean to pry."

"It's alright. I like to talk about him. It keeps him with me. I know, some people think I'm crazy — the Widow Dore and her cloak of sadness. But Mac was, we were, very much in love."

"How old was he when he died?"

"Thirty-two. Liver cancer. He suffered a great deal, but you'd never have known it, except for his physical appearance. He was —" Her eyes filled with tears, but she forced herself to go on. "Mercifully, he was taken before, I mean, it could have gone on for years, I suppose. He refused to stop teaching until the very end. Teaching was his greatest love."

Harry watched the color rise in her cheeks and thought, no way. The man might have loved teaching, but there was something Mac Dore had loved much more and she was sitting across from him.

"It was a very intense time when he got sick, but there were moments of happiness, too."

"You were lucky, Mrs. D. Love like that is rare. I believe we never completely lose those we love deeply. They remain in our hearts and become part of our souls. Your memories of your husband must bring you enormous strength and comfort."

"Why, yes, they do. Thank you." She sat back, regarding him with surprise. Was Harry Winthrop the first person since Mac's death who actually understood her or was it all an act to gain her trust? "And, please, do stop calling me Mrs. D. It sounds like a donut shop! My name is Bess."

"Bess it is." He picked up his menu with a flourish. "Now, then, shall I summon the fair Doreen?"

CHAPTER 31

Not long after Doreen disappeared with their orders, Bess looked up to spy Garrett Rollins and Darrell Rosen enter the restaurant. Garrett was busy staring at his reflection in the mirror behind the bar, but Darrell spotted them and waved. Bess waved back, praying they would not ask to sit down.

"Bess, Harry, good to see you again so soon." Darrell's eyes traveled from one to the other of them, questions on the tip of his tongue. By this time, Garrett had pulled himself away from the bar and joined them.

"Is this a formal interview?" Darrell asked, gesturing at them.

"Yes, you could say so," Harry said, sitting taller, taking command of the situation. "No harm in enjoying a good meal while we talk. I was going to call both of you this week to see when you're free as well."

"Not sure how I can help you, Harr, but sure, call away." Rollins' gaze roamed the restaurant, no doubt searching for someone more important.

"Thanks, Garr, I will. I'm sure with adjacent offices, you'll have many recollections about Milt that could prove useful."

For an instant, fire flashed in Garrett's eyes, but he soon regained his composure and look of feigned indifference. "Not sure if you're familiar with the life of an archivist, but I spend very little time in my office."

"So I've heard," Harry said, smiling as Doreen arrived with their salads. "So nice to see you gentlemen. I'll be in touch."

With that, Harry dismissed the two friends. As Doreen set down the salads, Rollins and Rosen stood awkwardly before making their way to the entrance to wait for a table. How did he do that, Bess wondered, grinning as she took fork to her salad.

"Couple of pompous you-know-whats, those two," he whispered, leaning forward. "Don't let's allow them to spoil our dinner."

She laughed. "Never. Tell me about yourself, Mr. Winthrop. I know you're a world traveler. Where have you been? What was it like?"

Throughout the meal, he regaled her with tales of his adventures abroad, people he'd met, his teaching, writing and occasional work as an investigator. "I've loved it all," he said, as they polished off the last of their fish and chips, a specialty at Ahab's. "I'm happy to be home for a while though. More time to write, be with Dad, get to know the village and surrounding area a little."

"Yes, you mentioned writing. What kinds of things do you write?"

"Oh, this and that. Travel pieces, the odd short story, poems, if the mood strikes."

"Have you been published?"

He shrugged, suddenly uncharacteristically evasive. After a few minutes, he said, "A few things here and there. I'll show them to you sometime, if you like."

"I would, very much. And —"

"Do you write as well?"

She laughed. "Me, no. Unless you count syllabi and midterm exams."

"And, you like to read mysteries, right?"

"Yes, I like history and biography, too. And any kind of fiction, really."

"Really like that Anne Greyson, do you?"

"Yes, do you know her?"

"Tried one of hers a few years ago, but it was a little silly for my taste."

"Oh?" She regarded him warily, wondering if he was making fun of her.

"I'm more of a Dorothy Sayers, Conan Doyle fan. Most mysteries seem so contrived. After a couple of chapters, you know exactly who did it."

"Not with Anne Greyson."

"Knew the whole plot by page 40."

"No, you didn't. Which one was it?"

"Some foolish farce about a nursing home. Knew it was the owner in the first chapter."

"You didn't!" Bess looked up to find his eyes dancing with mischief. Death of a Veteran was not her favorite, but the plot had twisted and turned enough to keep Helen and her readers guessing until the end. Foolish, indeed. She decided a change of subject was in order. "Ever been married, Mr. Winthrop?"

"Harry, please. Every time you say 'Mr. Winthrop', I look around expecting to see my father."

"Harry, then. You know all about my love life. What about yours? You must've left a string of broken hearts in every port." As she spoke, she noticed his gaze grow dark, eyes clouding over.

He smiled, pushing his plate aside. "I was almost married once. And, I've had women friends. I'm happy to tell you about it, just not now, okay?" As he spoke, he signaled Doreen for the check.

"Of course," she said, the chill between them palpable.

On the drive home, they talked about the village and local history, avoiding talk of personal matters and the murder. When they said goodnight, his affability had returned, but something was clearly troubling him. As he turned to go, his gaze was sad and unreadable. Perhaps love had not been kind to the charming Harry Winthrop, after all, although for the life of her, Bess couldn't fathom why.

CHAPTER 32

"Mornin' Mrs. Dore." Billy Blackburn waved to Bess as she headed to her first period class. The swarthy groundskeeper pushed a wheelbarrow laden with rakes, shovels, bags of manure and peat moss and several buckets of pruning tools.

Billy had once been a student in Bess' advanced painting class, a gifted artist who had dreams of attending Rhode Island School of Design. While he had excelled in art classes, his other academics had been a struggle. With support from many teachers, especially the Dores, he was passing all his courses until Lizzie died. After that, Billy gave up and his grades plummeted. Eventually, despite efforts to help and support him, Billy flunked out, completing high school at the district vocational school.

In addition to providing meals for Billy and Louie, Bess stayed in touch and took an interest in their lives. Sometimes, she invited Billy to come out for a day of painting with her, but he always declined. She always made an effort to stop and chat at least for a minute or two whenever they met, instead of treating them as invisible as so many on the campus seemed to do. This morning she was late for class and out of sorts, so a quick, "morning Billy," was all she could muster before disappearing into the art building.

The class was her art history elective, a raucous bunch of sophomores and juniors. As she fumbled with her briefcase, organizing her thoughts, they chattered away. Bess hated to be late. It threw off her entire day.

"Alright, everyone," she called above the din. "Take out your journals and get started. Please go over your notes on your impressions of Friday's slides, then spend a few minutes thinking about them before we start our discussion. Remember, we're zeroing in on the artists' use of light and texture."

Students reread and added notes to their journals, using this time to frame their discussion contributions. Tomorrow they would see another set of slides and the process would be repeated. Thursday's and Friday's classes had been spent viewing a series on the Flemish old masters which she had assembled with the express purpose of focusing on the artists' use of light. Vermeer, one of her favorite painters, had been well-represented. While they wrote, she read and reread her notes, trying to decide whether to guide their interpretations or allow a more open-ended discussion. She preferred the latter approach.

After this discussion, they would move to Spanish paintings of the same period. Feeling prepared at last, she set down her notebook and allowed her mind to wander back to the previous evening. She had been prepared to despise Harry Winthrop. In fact, she had not even considered another possibility. She had expected to dine with a boorish, self-centered fool, but Harry Winthrop was no fool, nor did he appear to be the slightest bit boorish or self-centered.

If someone had asked her to describe him, she would have said he was disarmingly kind and charming. In fact, she had not observed a trace of insincerity in anything he said or did, with the possible exception of his good-natured comments about Anne Greyson and her silly mystery novels.

By rights, she should resent and detest him. After all, he was here to snoop around, perhaps implicating her in Milt's murder. This charming stranger had invaded her peaceful, ordered world. He represented so many things she disliked, yet here she was daydreaming about him in the middle of class. Not only did she feel a traitor to Mac's memory, she also felt as if she was letting Roger down. She was certain Roger would not find the handsome newcomer half as charming as she did.

She made it through the rest of morning, banishing thoughts of Harry Winthrop from mind until she bumped into Kitty Bigalow in the lunch line.

"So, I hear you're hot and heavy with the playboy sleuth. Not giving the rest of us gals much of a chance, are you? The man hasn't even toured campus and you've already snatched him up. You're a sly one, Bess Dore. Decided to jump back into the dating scene with a splash, haven't you?"

"Kitty, what in the world are you talking about?"

Was the entire campus abuzz with tales of the Bridgham's dinner and her ride home with Harry Winthrop? Or, had Garrett and Will spread the word about their dinner at Ahab's?

"Don't play coy with me girl. It's alright, you're entitled, but don't expect to keep a wrap on that man of yours. All the girls are positively salivating. I mean, I'm married, unfortunately, so can't join in the hunt, but others are zeroing in. In fact, he's got a lunch date with Joan as we speak. Took her into town."

"Kitty, I'm not sure what you're talking about, but Mr. Winthrop and I barely know each other. Any time we've spent together was strictly business, related to the case. That is why he's here, remember? I'm a suspect, he has to interview me."

"Fine, fine, fine, if you want to play it that way. Ta ta!" Kitty waved in her best Miss Jean Brody imitation. She even looked a little like Maggie Smith in her sensible tweed skirt, silk blouse and paisley scarf tied jauntily round her long, thin neck. "If you want to call a cozy little dinner at Ahab's and your Romeo and Juliet act the other night business, go right ahead, dearie. We'll all play along. After all you've —"

"What are you talking about?" Diners at surrounding tables abandoned all pretense of eating and were now staring openly at the pair, hanging on every word. Lowering her voice, Bess continued, "What do you mean, Romeo and Juliet, for goodness sakes?"

"Well," Kitty hissed, eyes gleefully scanning the room. "I have it on good authority that our resident Hercule Poirot carried his lady fair into her little l ove nest."

"That is the most ridiculous thing I've ever heard. Who is spreading such vicious lies?"

"Calm down, Bess, dear. The Caseys saw you two love birds." Kitty referred to Bess' immediate neighbors, a husband and wife who were math teachers in the Upper School. The neighbors watched out for each other, taking in the mail, watering plants or watching over things if the others were away. Sylvia and Mark Casey were warm-hearted, wonderful neighbors, but also two of the nosiest people Bess knew.

"They saw the whole thing," Kitty went on gleefully. "They were driving by. Saw a strange car in your driveway and were concerned, of course. Who wouldn't be? Anyway, when they drove in to check on you, they saw Mr. Winthrop carrying you. Mark got out and called, but your Mr. Winthrop identified himself and reassured them that all was well. When you two disappeared into the house, the Caseys drove off. Described him as charming and gallant."

Mouth agape, Bess felt panic rising in her chest. What had happened Saturday night? Why couldn't she remember? "Excuse me, Kitty, I've got to go." She pushed past her colleague and ran from the room.

Except for monitoring a study hall, she had the afternoon free. Her seniors had gone on a field trip and field hockey practice had been canceled. She called the office and arranged for an upper school intern to cover the study hall. Then, gathering her things, she headed out. Before she could get to the parking lot, Jean Davol caught her on the steps of the arts building.

CHAPTER 33

"Bess, hi! Have you got a few minutes?"

"Oh, Jean, I, I, of course. Would you like to come back and talk in the studio?"

"You look like you're on your way out, my dear. Could I buy you a quick cup of tea in the Commons? We can talk in the Board Room. I promise, I won't keep you long."

Bess smiled, following Jean who was already 10 yards ahead, leading the way. Once they were settled at the long Board Room table, side by side, tea in hand, Jean began. "Thank you, my dear. I'm sure you're swamped, as always, but I wanted to speak briefly about an issue I'm having with Religious Life. I also wanted your advice about the memorial."

"It's rather a delicate issue, but I know you're discreet."

Bess regarded her companion, a Yankee through and through, her straight, shoulder length salt and pepper hair pulled back in a headband, sensible cardigan and matching skirt in muted shades of gray and blue. She liked Jean and Bill, her husband. They were kind, grounded people, Jean's always the voice of reason during often contentious board meetings. She smiled, setting down her tea. "Of course, Jean, how can I help?"

"You see, there's been a bit of awkwardness at meetings this year, what with Peter leaving and all. It's been difficult to get a handle on it, but I had a call the other day, and I didn't quite know what to make of it.

"As you know, since you cycled out of Religious Life, the Committee consists of myself, Darrell, who never attends meetings, Will McGuire, Jane Fellows and Kevin LeBlanc. First, there's the tension between Will and Kevin which, frankly, one could cut with a knife." Bess shook her head. "Not to worry, I'm not sure I even want to know what that's about. Then, Carrie Thurbert called yesterday and asked me to reconstitute the Committee as a personal favor to her. No explanation, no nothing, just asked if I, as Chair, had such authority. She wanted more staff to come on board as well as people whom I thought would be more sensitive to Peter during his final term at Old Harbor.

"I see by your expression that you are as surprised as I was. It's most extraordinary, don't you think? I hardly know what to do, but I don't feel it would be appropriate or politic to take such an action, do you?"

"Have you spoken to Peter?"

"Heavens no. I don't want to worry him with all this with Milt. Besides, I'm certain he would be mortified."

Bess agreed, but sat silent, unsure of what to say. She didn't know Carrie well and couldn't imagine what had motivated such a ridiculous and inappropriate request. Finally, she said, "Jean, I'm not sure what to say, but my best advice would be to do nothing. I suspect if you take no action, Carrie will not repeat her request. However, if she does, I think you should speak to Peter, mortified or not."

"Perhaps that is the best course. Thank you, Bess. Very sensible indeed. Now, about Milt's service. Any advice there?"

They spoke for a few minutes, agreeing that the simpler, the better. Finally, they rose to go. Bess wanted to hug Jean for the blessed few minutes of relief their conversation had provided in the midst of a strained and tumultuous day.

After Jean departed, she headed back towards the parking lot. In her car, just about to start the engine, she spied Peter Thurbert hailing her from across the lot. Not wanting to endure one more conversation about the previous night and Harry Winthrop, she gave him a guilty wave and drove off.

CHAPTER 34

Once home, she threw her bags on the front hall table and was headed to her bedroom as the phone rang.

"Damn," she said, running to answer it.

"Bess, it's me, Roger. Have you got a minute?"

"Oh Roger, this isn't a good time." She transferred the receiver from hand to hand as she shrugged out of her jacket. "Could you call back a little later or I could call you?"

"No, you couldn't. And, if you're all in a dither over your conduct this weekend, you should be. Now, shake it off, for Christ sakes, and listen to me."

He knows too. She groaned, sinking down in the armchair. I'm the laughing stock of the whole campus. "What is it?"

"It's about that Louie. I've just learned about a death a few years back, a student named Liz Mederois?"

"Lizzie, yes. She committed suicide, Louie found her. He adored her. Never been the same since." She wondered why Roger didn't remember the case.

As if reading her thoughts, he said, "Happened when I was in Germany."

"Of course," she said, recalling hearing from someone that he had been in the service. "Lizzie was a lovely girl."

"Look, I want to talk to Predo. Says in the police report from Mederois' file that Louie knows everything that goes on around campus. He might've seen something or somebody the night Wickie died. Can you get the guy to make any sense?"

"Not likely. He's pretty fragile and confused most of the time, I'm afraid. Perhaps if Billy were with him, coaxing him along? He trusts Billy."

"Ya mean the raven-haired Adonis, head of the grounds crew?"

"Yes, Billy Blackburn. He and Louie live together."

"Look, I'm coming to campus tomorrow morning. They trust you. See if you can learn anything, please. I need some kind of break here and I thought, if you run into Blackburn or Louie, you could probe a little?"

"But, I —"

"I'll check in with you before I try to find them."

"Roger, I don't know what I could possibly learn."

"Well, that's what you're gonna find out, okay?"

"I wouldn't know where to begin or what to —"

"And, you can fill me in on Junior Sherlock, too. That is, if you're not already engaged to the guy."

"That's not funny!"

"Hey, from what I hear you and him were practically--"

"Goodbye." She slammed down the phone, stalking to her bedroom, frantically beginning a search for the clothes she had worn Saturday evening.

In her diminished state the previous day, she had not given them a thought. Finally, she discovered the skirt, draped neatly over a wire hanger in the back of a closet, the wrong closet. He had put it in with her summer clothes in a closet she seldom used. Right beside it, hung the blouse and sweater.

"Oh, dear Lord, what have I done?" Rifling through the phone book, she dialed, heart pounding.

A distinguished voice answered on the second ring, "Winthrop Hall."

"Hello, is Mr. Winthrop, the younger Mr. Winthrop in?"

"I'm afraid Mr. Harry is out at the moment. Can I leave him a message? Tell him who called?"

"Yes, please ask him to call Bess Dore at his earliest convenience."

"Very good, miss."

Ringing off she grabbed her coat and headed out the back door for a walk in the woods. Fool, fool, fool, she thought as she trudged on. She certainly could not sit at home surrounded by photos of Mac, his soft, kind eyes staring at her in every room.

CHAPTER 35

Two hours in the woods had cleared her head and Bess felt better, ready to face the crisis head-on. If she could survive Mac's death, she could certainly survive this nonsense. As she came up the walkway, she heard the phone ringing. She ran to answer, breathless as she picked up.

"Hey girl, it's me. You okay?"

"Janie? Hi, of course, I'm alright, why?"

"Well, for one thing, you sound terrible. Then, there's the matter of you tearing out of school like you were at the Indy 500. Peter's worried about you."

"Whatever for?"

"My darling, I've heard the rumors and so has he. Wanta talk about it?"

"Oh, God Janie, I want to crawl into a hole and never come out. At least not until they find Milt's killer and Harry Winthrop is several continents away."

"Don't be an ass. For goodness sakes, Bess! It's not as bad as all that. Besides, your Mr. Winthrop's not going anywhere. When I was waiting my turn to speak to him, I overheard him telling Will McGuire that'd he planned to stay on in Old Harbor after the investigation."

"You spoke to him?"

"My dear Bess, practically everyone's spoken to him. He's investigating us, remember? He's been all over campus today, asking questions, getting to know people, peering into every nook and cranny. I tell you, if your Mr. Winthrop doesn't find the murderer, no one can."

"He is not my Mr. Winthrop!"

"Sorry. Anyway, he's making the rounds. Awful cute, isn't he? Has all the women swooning, making complete asses of themselves."

"Myself included, apparently."

"Don't be silly. I'm talking batting eyelashes and ludicrous come-ons. Enough to make a hooker blush. That's not your style. And, he's got the kids eating right out of his hand. I thought Amy Flathers was gonna faint dead away in his arms. What I observed today was blatant, uncensored flirtation, not the passionate romance you seem to already have."

"Oh for pete's sake!"

"Kidding, just kidding. Don't get all worked up. He's a nice guy, Bess. You could do worse, you know. And, we all lightening up after Detective Demaris. You have to admit, Roger is a touch gloomy."

She sighed. "Oh, please. Don't let's start in on poor Roger." Much as she loved Jane, she couldn't listen to another word.

"Want me to come over?"

"No."

"How 'bout if we meet at Pop's for supper?" Jane asked, referring to Pop's Diner in the village.

"No thanks, I just want to be alone."

"Sweetie, do you think that's wise? I don't like the way you sound. Why don't I just pop over and bring a pizza?"

"I'm fine, Jane, really. Just tell me one thing. What exactly did you hear today? About me and Mr. Winthrop?"

"Very little beyond the fact that he spent the night."

"Spent the night! Oh really, this is unbelievable."

"Bess, I knew it wasn't true. Everyone did, but you know how people love a good story. And, look on the bright side. This is a whole new image for you."

"That is not funny."

"Sorry, look, hon."

"Jane, I've gotta go. The doorbell's ringing."

"Call me?"

Careful not to slam down the receiver, she headed for the front door where she found a dejected Roger Demaris standing on her front stoop.

CHAPTER 36

"Hi, gotta minute?" He looked as if he hadn't slept in a week.

"I thought you weren't coming over until tomorrow."

"Changed my mind. Couldn't go home with this itch about that Predo fella. Thought I'd have a go at him. Can I come in?"

Stepping aside, she led the way back to the study. The room was icy cold, the French doors standing open, forgotten in her earlier dash to the phone. Shutting them, she shivered, hugging herself as she sat in the armchair beside him. "Want anything? Tea? Coffee? A soda?"

"No, thanks. I can't stay but a minute. I need you. I mean, I meant to say, I need your help. Your boyfriend's all over the place, nosin' into everything, trampling over witnesses, mudding up the waters to the point where we're never gonna —"

"He is not my boyfriend! And, I have no intention of getting into the middle of your sleuth-of-the-year contest. If you two can't work together, I don't want to hear about it. Now, if that's why you came, you'd better go. I've had an awful day and I'd like to be alone."

"I'm sorry, Bess. Look, no more bullshit. Your life and what you do with it is none of my business."

"Correct."

"So, let's forget it. It's not a contest either. I don't want your help to beat out your, I mean, our Mr. Winthrop. I just need you to talk to Louie."

"About what?"

"About anything. What he saw, what he knows, whatever. I just stopped by to see him and I'll be damned if I could make friggin' sense outta a thing the guy said. All a bunch of garble."

"Was Billy with him?" She studied him, wondering why he had felt it imperative to pounce on Louie tonight. What was so important that it couldn't have waited until morning like they planned? Of course, she knew the answer. He wanted to get the jump on Harry Winthrop.

He nodded. "Blackburn practically held his hand, but it didn't help. Every question I asked, he'd spout off about how he'd seen her or he'd ramble on about being safe. Crap like that. Same stuff he was goin' on about the day I crashed into him."

She nodded. "Lizzie, that's who he's talking about, when he says 'I saw her.' He means Lizzie. He's remembering when he found her, just after she died."

"Talk to him. Try to catch him in a lucid moment, will you? He likes you, he knows you. You guys sit around and shoot the breeze sometimes, don't you? See if you can get anything out of him about the day Wickie died, okay?"

"I don't think Lou has much of a temporal awareness. The passage of time means nothing to him."

"Give it a try. That's all I'm asking, okay?"

"Well, I suppose I could have a talk with him. I'll try."

He rose. "Thanks. Now, to check Susan LeBlanc's alibi. She's one slippery broad, that one. Haven't managed to pin her down worth shit. Loves to talk, but, it's all in circles, like she's spinning a web."

"Should you be discussing this with me? Me being a prime suspect and all?"

"Yeah, right."

"I can't imagine Susan hurting anyone."

"Humph. You probably can't imagine anyone hurting anyone. There's another side to everyone. I'm betting you've never seen the Susan LeBlanc I met when I visited the lady in her lair. A real vixen, and, none too happy with Wickie either.

He had somethin' else goin' on when he died and LeBlanc knew about her. Tried to make out like she didn't care, but that's bullshit. She cared plenty. Left her husband, who she still loves, by the way. What does she get — Milt, the lech. That lady is hurtin' and she's none too keen at being left on her lonesome."

"What could she possibly hope to gain by killing Milt?"

"Who knows, but my money's on her or that bitch Richards. 'Course it could be your buddy, Thurbert, but I haven't figured out a motive for him yet. I will though. Wickie had somethin' on him, I'm sure of it. Don't 'spose you'd like to help me out there?" She glared in silent reproach. "Oh well, maybe it'll turn out to be that puffed up pomegranate Parmenter. God, I hate that guy. Think Milt mighta been boffing old Muriel? Goin' fer the mature ladies fer a change?"

"Roger!"

He laughed. "Hey, it's just a theory. Gotta smile outta you, at least. Take care of yourself, Bess. You look like shit. You're not the first woman to be caught in a compromising position, ya know."

"Don't start, Roger. Please."

"Okay, okay, I'm goin', but, lock the door behind me. You keepin' things locked up tight?" She nodded, closing her eyes. "Good."

CHAPTER 37

As Roger showed himself out, Bess sank into her chair, closing her eyes. What could she do? How could she possibly go back to school and endure the stares, the snickers, the whisperings, the teasing? And the students. If the campus was abuzz, chances were very good that the students had gotten wind of it, too. Oh, Lord, what could she do?

The phone rang and she picked up the den extension to hear Peter's voice. "Bess? It's me. I'm calling to see. Well, how are you?"

"Oh Peter, I wouldn't know where to begin. I assume you've heard it all?"

"Yes and I don't believe a word of it, so put the whole ridiculous business out of your mind."

"How can I?"

"It'll die down in a day or two. These things always do."

"These things, oh, Lord. And, what do you propose I do in the meantime?"

"Rise above it all."

"Well, you're sweet to call."

"Actually, I've another reason for calling. It's about the Search Committee." He referred to the committee formed to seek his replacement. Bess along with two other faculty members had been asked to serve.

"Oh?"

"I wondered if the school finances had come up in your discussions."

"Well, we've only had two meetings," she began, hedging already. The subject of Carol Richards had come up several times, but the committee had been given strict instructions to keep all discussions confidential. She hadn't told a soul and she knew she should not begin now.

"I know, Bess. I wouldn't ask unless, well, it's terribly important."

"The business office has come up, but that's all, in discussions about how much of a business background we should look for in a new Head and so forth. Why do you ask?"

"I can't say, except that Mr. Winthrop, who it seems has a fair bit of business experience himself, has been checking into things and has found some irregularities. I just wondered if the Board members on your committee had mentioned anything."

Mr. Winthrop moves fast, she thought. How long had he been here, three days? "I'm sorry Peter. I can't think of a thing. You'd better speak to Cornie. He hasn't been to any of our meetings yet, but I'm sure he'd be aware of anything like that." Why was she telling this to Peter? As headmaster he knew Cornie and the Board infinitely better than she did.

"Yes, yes, I will. I'll let you go. And, Bess don't worry about the gossip. It'll die down. If I'm not worried, you shouldn't be. Everyone knows it's hogwash and Harry himself has given me a full accounting of the situation."

"How very considerate of him," she snapped, seething with indignation.

"Now, Bess, you know what I mean."

"Yes, I understand perfectly. By all means, go right to the source. Don't bother to ask your friend of many years, your own faculty member. Don't waste time hearing her side of the story, just ask Harry. He's sure to give you the truth."

"Now, Bess that's not fair. I tried to speak to you, but you tore out of the parking lot like you were on your way to a fire. I ran into Harry this afternoon and he —"

"Never mind, Peter. It's fine. Listen, I've got to go."

"Would you like to take a couple of days off?"

"No, thank you, I'll be fine. You're right of course. I just have to face up to this and go on. I'll see you in the morning."

Clicking down the receiver, she headed for the kitchen to heat up some soup. Not the slightest bit hungry, she felt she should eat something to keep up her strength. She had just settled down with a bowl of vegetable soup and toast when the doorbell rang.

"Oh for pete's sake, what now?" Never in all her years in the house had she had so much activity, so many phone calls, so many unexpected visitors.

'What now?' turned out to be Harry Winthrop standing on her doorstep with an armful of daisies. "Can I come in?"

CHAPTER 38

Bess shrugged, stepping aside. "Why not? Come right in. Did you make sure the Caseys saw you drive in? Wouldn't want them to miss the latest tryst, would we? In fact, why don't you get back in your car, back up the driveway, beep the horn a few times, just to be sure."

"Bess, I —"

"Gotta keep the rumor mills going, don't we?"

"Bess, I'm sorry. I should have said something last night at dinner." He stepped inside, closing the door.

"Yes, you should have." Angry tears clouded her vision as she stood, limp and helpless. "Look at me, I'm a complete wreck!"

"I'm sorry, did I get you up?"

"It's only six o'clock. I don't go to bed quite that early. I was having some soup, would you like some?"

"Yes, I would. If you're sure it's not too much trouble."

They ate in silence. Afterwards, Bess made a pot of herbal tea and suggested they drink it in the study.

His eyes watched her every move, as they sat surrounded by reminders of the man she had loved, still loved. "Rough day?"

"I've had better." She smiled wanly, the steaming chamomile tea helping to sooth her frayed nerves.

"I've heard of small town gossip before, but this place is in a class by itself."

Swallowing a large gulp of tea that burned in her throat going down, she sat up straighter. "I want you to tell me exactly what happened Saturday night. I want the truth, please. And, leave nothing out."

"Well, as you said, you were very tired. A little too tired, I'm afraid to get out of the car. You were, asleep when we got here."

"Passed out, you mean. I said, I want the truth."

"I'm trying, but don't forget, I'd just met you. Anyway, tried to wake you up, but when that failed I carried you into the house and put you to bed. End of story."

"But I was —"

"Your clothes were damp and I didn't want you to catch cold. I just pulled them off, keeping my eyes closed the whole time. Then I hung everything up, turned out the lights and was gone. Locked the door on my way out."

"And, we didn't? You and I didn't?"

"Not a thing."

"You wouldn't lie to me, to make me feel better, would you?"

"Let me ask you something. Have you ever slept with someone you hardly knew? Hopped into bed on the first date? That sort of thing?"

"Of course not."

"Then, what makes you think you'd suddenly jump in bed with me just because you had a little too much to drink? Not that I wouldn't be flattered, mind you, but I make it a practice never to take advantage of inebriated women. Never."

Blushing, she smoothed back her hair, noticing her wrinkled beige skirt, one of a whole closetful of sensible wool skirts. It matched her drab beige cardigan. How dowdy I must look, she thought miserably. How dowdy and dull.

Harry watched her, reading her thoughts as if she'd spoken them aloud. Bess Dore, if you only knew how lovely you are. "What a silly fool, I am." She sniffed, mortified to find herself crying in front of a man she hardly knew. "I've made such a mess of things. I don't know what I was thinking of, drinking like that. I hardly ever drink and if I do it's no more than a glass of wine."

"I'd never have guessed." He smiled, handing her his handkerchief. The letters "H & S" were embroidered in the corner in delicate, curling stitches. "Don't beat yourself up. Everyone's entitled to a lost night once in a while."

"Why didn't you say anything last night?"

"You already looked suicidal and I wasn't about to add to your misery. Fact is, I would never have mentioned it. It was no big deal. If it hadn't been for those snoops at the end of your driveway no one would've been the wiser."

He was rewarded with a glimmer of a smile. "It really is too ridiculous for words, isn't it?"

"That's the spirit. Now, let's forget it and start over, shall we?"

"Yes, I'd like that."

"Bess, I'd like to know you better. If you'll let me."

"I'm not interested in a romantic relationship," she blurted, suddenly realizing that he might have meant something completely different. "What I mean is —"

"Whatever you say. But, can we at least be friends?"

"Yes, yes, I should think so."

"And, while we're on the subject of friends, I've met your friend Demaris and I don't think he likes me."

She laughed. "Roger's not so bad. He just takes a while to warm up to people."

"I'll say."

"He's a good policeman. He knows what he's doing and he doesn't like others getting in his way."

"I'm sure he's great. Very protective of you, by the way. Have you known each other long?"

It was on the tip of her tongue to say none of your business, but she replied, "All my life. Where did you see him?"

"In the business office this afternoon. Went up to see Ms. Richards, but she gave me the slip. Him, too, apparently."

She smiled. "Yes, I expect Ms. Richards would avoid Roger like the plague. She's not very happy with him."

"Not a friend of yours, is she?"

"No, but then I don't think Carol has many friends on campus. She keeps to herself."

"She's not one of your favorite people, is she?"

"Not really, but truthfully, I don't know her well. She could be a lovely person for all I know."

Bess thought back to her earlier conversation with Peter and the Search Committee discussion about Carol Richards and the state of school finances. She raised her hands. "And, I know nothing about the school's finances."

"Okay. Good to know. I am, however, curious about the elusive Ms. Richards. The books don't add up. Maybe you can help me track her down tomorrow?"

"Don't count on it. As I said, we're not close."

"Can I check in with you? I have an appointment with Susan LeBlanc early in the morning, but then I'll be at school for the rest of the day. If I come by and carry your books between classes, will you help me get in to see Richards?"

She laughed again. "I suppose that would be fine, but I can't imagine why you need me."

He gave her a soft smile, rising and apologizing for keeping her up on a school night.

Soon after Harry's departure, Bess slipped into a hot bath, then bed. Despite the chaos of the day, she fell into a deep, restful slumber, the most peaceful night's sleep she had experienced in years.

CHAPTER 39

The temperature dropped during the night and hovered for most of the day in the mid-forties. Eschewing Mac's threadbare wool overcoat, Bess left the house early wearing her own, navy parka. She alternated between the two coats in cold weather, but this morning she felt guilty pushing the old herringbone aside as she reached for the parka. Ten years married to Mac's memory and suddenly her whole world had been turned upside down. Try as she might to focus on her classes, the only thing she could think about was her meeting with Harry Winthrop.

During lunch, she called the Business Office and arranged to meet with Carol Richards at four thirty. A little before four she straightened up, stopped at the Coop for donuts and hot chocolate, and headed across campus. Long, afternoon shadows stretched over the lawns and fields as she spied the old gardener raking along the stone walls bordering the orchards.

"Hello, Lou," she called.

"Hey Missus D." He stopped, leaning on his rake, grinning from ear to ear.

Holding up the bag, she called, "I stopped at the Coop for hot chocolate and doughnuts. Come join me, will you? Must be close to quitting time?"

"Can't, not yet."

"It's okay, five minutes won't hurt. I'll say it was my idea, that I made you. Okay?"

"Okay." Louie needed little persuasion when doughnuts were involved and he loved 'Mac's lady.' Bess often brought him a mid-afternoon snack and so they had played out this conversation many times over the years. They would sit and chat, sometimes joined by Billy Blackburn.

For several minutes, they sat in companionable silence. When he started on his second doughnut, she began. "Lou, have you met Mr. Winthrop or Detective Demaris, the policeman?"

"Saw the cop. He talked to me."

"How 'bout Mr. Winthrop?"

"Nope."

"I bet you've seen him. He's the new man who' been walking around campus the past few days. He's been talking to people, asking lots of questions. He's tall, with hair about my color."

"Haven't seen him."

"So, how'd you get on with the policeman?"

"Good."

"Was there something you wanted to tell him? Maybe something secret you knew about Mr. Wickie? Or something strange that might have happened the day he died?"

"Saw him. Saw her. I'm safe, I'm safe."

"Of course you're safe." She reached over, patting his arm. "Don't be scared. I won't let anything happen to you. You believe that, don't you?"

"Won't get you, won't get you."

"What won't get me, Lou?"

"Monster."

"What monster?"

"I'm safe, I'm safe," he moaned, rocking back and forth.

"I'm sorry, Lou. I frightened you. Forget the monster. Let's talk about the police man and Mr. Winthrop. They're your friends. I wanted you to know that. You're perfectly safe with them just like you are with me, okay? They're here to help make the school safe again after Mr. Wickie's death. You remember Mr. Wickie, don't you?"

"Don't like Milton."

Suppressing a smile, she said, "Many of us didn't care for Milton. Why didn't you like him?"

"Don't like Milton."

"Do you ever go up to Milton's office? To clean or anything?"

"No, don't like Milton!"

"I'm sorry, Lou. I just thought maybe, I mean I wondered if you might have seen anyone visiting Milton last week? Late in the afternoon when you and Billy were packing things up? You do understand that Milton was killed, don't you?"

Suddenly he jumped up, upsetting his cocoa. "Don't like Milton! Don't like Milton! I'm safe! I'm safe! I saw her! I saw her!"

"Oh Lou, I'm sorry. I didn't mean to upset you."

"Mac's lady better watch out. Not safe, not safe."

"What's not safe?" said a familiar voice behind them. Harry stood behind them, concern in his blue eyes. He was dressed in blue jeans and a ragg wool sweater, an Old Harbor Friends navy warm-up jacket slung over his shoulder. Crablike, Louie scuttled sideways.

"Lou, this is Mr. Winthrop, Harry." But, the gardener was already halfway across the common, rake and bucket in hand.

"Oh, dear. I'm afraid you've scared him off."

"Sorry, I could disappear? Were you having a heart to heart?"

"No, never mind. He's too upset. I wasn't able to make much sense, except that he disliked Milt."

"Who didn't?"

"Yes, well."

"I heard him saying 'I saw her', or somethin' like that. Does he think a woman killed Wickie?"

"No, I mean, I don't know but, you can't go by what Lou says. He's been talking like that for years. When he says 'I saw her', he's usually referring to a former student, Lizzie Mederois. Louie was very attached to Lizzie. She committed suicide. Took some kind of poison. Poor Lou found her. He's, well, he's never been quite the same. Shall we go up? Wouldn't want to keep the dragon lady waiting." She started towards Commons Hall.

CHAPTER 40

"How was your day? Any better than yesterday?"

"Much. Plenty of stares of course, and lots of talk, but I did my job, held my head up and looked straight ahead in the lunchroom. Somehow I got through it."

"That's the spirit. By the way, the LeBlanc woman gave me the slip again. That's three times I've made appointments and she's dodged me."

"Roger, Detective Demaris seems to have the same problem. I believe he had to dispatch one of his officers to stake out her house. Funny, it doesn't seem like Susan. His description of their meeting together didn't sound at all like the Susan I know.   Where have you tried to find her?"

"Home, shop, you name it."

"She spends a lot of time at the gym. Teaches classes and so forth. Did you try there?" She led the way into the Commons Building, pointing out the study hall as they went by, realizing after the fact that he'd probably seen it and every other inch of the school already.

"Where is this gym?"

"In town, the Harbor Gym. It's a small place. I've been a few times with my friend Jane, I think you've met her, Jane Fellows?"

"Ah yes, Jane. A real spit fire that one. Pretty too." Bess nodded. "What're all these beautiful, unmarried women doin' hidin' out here?"

"We're —" she started, then blushed crimson.   "I mean, they're not —"

"'We're is fine, Bess. You were right the first time. You're most definitely one of the beautiful women. In fact, you're the only beautiful woman I'm interested in and I'm not talking about the case."

"As I was saying," she stammered, weak-kneed as they started up the steps. "If you ask Jane, I'll bet she can tell you exactly when Susan exercises and teaches."

It wasn't that a man hadn't been interested in her. Several men, including Milt, had asked her out since Mac's death, but Harry Winthrop was the first and only man since Mac who attracted her. The idea was terrifying.

They stopped on the landing and found him staring at her. "Will you have dinner with me?" The question came out of nowhere and she heard herself responding, "yes" before she could conjure up all the reasons why she shouldn't or couldn't.

"Good, let's get this over with so we can be on our way."

They found Carol Richards' door ajar and Bess tapped lightly, receiving a clipped, "come" in reply.

The business manager sat behind a massive cherry desk, girded and ready for battle. Bess forced a smile. "Carol, hi. I'd like to introduce Harry Winthrop. He's the investigator that the Board —"

"Oh, do hush, Bess! What do you take me for, a complete moron? I haven't been hiding under a rock for the past week, you know. I know perfectly well who Mr. Winthrop is. Now, come, sit." Swinging out of her seat, she sidled across the room to a round conference table, waving Harry into a chair, dismissing Bess with nary a glance.

While one would never call Carol Richards beautiful, she did have a certain style. In a frenetic, staccato way, she was a striking woman. Her thin, pinched face, framed by blonde, perfectly dyed, perfectly coiffed shoulder-length hair, was heavily made-up. Bright red lipstick, freshly applied, stood in sharp contrast to the ghostly pallor of her cheeks. She wore an expensive, gray silk suit with a cream colored blouse its neckline revealing more than a hint of cleavage. In her two-inch heels she stood just under five feet tall. A midget, Harry thought, smiling.

"I've been waiting with baited breath to meet you, Mr. Winthrop." She slid her chair forward until their knees were touching. Surprised at this new side of the Business Manager, Bess watched Harry's reaction as the other woman leaned closer, almost falling out of the front of her blouse. For a petite woman, she was well-endowed.

Harry inched closer, if that was possible, and purred right back at her, "And I you, Ms. Richards. I've heard a lot about you." Bess rolled her eyes, wishing she were anywhere but watching the two of them.

"All of it good, I hope," she said, batting her eyelashes.

"Absolutely."

"So, what can I do for you?"

"Well, as you know, I'm looking into Milt Wickie's death at the Board's request and I wondered what light you might shed on the matter."

"Where I fit in? Where was I when he was killed? Why did I want the sonofabitch dead? That sort of thing?"

"Exactly."

"Well, at least you're an improvement over the policeman from hell. I'm afraid my account of the evening in question is a trifle boring. I was home alone all evening, no calls, no visitors. I watched a little television, then went to bed with a book, Danielle Steele's latest."

"Too bad." His voice dripping with sympathy.

"Why? Don't you like Danielle?"

"No." He laughed. "I meant, too bad, no alibi."

"Oh, don't you go worrying yourself on my account." She patted his knee. "I haven't a single reason for wishing Milt dead unless bosses have started killing employees that are pains in the butt and lousy at their jobs."

"Why didn't you fire him?"

"Because Peter Milquetoast Thurbert is a wimp. Peter's been a great head-master, but let's face it, everyone needs to move on sometime. He's gotten too soft. Hired Milt, then thought he owed the little weasel. Intolerable situation really, but then, Peter has always been a spineless jellyfish."

"Correct me if I'm wrong, Ms. Richards, but aren't you? I mean, weren't you Milt's boss?"

"Yes."

"Then why didn't you fire him yourself? Or don't you have that authority?"

"Ask Peter Thurbert that question, not me." She sat up, straightening her collar.

"Peter handles the hiring and firing of your staff then?"

"Let's talk about something else." Her voice silky again, she leaned forward. "How long will you be staying in Old Harbor, Mr. Winthrop?"

"Harry, please."

"Of course, and please, call me Carol." More eyelash batting. "Call me anytime," she whispered, leaning forward as Bess watched certain this time that she would fall right out of her blouse.

"Carol, tell me, if you didn't kill Milt, who did?"

"Well, you've got a prime suspect sitting right behind you, hon. Bess had a great motive, as you're no doubt aware. Unless of course you two are so chummy now that she's above suspicion?"

Bess gasped, but Harry continued cordial as ever. "No, no, I'm 'fraid we're looking beyond Mrs. Dore for this crime, Carol. You see, she doesn't really have a motive, except of course, the same sort of annoyance you, yourself, felt for the man. And, unlike yourself, she has an airtight alibi."

"Oh, do shut up. Of course, I know our boring little schoolmarm had nothing to do with the dirty deed. She doesn't have the guts to squash an earwig. Now, if you two will excuse me, I have work to do."

"Just a few more questions. Then, I promise, we'll get out of your hair."

She stood up, crossing the room to gaze out the window. "If you want a suspect, I'd put my money on that lunatic gardener. He's certainly capable of it and I saw him acting even more bizarre than usual the afternoon of Milt's death. Didn't think anything of it at the time. After all the man's certifiable. He's always doing kooky things, but now, I'm not so sure."

"What exactly did you see him doing?"

"I was standing right here at this window when I spied the demented little fool rummaging around in the bushes. Right down there." Harry and Bess joined her at the window. "Rummaged around, pulled out a green bookbag and looked inside. Then, he screamed, threw it back into the bushes and ran off. His behavior was so odd I searched the bushes myself on my way home and I got a run in my new, very expensive stockings for my trouble, too. "

"And?"

"It was gone."

"You think it was his?"

"How should I know. But, who else would be foolish enough to toss their belongings into the bushes? Think, Harry, think!"

"We'll check with Louie later, thanks."

"Oh, so it's we, is it? How very cozy. What are you playing — Nick and Nora Charles now?"

"Back to Mr. Wickie," he said, cutting her off with a smile. "I'm in the midst of a quiet audit of the school's books and so far things don't seem to be adding up. Do you suppose Milt was dipping into the till?"

"I wouldn't know, but I wouldn't put it past him."

"Could we talk more specifically about certain accounts? I'm especially interested in —"

"Excuse me, Harry dear. We cannot talk about any accounts with her present."

"But Mrs. Dore has —"

"Look, let me spell it out, honey lamb. I've been told to cooperate with you and I'm cooperating, but I am also the Chief Financial Officer of this institution and I will not discuss confidential financial matters with a member of the faculty present."

"Now just a minute."

"It's alright, Harry," Bess said, hopping up, glad of an excuse to leave the room. "Carol's right, it's not appropriate. I'll wait downstairs."

"Shut the door on your way out," the business manager called, rising. As she closed the door behind her, it looked to Bess as if Carol Richards intended to sit in Harry's lap.

CHAPTER 41

Dismissed from Carol Richard's office, Bess taped a note for Harry on the study hall door and walked over to the Meeting House to wait. As she reached the door, Will McGuire stepped out. His expression belied the silence from which he came. He was clearly upset, his eyes red rimmed. "Will, is everything okay?" She stepped forward, resting a hand on his forearm.

"No, everything is not okay, but it will be as soon as I straighten out a few things. I never meant to —"

"Bess?" Kevin LeBlanc emerged from the shadows at the side of the Meeting House. "Is everything alright?" He stepped between Bess and Will, arms akimbo.

Will shook his head. "Who are you kidding, LeBlanc? See you later, Bess." With that, he trod off, leaving Bess and Kevin staring after him.

"What's going on between you two, Kevin? You've been at each other's throats every time I've seen you lately."

"Ask Mr. Perfect, why don't you? His behind the scenes meddling has hurt a lot of people around here."

"Like who?"

"Like me, for one, and your friend, Peter, too. Look, I've gotta go. Are you sure you're okay?" She nodded and he stepped back into the shadows and was gone.

Closing her eyes, she decided to let speculation about Kevin and Will's feud wait. She craved the stillness that lay inside, the stark peacefulness of the Meeting House in the early evening.

Bess often came in after classes to sit and reflect on the day before heading home. Straight-backed and silent, she sat in the darkened room. A hallway lamp sent a narrow shaft of light through the partially opened door, bisecting the flickering rays of the dying day shining through the windows.

Tonight, her thoughts drifted back to Mac's final days. In her frequent reminiscing, she rarely dwelt on that period. It hurt to think of his suffering and memories of their last conversation still grieved. She had not kept her promise, and had, in fact, blocked it from her mind until the past week. Now, her dear husband's words crept back, unbidden, to tear at her heart.

She closed her eyes and saw Mac's wan face lost among the eiderdowns she had piled high over him. No matter how many quilts and blankets she wrapped around him, Mac's skeletal frame shook, delirious from the cold and pain. Her grandmother's patchwork quilt, dark velvets and satin embroidered with delicate, golden stitches, was pulled right up to his chin. Against the dark velvet, his skin appeared translucent, as if he were slowly fading away, as if one day she would look and find him disappeared altogether.

Gently, she had reached down to stroke his cheek and forehead, brushing hair from his eyes. Tiny, strawlike wisps were all that remained of the once-thick sandy hair. She had brought a cup of broth, but he couldn't swallow. "I'm sorry, my love." His voice was a whisper, a weak, valiant smile lighting up his face. "I don't seem to be able to take any right now. Maybe later."

Bess felt the familiar ache, the deep, restless throbbing in her heart, as she set down the tray and came to sit beside him, kissing his forehead. "No worries, my darling. I'll reheat it when you're ready."

"Bess, my love, I want to say something."

"Mac, please. Don't try to talk. Shall I read to you?"

"No, Bess, please." He grasped her wrist. "This may be my last chance."

"Don't be silly, darling," she said, touching the cold, dry cheek, willing her warmth into him.

"You'll be better in —"

"Bess, please." His tone silenced her. "I've been thinking about you a great deal, my lovely, sad-eyed friend, my astonishing, passionate lover. It pains me to see you unhappy, my dearest. I'm worried about what will happen to you when I'm gone."

"Please, don't talk like that Mac."

"We've had some glorious years together, my beautiful Bess. The happiest of my life. You taught me to love, in ways I never thought myself capable. Believe me, my darling, I die knowing that I have been the luckiest of men."

Sobbing, she'd taken his hand. "Mac, please don't talk anymore. I know how you feel, my dearest, you don't have to tell me."

"Let me finish. You are only thirty-two, you have your whole life ahead of you. It is my most ardent wish that you not spend your life alone."

"Let's not talk about it now." She had jumped up, gathering the tray, straightening his bedside table.

Clawlike fingers grasped for her. "Bess, listen to me. I cannot die in peace without your promise that you'll keep your heart open and marry again if the right man should come along."

"No, please don't, Mac. I couldn't possibly."

He laughed, weakly, then squeezed her hand with what, she knew, had taken tremendous effort. "I'm not asking you to run off with the first unattached male that crosses your path, but I want you to promise me that if someone comes into your life. Someone good and decent. Someone who will love you, laugh with you, work beside you, help you. If that someone comes along, I want you to promise me that you will not shut him out."

"Oh, Mac." Still sobbing, she had buried her face in the quilts piled high over his chest.

"Please don't cry, my darling. I need your strength right now more than ever. I also need your promise. It's the last thing I will ever ask of you and it means everything to me. I cannot rest peacefully until I have it."

"No, no, no! I can't."

"Bess!" His sharp tone made her sit up and she stared at him in surprise. "This is very important to me!" For an instant, the old Mac returned to her, the champion of lost causes, the righteous fighter for the underdog, for the things he believed in, his eyes blazing with passion. Then, he collapsed, closing his eyes, lost in a spasm of pain and exhaustion.

"Mac!" Terrified, she watched until the spasm of pain subsided and he opened his eyes. They were filled with tears. Clearly, he was too exhausted to speak again, but his gaze held hers, the same plea reaching out to her as if he were shouting the words.

"Oh, my darling, of course I'll promise. How selfish I've been. When you, who've never asked me for a thing, lie here so desperately ill and are only thinking of me and my well-being."

"Good." He whispered, smiled, and closed his eyes.

He never woke up. Three hours later, his wife lying beside him, Macomber Dore died, the cold broth still sitting on the bedside table where she'd set it down.

His memorial had been held in the Meeting House, a joyful celebration of a short life, well-lived. A life in service and commitment to others. Mac had specifically asked his friends and colleagues to say their goodbyes with a smile, even a joke if they could think of one. Out of the silence, many spoke of what he had meant to them and the community. She remembered Peter's words as he'd stood in the room filled to bursting, "A friend, a deeply passionate teacher and a loving husband, Mac was a person who brought out the best in people. His abiding faith and tireless devotion to his fellow human beings will never be forgotten."

CHAPTER 42

Bess was weeping, lost in time when she felt his touch on her shoulder. She reached back, expecting to grasp Mac's emaciated fingers in her own. Instead, Harry's firm hand clasped hers, startling her back to the present.

"You okay?" he asked, knowing full well that she wasn't.

Jumping up from the bench she let out a tiny yelp.

"Oh, Bess, I'm sorry. I didn't mean to startle you."

"No, it's fine. I'm fine." She walked out, ahead of him, drying her eyes.

Once outside, she walked even more briskly. "Hey, hold on a minute, will you?" He reached out, taking her arm.

"Please, let go, Harry. Can we just go? I can't, I don't feel like talking right now."

"Want to skip dinner?"

"No, I'd like to go. Didn't you want to stop by the gym to see Susan?"

"Bess, stop a second, will you? I'm not blind. I heard you crying. I know you're upset. I want to help."

"You can't help, so let's just drop it. Maybe you're right, maybe dinner is a bad idea."

"Okay, okay." Hands up, he stepped in front of her. "Can we just start over, please? I'll drop it. Not another word, okay?" She nodded mutely. "Good. Now, let's take my car. It's right next to yours."

"Could you follow me home, please? I'd really like to change."

"Of course."

While Harry waited, Bess changed into jeans and a sweater. In her comfortable clothes, her spirits began to lift as they drove into the village. "Did you learn anything helpful in your chat with Carol?"

"Precious little, but something's fishy in that office and I intend to find out what it is. That lady doesn't know it, but I've just begun to dig. My guess is that she held all the purse strings.   Milt probably couldn't have stolen a dime even if he'd wanted to. She sure doesn't impress me as someone who'd turn the reins over to an underling, especially someone she hated as much as she did old Milt."

"How could you find out?"

"Dad's got lots of contacts with the local bankers. They love him as you can probably imagine." He grinned sheepishly. "What can I say, the man's loaded. All the information will be off the record, you understand, but then, I'm only interested in the murder, not embezzling or anything else the ice princess may have been up to. Here we are." He swung the Mercedes into the parking lot of the Harbor Gym. "Time to give Ms. LeBlanc a work-out."

As they approached the gym's front entrance, the door swung open and Demaris stepped out. "If it isn't the happy couple." He swaggered towards them. If Bess hadn't known better, she'd have sworn he'd been drinking.

"Hello, Roger." She smiled, bracing herself.

"Detective," Harry nodded.

"So? What brings you two here? Starting a partners' exercise program? Two for the price of one?"

"Don't be ridiculous, Roger. We came to speak to Susan."

"Whoo-ee, Miz LeBlanc's popular tonight. First, a cozy little chat with yours truly, now a rendezvous with the Mod Squad."

"Look Demaris. We can work together on this, you know. I'm happy to sit down with you."

Demaris ignored him, drawing Bess aside. "Whatd'ya learn from the loonie?"

Shocked at his cruelty, she replied icily. "If you're referring to Louie, very little, I'm afraid."

"Well, keep after him. I know that nutzo saw something and it's just a matter of getting him to —"

"Roger!" Embarrassed by his insensitivity, she refused to allow him to continue, recognizing the pathetic display of bravado for what it was. Anxious to be gone, she added, "And, Harry's right. You two should be talking, sharing information."

"Give it a rest, Bess." His dark eyes flashed fire. "Before this Bozo arrived you were, we were, shit, why am I bothering? Look, this is a police investigation, in case you'd forgotten. I can't share a fuckin' thing with you even if I wanted to. Now, if you'll excuse me, gotta go." Pushing between them, he strode off, calling over his shoulder, "Good luck with Jane Fonda, you'll need it!"

CHAPTER 43

Harry followed Bess into the Harbor Gym, wondering again about her past with Roger Demaris. Moist air, laced with sweat and Ben Gay, assailed them as they stepped over the threshold, driving speculation about Bess and the irascible policeman from Harry's mind for the time being. A slender, young man in his early twenties, directed them to Studio B, "two doors down on the left. Class is just beginning, but Susan can probably spare a minute or two." As they started down the hallway, he called, "Cop was just here you know!"

Cracking the door of the studio, they spied a roomful of leotarded women, arms stretched high above their heads, bending first to one side, then the other, most in synch with the music. Must be an advanced class, Bess thought, remembering her own gangly group, constantly bumping into each other, not one of them in step with the teacher, never mind their neighbors. At the front of the group, back to them, a lithe figure, her long, black hair tied back in a pony tail, called out the steps, her booming voice just audible over the blaring music.

"Susan!"

She turned. "Bess, what are you doing here?" As she walked towards them, the picture of health in tricolored spandex, the class continued the dance in a slightly less synchronized fashion. Foxy, was Harry's initial impression and Roger was right. The body most definitely gave a young Jane Fonda a run for her money. He stepped from behind Bess.

Susan's expression changed instantly. "What can I do for you?"

"Can we go somewhere to talk?" Bess asked. Once again, it was clear — three was a crowd.

"Sure, hold on." Susan tore her eyes from Harry long enough to call out to a woman at the back of the room. "Betsy, come up and take over, will you?" Turning back, she ushered them from the studio, leading the way to a small office down the hall. "So, what's this about?" she asked, as soon as the door closed behind them.

"This is Harry Winthrop, Susan. He's looking into Milt's death."

"Bess, for Christ sake, a cop just finished wasting half an hour of my time. Haven't we all answered enough questions? Who the hell are you, his deputy?"

"My fault, Ms. LeBlanc. I asked Bess to bring me. I should have introduced myself. I've been trying to set up a meeting with you for several days, remember my calls?"

"Look, Mr. Winthrop."

"Harry, please."

"Harry, then... I know I don't have to answer a single one of your goddamn questions, but I'm gonna be nice, okay? Here it is, and this is the last time I'm sayin' it. Yes, I was Milt's lover. Have been for more than a year. I've left my husband and don't intend to go back and that's it."

"Where were you the night Milt died?"

"Right here, from four to ten. Teaching and manning the desk. Couldn't even leave for supper so I grabbed a yogurt between classes."

"How'd your husband feel about this arrangement with Mr. Wickie?"

"How the hell do you think he felt? He didn't like it, but there wasn't a damn thing he could do about it. Milt wasn't the reason Kevin and I split up, despite what you may have heard to the contrary. He just came along at a convenient moment. Our separation was mutual, believe me. Whatever you do, don't waste your sympathy on Kevin. You know him, Bess. He was a bad boy many times over the years. Now, if you don't mind, I've got to get back to class."

"What about last Thursday? Did you, perhaps, leave your class like tonight?"

"Last Thursday's class is my ultra advanced students. It's a two-hour class, very intense, very teacher directed. No one can teach it but me. No one."

"Of course." Harry stepped back, thinking that Ms. LeBlanc wasn't quite as attractive as she had first appeared. "Thank you, we'll let you go."

As they drove out of the parking lot, he whistled. "That's one tough cookie."

"Susan's been through a lot." Bess leaned back, resting her head against the soft, leather headrest, suddenly very tired. "And, she's right. Living with Kevin was no picnic. He's had a roving eye for as long as I've known him. Sad thing is, Susan deserved a lot better than Milt."

"Well, she's rid of him now. And, we're rid of her and the whole mess for tonight at least. Shall we dine, m'lady?"

"What kind of food would you like?"

"Oh, didn't I tell you? I have the establishment all picked out." He was smiling over at her in the growing darkness. "I hope you like Indian food?" She nodded. "Good, it's a specialty at Chez Winthrop!"

CHAPTER 44

Bess had met the elder Winthrop once or twice and had seen him around the village or touring the campus on Peter's arm. Usually such tours preceded an announcement of a new building or project made possible by Winthrop millions. Occasionally, Harry Winthrop also appeared on the podium at convocations or graduations, and, of course, building dedications. Despite these many sightings, Bess had never had a conversation with the school's most generous patron, much less sat down to dinner with him. As Harry ushered her into the cavernous foyer of Winthrop Hall, she wasn't sure how she felt about it.

They proceeded onward into a lavishly appointed study, three of the room's four walls lined floor to ceiling with bookshelves. Polished cherry trim framed thousands of beautiful leather bound volumes. Two long sofas, covered in soft leather, festooned with piles of bright kilim pillows, dominated the room's center, a massive round coffee table between them. On the table, sat an enormous vase of autumn flowers, mums, daisies, gerbera and sedum. Smaller arrangements of the same flowers were scattered about the room. A fire blazed in the fieldstone hearth, armchairs covered in soft, green plaid on either side beckoning one to sit in the warmth.

"Not nearly as imposing as it looks," Harry said, leading her to an armchair by the fire. "We spend our evenings here — television's hidden behind mysteries." Pushing a button on the end table to the left of one of the couches, he stood back watching her expression as the wall of books opened a crack, then slightly wider until the whole partition started turning, making a complete revolution. The bookshelves slowly disappeared as a floor to ceiling entertainment center slid into place. "Dad's eyesight isn't what it used to be." He pointed to a huge television screen spanning the wall.

Speechless, she sat down.

"This room is his one extravagance. Honest. He, we, really do live quite simply."

"Yes, I can see that."

"What can I get you?"

"White wine would be nice, if you have it."

"Coming right up." He left her alone and disappeared through a door at the opposite end of the room.

No sooner had Harry vanished and a door at the opposite end of the room opened and the master of the house stepped in. He was wearing a long, scarlet bathrobe. In his trembling, left hand he clutched a large, crystal goblet filled to the brim with what appeared to be sherry. "Why, Mrs. Dore, what a pleasure." He shuffled to meet her as she rose shaking the gnarled hand. "Gracious, my dear, do sit down. No need to pop up on my account." He plopped into the chair opposite her own, spilling some of the sherry on the carpet.

"Macomber Dore's widow, aren't you?" She nodded. "Fine man, Mac. I remember him well. A fair sort of person, as I recall. Never one to make snap judgments, never looked at things superficially, did he?"

"No, he didn't. How did you know him, Mr. Winthrop? I thought, I mean, Mac died before you moved to Old Harbor?"

"Knew him from the settlement house, St. Louise's, in Cambridge."

"But, he hadn't been there since —"

"College, yep, you're right, that's when I knew him when he worked over the summer. Had a fire in his eyes in those days, I can tell you. Been dead quite a while, hasn't he?"

"Ten years."

"Long time. Pity to lose a man like that in his prime. I hadn't thought of him in twenty years until recently."

"Oh?"

"My son seems to have taken a keen interest in him, why just the other day he —"

"He what?" Harry said, appearing in the doorway, two glasses of wine in hand.

"Ah, my boy, I was just telling Mrs. Dore here about your keen interest in her late husband."

Harry blushed, handing Bess her glass and stepping behind her chair. What a devil, Bess thought regarding the old man whose eyes were dancing with glee at the mischief he was causing. "Thank you." She turned, smiling at Harry.

Drawing up a chair, he kept his eyes averted. "So Dad, what have you been up to today?"

"Well, let me see. There was breakfast, then a little stroll with Percy. Percy is my cocker spaniel, my dear. Can't imagine where he's gotten to? Loves the fire. Do you have a dog, Mrs. Dore?"

"No, and please call me Bess."

"Bess, nice name that. Short for?"

"Short for nothing. Just Bess."

"Now, where was I?"

"You were rambling on about your day knowing full well why I asked you in the first place."

"Now, now sonny, no need to get testy."

"Dad, can we please skip over the hour-long description of the rug rat's antics and move straight to the point?"

"Oh, yes, I see. You must be referring to my trip to town, sonny. Well, I'm sorry to report that it's not nearly as interesting as Percy's day, but all right. Let's see now. Chatted with Zelma, she's down in the trust department at Old Harbor Savings, my dear." He winked at Bess. "She and Bob Ashford handle all of the school's accounts. Bob's away, be back tomorrow. She said he knows more than she does 'bout the figures. Now, this is off the record, you understand," he paused, eying his son. "Actually sonny, better tell you later." Taking a huge gulp of sherry, he sat back in his chair.

"It's okay, Dad. Bess won't tell."

"It's alright, Mr. Winthrop. I'm happy to step out and you two can chat for a minute."

"Don't be silly, my girl. 'Course I'm gonna tell you, I'm just building the suspense a little. Sonny never lets me have any fun."

"'Cuse me, sir." The door opened, a plump, gray-haired lady in a long, white apron peeked in.

"Come in, Molly."

"Just checkin', sir." She remained behind the door. "What time will you be wantin' dinner?"

"Oh Moll, I'm sorry," Harry said, crossing the room to stand beside her. "This is your night off. I am a dope. We're keeping you and I'm home late besides."

"Quite alright, dearie. I was just checkin' as it's all ready."

"Come in and meet Bess. Bess, this is Molly Pierce, best cook in the world."

Beaming, the woman turned red from ear to ear as she stepped forward to shake Bess' hand. "Glad to know you miss."

"Hello, Molly. I'm looking forward to your supper. I'm sure it will be delicious."

"Thank you, miss. A curry it is, shrimp. I hope you like it hot and spicy. Been cooking for these two for so many years, but I don't think I ever get it hot enough for Master Harry."

"Moll, you go on. We'll serve ourselves when we're ready."

"Don't be daft, sir, 'course I'll stay, what with your company."

"Pierce, off with you! You heard Sonny — not another bloomin' word. "We'll serve ourselves and that's that. Do it most every night anyway."

"But sir, I —"

"Off you go Moll," Harry said, gently nudging her out the door. "We'll be fine, really. Have a good evening."

Closing the door, he and Bess returned to their seats. "Now Dad, you were saying?"

"What the devil was I talkin' about sonny?"

"Dad, if you don't tell me what Zelma said before —"

"Oh, yes, hold yer horses. Zelma sends her love, by the way. She's very hurt you haven't been down to see her. You've been home a week already."

Harry looked as if he might explode. "I went to see her two days ago and she was out. Now, give."

"There's nothing definite, unless we could get a hold of school books to verify, but over the years there appear to have been a number of inconsistencies. Things Zelma and Bob questioned Mrs. Richards about. I never liked that woman. She puts me in mind of a lizard. One of those, what'dya call 'em? Gila monsters. Always expect a long, skinny tongue to zip outta those red lips of hers, don't you?"

Bess giggled.

"I see we think alike, my dear." Another wink. "Anyway, the reptilian Miz Richards hasn't exactly run a tight ship. Every major fund drive, every tuition increase, large bequest, you name it, every time a big gift comes in, something goes missin'. How she does it, Zelma couldn't say. She can't skim off my money, 'cause all of it comes directly from my accounts to the contractors or whatever for each project. Never goes into the school's coffers. Even the scholarship money is controlled by my trust accounts. No wonder the woman's not very cordial to me."

"How does Zelma know money's missing?"

"Well, sonny, her hubby, Bruce is an alum and gets the bulletins, sees the numbers. He also knows what gets deposited, through Zelma, unofficially, of course."

"But, wouldn't that be rather foolish, Mr. Winthrop? I mean, anyone could add things up. Why didn't Carol just report different figures to the bulletins?"

"That's tricky business. Alumni know to the penny what they've given and they notice mistakes in the report before the ink's dry. They always check, that's half the reason they give. They want to see their names up there in the President's

Club and so forth. Could fudge a little on the anonymous gifts, but they check that too, believe me."

"How much we talkin' about Dad? Couple of hundred a year?"

"'Fraid it's more than that sonny. Zelma suspects there may be thousands stashed away since Bruce started keeping track."

"Why hasn't the bank ever told anyone?" Bess asked, incredulous at what she was hearing.

"Oh, they've taken the matter up with Peter Thurbert many times. Says he's gonna look into things and never does, or if he does, he's not sharing it with them."

"Maybe he's the culprit?"

"Never!" Bess cried. "Peter wouldn't steal a dime from the school. I'd bet my life on it. He's as honest a man as —"

"As yer husband, you were gonna say, weren't you?" Harry Senior said, regarding her. "Don't even speak of them in the same breath, my dear. I know Peter's a friend of yers and he's always been perfectly pleasant to me. He'd be a complete idiot to be otherwise, of course, but he's, well, let's just say it's time for him to move on. School'll be better off without him and that goose of a wife of his, too."

"I'm sorry, but I can't let you —"

"I'm starved." Harry leapt from his chair. "Let's eat."

CHAPTER 45

Whisking his father's empty goblet from the table, Harry grabbed Bess' hand and pulled her up. She waited at his side while he poured another glass of sherry from a crystal decanter on a side table, then glanced up to spy her reflection in the mirror. Her cheeks were still flushed, but the scarlet glow was receding.

"I apologize, my dear." Mr. Winthrop came up behind them. "I didn't mean to upset you."

"It's alright," she replied, without much conviction, recalling Peter's recent call querying her about the search committee's interest in the Business Office. "I just know how Peter loves the school, that's all and I can't imagine him stealing from it."

"I'm sure you're right, my dear. My late wife was always right, but there's something funny goin' on over there and I'd sure like to know why Thurbert hasn't gotten to the bottom of it."

"Let's drop it for now, Dad," Harry said, giving his father a stern look as he lead Bess into the dining room.

As they ate, conversation turned to other things. "What about the Predo fellow?" the elder Winthrop asked, draining his fourth goblet of sherry without so much as a slurred syllable. His plate of shrimp curry and hearts of palm salad sat largely untouched in front of him. "Anyone gotten anything out of him?"

"Not much," she said. "Louie's very confused and scared, poor thing. He's always been frightened of newcomers and Harry's and Roger's presence has been quite unsettling for him, I'm afraid."

"Roger?"

"Detective Demaris, he's the local policeman who's been —"

"Yes, yes," his father cut him off. "I know him. Brusque sort of person, isn't he?"

Harry winked at Bess. "This would be the pot calling the kettle black."

"Speak up, can't hear ya." Bess watched the two, clearly enjoying themselves and each other's company. She envied Harry, thinking of her own mother and their relationship.

"As I was saying, Harry Senior went on. "I know that Demaris fellow. Had a run-in with him myself last year. Not nearly as personable as Chief Sisson. Why isn't the chief handling this investigation anyway? That sergeant'd scare a bear off, never mind a poor half-wit like —"

"I scared him too, Dad."

"Well, that's no surprise."

"And, he's skittish, not half-witted."

"Thurbert told me a little about him. Ever since that unfortunate business with that girl's death, what was her name? Before my time. Anyway, poor man hasn't been the same since."

Bess nodded in agreement as Harry asked, "Who was the girl?"

"Lizzie Mederois. Remember, I told you about her? She's the student who committed suicide. Twelve years ago. Louie found her. There was some speculation that he might have actually been with her when she swallowed the poison. No one has ever gotten him to speak clearly about it, not even Billy. Louie worshipped Lizzie. He was devastated when she died."

"What's Billy Blackburn's story?" Harry asked.

"Ah yes, Blackburn," his father answered. "The blackguard of the case, as I recall."

"How so?" Harry asked, alarmed to see the color rising in Bess'cheeks again.

"Got the poor girl pregnant, didn't he?"

"That was never proved!"

"According to Thurbert, the boy as much as admitted it."

"He admitted no such thing. Billy Blackburn was a responsible, promising student."

Harry looked from one to the other. "The groundskeeper? What happened?"

"Billy and Lizzie were best friends. Both on full scholarships. They studied and worked together. She was a much stronger student and she gave him a great deal of support. The Mederois family had never had anyone go past the eighth grade. All their hopes rested on Lizzie. You can imagine the pressure she was under. Billy helped lighten her spirits, gave her a bit of fun now and then.

"What no one realized, until after Lizzie's death was just how much she had supported Billy academically. His grades plummeted immediately. He gave up, began skipping classes, and finally dropped out."

"Still loved the school, I guess." Mr. Winthrop said. "Twas on the grounds crew full-time straight from graduation from Diamond Voc, right? It's Blackburn keeps Louie Predo together, according to Thurbert. Without him, the man would have been committed long ago."

"Sometimes I think it's the other way around," Bess said quietly.

"What was she like?"

"Lizzie? She was a lovely girl. Kind and thoughtful, not an ounce of malice in her. She worked desperately hard, holding down two jobs and always keeping up with her studies. The other girls were not always kind. We tried to intervene when we could, but it's impossible to catch every slight. She had a few friends, mostly other girls from the village, but, for the most part, Lizzie was alone or with Billy."

"Was Louie on the grounds crew then?"

"Yes, he was head groundskeeper. As he's gotten older and more confused, they've pared back his duties. He's still a hard worker, though."

Harry rose to clear the table.

"So, Bess, what do you do in your spare time?" the elder Winthrop asked.

"Well, I like to read, hike, and I enjoy my garden. Season's over now, but I love the spring."

"What'do ya like to read? Highbrow or lowbrow?"

"Mostly low, I'm afraid. Novels, I love Jane Austin, Dickens, Barbara Pym. Like many people I go through stages where I'll read through an author. I've had an Edith Wharton stage and a long siege with Faulkner. Some more recent stuff although I'm afraid I don't keep up with the best sellers, unless they're mysteries. Mysteries are my favorite pleasure reading."

"Ah, a woman after my own heart. Love 'em. So does Harry, don't you sonny?" He glanced up at his son. Harry stopped clearing, his eye trained on his father. "That wall behind the television is full of mysteries."

"Yes, Harry showed me. Very impressive."

"So, who do you like? Who're your favorites? Me, I like mostly hard-boiled. None of this cozy stuff. Don't read many women either except for that Greyson woman. She's —"

Bess clapped her hands. "Why she is one of my favorites."

"'Course, it's all a load of poppycock. Why she —"

"Alright, Dad. Time for you to go to bed. I'll clean up. Now off you go."

The elder Winthrop winked at Bess, his eyes lingering thoughtfully on her for several minutes. She sensed that he had more to say, much more, but he simply nodded and turned away. As an afterthought, he called over his shoulder, "Come back and see us again soon, my dear."

After they cleaned up, Harry drove her home. Both of them were quiet until they'd reached her door. "Hope Dad wasn't too much for you. He does go on and on. Drinks too much, too, but he's a good sort. Evenings are the worst since Mother died. We don't get much company and I fear he's forgotten the few social graces he once possessed."

"Don't apologize, please. I enjoyed your father very much. You haven't met my mother. If you had, you'd count yourself lucky. They'd make a good pair, actually. I had a wonderful evening."

They stood on her front stoop now and Harry whispered, "Well, good night, then," pulling her to him, kissing her.

And then he was gone, Bess staring as he hastened down the walkway. She stood watching as his car pulled away. When his headlights disappeared, she turned to go inside, closing the door.

Feeling light-headed, knees wobbling, she grasped the edge of the hall table and gazed at her reflection in the mirror. It had been over ten years since she'd been kissed and a good deal longer since she'd been kissed like that. Despite a flood of warring emotions, she found she was smiling, her eyes sparkling with a light she thought had been extinguished forever. It was happiness staring back from the mirror.

CHAPTER 46

The evening spent with Bess and his father had unnerved Harry more than he cared to admit. His feelings for Bess surprised and unsettled him. What would she think of his father's revelations about his sudden interest in Mac Dore? And what would she think, if she knew about Stella? He wondered if his unease came from self-preservation or fear of scaring her off. Every time they met, she looked ready to dart off at the slightest provocation.

A morning trip to the bank had proved fruitful, satisfying his curiosity on one count, at least. His father's trust officer, Zelma, had grown up in the village and remembered Bess and Roger Demaris in their younger days. "Guilford was her maiden name," Zelma told him. "I was two years ahead of her." She had rooted around in her office closet, then given up. "Thought I had some old yearbooks here, but guess not. Anyway, they were good friends, I believe, nothing more. There were rumors of a brief romance after graduation, but if there was such a thing, it was short-lived. Wasn't long after that she was bringing Mac to town, and that was that."

Resolute, Harry drove through the village, headed for the police station. So, they had been involved. The first time he saw them together, it had been obvious. Demaris was still in love with her. Love or not, Harry was determined to have it out with the stubborn sergeant. As he pulled into the station lot, he was not sure what he planned to say, but it was time to clear the air.

After he passed through security, a Nordic woman greeted him at the front desk and directed him down the hall. "Last office on the left. I think he's in."

Harry made his way as directed, pausing to peer through the office's glass door before knocking. He spied a beefy young man with carrot red hair lounging in a side chair reading the paper. No Demaris. Pete Dugan, the assistant.

Harry knocked softly, hoping not to startle Dugan, but was unsuccessful. Pete jumped up, thrust paper behind the chair, and came red-faced to open the door.

"Your boss around?"

Dugan straightened his belt, struggling to regain his composure. "Who wants him?"

Harry knew Pete recognized him, but played along. "Harry Winthrop. We met at the school? I'm helping with the Wickie murder investigation."

Harry watched the younger man, arms akimbo, staring him down, silent, pugnacious. What had he heard about Dugan? Fiercely protective of his boss, a good officer.

"Look, I need to talk to your sergeant. Is he around?"

"He's in a meeting."

"How long will he be?"

"No telling. Could be five minutes, could be two hours."

"Well, I'll wait a while then, if you don't mind."

"Look, Mr. Winthrop. He's really busy this morning. You'd better call back and make an appointment. He has to go right out after this meeting."

"And when will he be back?"

"Can't say. We're in the middle of a murder investigation and this isn't our only case, you know. He doesn't have time to stand around talking to anyone when we're this busy."

"I only need a few minutes so I'll wait. Maybe I can walk him out to his next meeting."

Dugan barred the door, his left hand resting on his holstered gun. "If you leave your name I'll tell him you were in and he can —"

"Okay, okay, Pete. Down boy." Demaris appeared behind them, chuckling softly.

Clearly there was a great deal of affection between these two men, which said a lot about Demaris, Harry thought watching the exchange. "Detective, hello. Would you have five minutes?"

"Rodge, I tried to —"

"It's okay, Pete. Beat it, will you? I'll be out in a few minutes. Why don't you grab us some coffee, okay?"

"But —"

"Outta here. And close the door behind you."

Reluctantly, Dugan retreated and his boss motioned Harry to sit. Instead of taking the chair beside him, he walked around and sat behind the massive gray metal desk, its top littered with papers, files and empty cups. "My deputy seems to have taken a dislike to you, Mr. Winthrop."

"Harry, please. Doesn't appear that the apple falls far from the tree."

"I'm glad you came by. I've been meaning to call you."

"We're on the same wavelength then."

"I doubt it."

"Look, Detective, I'd like to clear the air. I believe we can work together on this investigation. I will try very hard not to get in your way, I just want to help. The school's hired me and I feel an obligation to do my best for them. I know you think I'm nothing but a pain in the ass, but I am not a complete novice at this. I've done some investigative work and I know what I'm doing."

"Are you finished?"

"Excuse me?"

"I mean, is that the end of your boy scout of the year speech or is there more?"

"Look, Demaris, I came here in friendship."

"I'm not your friend, Mr. Winthrop. I'm a public employee hired to do a job."

"That's exactly what I'm talking about. This attitude of—"

Dugan opened the door, carrying Styrofoam cups of black coffee. The two men accepted the coffee, nodding thanks. Pete went as if to sit and Demaris waved him out. As the door closed, he set down his cup, glaring at Harry. "What the hell are you talking about?"

"Is it because I'm wealthy that you despise me? Is that it? Spoiled, rich boy coming in, taking over your investigation? Is that what this is all about?"

"Damned if I know. You're the one in such a huff. I'm just tryin' to do my job and it's not easy with a bunch of armchair sleuths runnin' around trampling all over the evidence."

"And, you've made so much progress."

"How would you know if I've made progress or not? Your girlfriend tellin' stories?"

'If you're referring to Bess, no. But, while we're on that subject, I know about you two."

"What the hell does that mean?"

"I know you were involved."

"Buddy, I don't know who your sources are, but that's ancient history. So ancient, it's friggin' laughable."

"I don't see you laughing."

"Look, leave Bess outta this, will you? She's none of my business and shouldn't be yours either."

"You're the one who brought her up, and I'll decide whether or not she's my business."

"If you were half as decent as you claim to be, you'd leave her alone. She doesn't need some rich prick waltzing in, messin' around with her head, then taking off."

"You're still in love with her, you bastard. That's why you don't want me messing with her. I don't know what you've heard, Detective, but Bess and I are friends, nothing more."

"Yeah, and I'm the Easter Bunny."

"Look, I came down to try and reach some sort of agreement that would allow us to work together, but—"

"The only agreement we're gonna reach is for you to butt out and let me get on with this investigation. You shouldn't be anywhere near it. I've done some checking up on you, Mr. Ace Private Eye. I know all about your DWI, death resulting."

CHAPTER 47

Harry reeled back, Demaris' words like a kick to the chest. Stella's beautiful face flashed before his eyes, head thrown back in laughter. She had looked especially lovely that night, the last of her life. Dressed in floor length, shimmering silver for the Jacobson's party, her dress fit her like a second skin. Bill Jacobson had been Harry's roommate at Harvard. He had married Lenore right after graduation and their tenth wedding anniversary united many old friends.

Excellent wine had flowed freely throughout the seven course meal, preceded by a long, spirited cocktail hour and several rounds of cognac after dinner. Then, the friends had begun playing pool, shots of tequila the penalty for missing a shot. Bill had begged them to spend the night, but Harry and Stella, newly-fianced, had other plans.

Stella insisted they go home, to their apartment on Beacon Hill, two blocks from the three-story brownstone where Harry had grown up and where his parents still resided. "We can slip into the Jacuzzi and have a nightcap," she had purred, leaning on him as they made their exit.

Harry remembered catching her reflection in the hall mirror. Almost as tall as her fiancée, Stella Lang had been rail thin, her bare arms, swan-like and supple draped languidly round his neck. Her shoulder length blonde hair was drawn back in a thin, diamond crusted tiara. Only Stella could wear a tiara and get away with it.

Harry never understood why he had fallen in love with Stella. She represented everything he had spent his life trying to escape. Glamorous, wealthy and sophisticated, she was a Bostonian's dream girl. A Radcliffe graduate, politically savvy and passionate, she would make the perfect wife for a man of power, a master of the universe type.

Harry had succumbed on their first meeting, at another of Bill and Lenore's parties. If he closed his eyes, he could almost feel the warmth of her skin, incredibly soft as her arms brushed his cheeks.

"Mr. Winthrop, did you hear me?"

Harry realized the detective had been speaking for several minutes and he had not heard a thing. If he had, he would have heard how Demaris had learned that a truck had come out of nowhere, and about Harry's frantic attempts to avoid the crash. About their car flipping over the guard rail and into the path of oncoming traffic.

What Demaris hadn't mentioned was Stella's screaming, as she called his name over and over as they waited, pinned beneath the car, waiting to be rescued. "Harry, Harry, Harry — I can't feel my legs, my legs, my legs!" By the time, the fire department arrived the screams had stopped. When they lifted the car, Stella was dead, severed at the waist by the jagged sheet metal of the car's collapsed roof.

Mercifully, Harry had lapsed into unconsciousness by then. When he woke the next morning, Stella's body, in one piece again, thanks to the undertaker's magic, lay in an open casket which her fiancée would never see.

"Mr. Winthrop, hello?"

"You had no right." Harry stood, struggling to regain his composure.

"I had every right. This isn't a garden party, it's a murder investigation. Look, I'm not out to get you, but this is a police case, not yours, and I'd like you to butt out. As far as Bess goes, she's her own woman and none of my business. But, as an old friend, I don't want to see her hurt and I sure as hell don't want to find her DOA on one of our winding country roads."

"Fuck you, Demaris. I have to live every day with memory of my fiancée's death, but I sure as hell don't need you throwing it in my face. It has absolutely nothing to do with my competency to assist in this investigation. And, as for Bess — you needn't worry yourself. I rarely drink and then never more than a sip of wine. If you think your insinuations are going to warn me off seeing her or continuing to help the school, you're sadly mistaken." He slammed the door on his way out, failing to acknowledge Pete Dugan who stood in the hall, two feet from his boss' door.

As Harry drove out of the village, his eyes blurred with tears. Would he ever be free of the guilt and pain? Stella's death had followed him halfway around the world, and now it had caught up with him again. As he headed towards the school for yet another unnecessary appointment with Joan Nettleman — she phoned at least three times a day with new and vital information which always turned out to be useless — he thought about how long it had been since he talked with Bill and Lenore. He resolved to call them soon. Then, endeavoring to put the encounter with Roger Demaris out of his mind, he braced himself for another hour of Joan's kerfuffle.

CHAPTER 48

In the hushed silence, downy snowflakes fell as Harry and Bess headed across campus to Louie's apartment above the maintenance barn. Several inches of snow already covered the ground, the campus whispering under its white eiderdown. Silence, punctuated by the occasional door slamming, was all they heard.

They were discussing Roger Demaris.

"Harry, he's angry."

"Tough shit. There's no reason for him to be and if he weren't such an ass, we could be making twice the progress."

Bess stared at her companion, wondering about his anger. What had triggered such strong feelings in this usually affable man? "Not surprisingly, that's not the way he sees it. And, please don't yell at me. One snarling sleuth is quite enough, today, thank you."

"Sorry."

"Is something wrong?"

"No."

"What did Roger say?"

"Let's just leave it that we don't see eye to eye."

"So I gather."

"Did he tell you what we talked about?"

"No." She walked ahead, surprised and frightened by the bitterness in his voice and unable to believe that Roger's barking had aroused such a reaction. She decided to let it go. "Anyway, the reason I brought Roger up was to propose a way to end all this. I suggest that you both come to dinner at my house, tomorrow night, if you're free. We can discuss the case or just talk, I don't care, but this bickering has got to stop."

"It's his problem, Bess. I'm —"

"Completely innocent. Yes, I know."

"Bess, wait a minute. There is something that we talked about. Something I want you to know. I will tell you, I promise. And, I would like you to hear it from me. Just not this minute, okay?"

They had paused on the path and she nodded, searching his expression. Then, he smiled. "You look beautiful right now." Gently, he brushed snowflakes from her hair, from her soft, gray beret. "Like a snow maiden from a fairy tale."

"Harry, please, I'm trying to be serious."

"I'm completely serious. I'm falling in love with you, Bess Dore. There, I've said it. I swore I wouldn't, so I wouldn't scare you off, but there it is. I love you and I want —"

"Harry, please don't." She shook her head.

"Shit, I'm sorry, Bess. I swore I wouldn't say anything, but then I looked at you and it just came out. I'm moving too fast, aren't I? It's just Demaris is such a jerk, so protective of you. I guess I'm a little jealous of him."

"Jealous of Roger? That is ridiculous. There is absolutely nothing between Roger and me. Nothing."

"Maybe not in your mind."

"I can't talk about this right now." She turned away. "I don't want to be in the middle of the squabbling anymore, that's all. So, you'll come to dinner tomorrow night? Maybe you'll discover you actually like each other."

"Hoping for a miracle, are you?"

"Something like that." She knocked at Louie's door. Immediately, they heard footsteps and Louie opened the door.

CHAPTER 49

Louie Predo stared at Bess and Harry as if they were strangers. "Lou, hi," she said, placing an arm on Harry's sleeve. "This is Harry, remember?"

The gardener grunted, stepping back inside the doorway. "Lou, we're sorry to bother you, but can we come in and talk for just a few minutes?"

"Not clean. House dirty."

"That's okay, so is mine. We won't look. Please. Can we just come up for a few minutes?"

"Wait here." He scurried back up the stairs and reappeared a few minutes later with his jacket. "We can talk outside."

They followed him out and the trio took the path towards the classroom building. "Lou, we don't want to upset you, but there's just something about the day of Mr. Wickie's death that we need to ask you."

"No."

"Now, Lou. Please don't be upset. We know you didn't do anything wrong, but we need your help. We want to know if you saw anything or anyone." Bess took his arm, patting his hand and wiry, twitching body relaxed slightly. "It's okay. You know I'm your friend, don't you?"

"Yup."

"Then, help us."

"Don't know anything. Didn't see anything," he stated matter-of-factly. Harry watched her, marveling at her gentleness and its effect on the frightened gardener.

"Lou, Carol Richards says she saw you take a green backpack from the bushes. Right about here." Bess stopped by the bush that Carol Richards had identified. "Do you remember?"

Frozen, Lou stared into the shrubbery, eyes now wild with terror. "Lou, please, I don't want to frighten you, but this is important." She gripped his forearm, staring straight into his eyes, pleading. "Was it your backpack?"

"No!"

"Do you know whose pack it was?"

"No!"

"Did you see how it got there? In the bushes? Who put it there?"

"No!"

"But you saw what was in it, didn't you?"

Louie swayed as if he might topple over and Harry put out his arm to catch him. We're losing him, he thought, watching as the man's eyes rolled back and glazed over. Louie's body went rigid. "I'm safe. I'm safe. Mr. Mac knows I'm safe!"

"Lou, please, Mr. Mac would want you to tell us. What was in the bag? Please."

"Mmm, monster! Mac's monster! The sea monster! Keep away! Keep away!" he shrieked, turning and running off.

Harry started to follow, but she held him back. "Let him be. He's too upset. He won't tell us anymore."

"What the hell was that all about? Mac's sea monster?"

"He means the knife," she replied, remembering Louie's fascination with her husband's scrimshaw collection. The monster he referred to was almost certainly the sperm whale depicted on the knife sheath, its huge jaws crushing a long-boat full of helpless sailors. "He may know more, but we'll never get it out of him now."

"So you don't think he put it there?"

"No. Ordinarily I think he would have brought the knife straight to me, but something was wrong. He's hiding something. Why else would he throw it back like that?"

"Unless Miz Richards made up the whole thing and swiped the bag herself."

"Then why tell us about it? It doesn't make any sense."

"You're right. Where to next Miss Marple? Think Kevin LeBlanc'd be in?"

"Probably, unless he's coaching. We can check. I just have to make a quick call."

CHAPTER 50

When Bess joined Harry a few minutes later, he regarded her curiously, but didn't ask about the phone call. She volunteered the information herself as they headed to North House, the senior boys' dorm where Kevin LeBlanc was dorm master. "I called Billy to tell him Louie was upset. I didn't like to leave him like that."

"Did you tell him why?"

"No, should I have?"

"Probably not. Best to keep it to ourselves for now until we can consult with the good detective."

"That's the spirit." She laughed, taking his arm.

As they neared the front steps of the dorm, a group of senior boys burst through the door, laden with gym bags. Bess called to one, "Jack! Hold up. Is Mr. LeBlanc in?"

"Haven't seen him Mrs. D., but he's probably around. Unless he's already over at the Field House. We have a practice in fifteen minutes."

"Thanks, we'll check."

Jack waved and ran off to join his friends.

Harry opened the front door. "After you, Mrs. D."

Kevin's apartment was on the ground floor at the rear of the two story building. Each floor had ten rooms, two or three boys to a room except for two tiny singles on the first floor. The walls of the hallway were painted a soft green, edged with dark oak trim and bead board wainscoting, the latter scuffed and marked with the passage of thousands of boys, backpacks and sporting equipment.

Although well-worn, the gray wall to wall carpeting was relatively clean and well-swept. Kevin's door was covered with posters, flyers, calendars and schedules. On the wall to the right was a small white board with a marker dangling on a string, and beside it a bulletin board. A huge calendar listing of all upcoming school events was tacked to the boards along with posters and notices covering every inch of space.

The white board was blank, no message indicating whether the dorm master was in or out. They knocked.

"Come in," a voice called.

Harry pushed open the door.

"Kevin, it's me, Bess!"

They stepped into a Spartan living room, a folding chair and card table with a computer, the only furnishings.

"Hey, Bess." He poked his head out of a room at the end of the hall. "Just got out of the shower. Be right out."

She felt like a traitor. He was her colleague and friend. A friend who had had a painful year and now lived alone, stripped of most of his possessions. Over the years, she had spent many evenings in the LeBlanc's apartment. Susan had a real flair for decorating and most of the furniture had been hers, family pieces and beautifully crafted reproductions. She favored the stark simplicity of the Shakers, but their sofas and chairs had been comfortable, covered in bright fabrics and throw pillows Susan had embroidered. Clearly, she had taken everything. Nothing remained of the warm, inviting space they had co-habited for so many years.

There'd been rumors of his dalliances, but Bess hadn't put much stock in them. The introspective chemistry teacher didn't seem the type. Now, she didn't know what to think. She remembered Kevin bragging about his wife and her skills as a decorator, her new craft business, her athletic ability and how lucky he was to have her.

"Maybe you'd better talk to him alone," she whispered, inching her way towards the door.

Too late. "Here I am." Kevin appeared, a folding chair under one arm. "Uh-oh, didn't know there were two of you. Hold on, I'll get one more chair."

"No need," Harry called, but their host had already disappeared.

"Sit," he commanded upon his return, unfolding the two chairs, "auditorium" stamped on their bottoms.

"Don't worry," he said, noticing her stare. "I've got permission. Peter let me borrow these till I can get around to buying some furniture. Not sure what I want yet, so I'm just making do. What can I do for you two anyway? Are you sleuthing or is this purely a social call?"

"I'm sorry, Kevin." Bess wished she were a hundred miles away.

"No need for apologies. And please, let's not do the poor Kevin thing, okay? I've had enough of that to last two lifetimes. It's getting old. I'm over Susan. Well, almost, anyway. It's taken a while, but I'm getting there."

"Look here, LeBlanc. Bess and I don't want to bother you, but in going back over this Wickie murder, you do seem to have a motive for wanting him dead."

"Couldn't agree more."

"So?"

"So what? You want to know if I stabbed the philandering bastard? The answer is no, but I would have, if I'd had the nerve. Only kidding, Bess. Am I glad he's dead? I know that's not Quakerly of me, but it's true."

Shocked, Bess remained silent as Harry continued.

"So where were you last Thursday in the late afternoon?"

"I'm sure you've already checked my movements very carefully." Bess looked away, thinking how little she cared about Milt Wickie's death. How many lives had the horrid man ruined?

"Humor me."

"I was an hour away, at the Abbey, coaching a soccer game. That's a school in Bay Point, just down the coast. We left at two-thirty and didn't get back till after eight."

"Know of anyone else that wanted him dead?"

"Everyone as far as I can tell. The guy was a bastard."

"What about your wife?"

"Susan?" He paused, his expression guarded. "No way," he replied without conviction. "Don't know how she felt about him, but Susan wouldn't hurt a fly. Nope, if she'd gotten tired of him, she'd've just left, like she did with me."

Harry rose, folding his chair. "Well, thanks. We'll get out of your hair. Mind if I use your facilities while we're here?"

"Sure, down the hall."

Bess stood briefly, then sat back down. "Kevin, can I ask? What's going on with you and Will?"

"Nothing. He's a horse's ass, that's all. Made a pass at Susan a few months back, the bastard. Right after our split up when she was hot and heavy with Milt. She told me about it because she was so surprised. Came out of the blue.

"I know, what did it matter to me, since we'd already split up, but it did. Will was a good friend. Will had a girlfriend, or lover, more accurately. Why'd he have to go after Susan, too?"

Harry reappeared at Bess' side. "And that would be whom?"

"Thought everyone except our clueless headmaster knew. Will and Carrie have been at it for years."

Bess reeled back as if she'd been slapped, distressed for her friend, and flabbergasted at the complex web of deception that operated in a community she thought she knew well.

Harry whistled. "Talk about a Peyton Place. Listen, we've got to get going, but if you think of anything else I should know, here's my card with my cell number."

"Don't hurry off on my account. I've got practice soon, but the guys can wait a few minutes. Want some coffee or something? I don't get many visitors, adult visitors anyway. With Susan gone, no one's been brave enough to face my cooking."

"Thanks Kevin, but we've got to go." Bess rose, folding her chair as well.

"I'm headin' over to the Field House. Bess, do you want to walk with me? You have practice too, don't you?"

"Thanks, but Meredith's taking it. We've switched off for a few weeks. I hemmed and hawed and acted guilty for a day or two, but then I let her convince me. I'm going to cover her basketball schedule in January for three weeks when she's in England."

"Okay, well, stop by again, anytime. Remember, no sympathy. I can see it in your eyes. I don't mind your questions and don't mind the visits. I don't even mind if you accuse me of murder, but please, for God's sake, don't pity me."

As Harry led the way, she waved over his shoulder.

"Remember, no goddamn pity!"

CHAPTER 51

As Harry and Bess walked back across campus, darkness was already closing in. "I'm sorry I have to head out," he said, brushing against her as they headed for the parking lot. "I would have liked to take you to dinner."

"Not to worry. I'm exhausted. An early evening is in store for me."

"Tomorrow's that special meeting, isn't it?"

"The Forum, yes. It's at two. Are you coming?"

"Thought I would. Any chance you could have lunch with me before?"

"As it turns out, I have a free period before. My class ends at 12:30. What did you have in mind?"

"I was thinking a picnic in my car. I'll pick you up and we can drive somewhere close by. Might be a little cold for blankets on the ground."

"Shall I pick us up some sandwiches from the Coop?"

"I have it covered, never fear. Molly is on the case. She'll make us more food than we could consume in five picnics."

"Sounds wonderful, thank you. Shall I meet you in the parking lot at 12:30 then?"

"Unless you'd like me to come to your room and carry your books?"

She smiled. "That won't be necessary. Oh, by the way, I forgot to ask. How did your meeting with Joan go today?"

"You mean my fifth meeting with Ms. Nettleman, don't you? Or, Meddleman, as I like to think of her. Another complete waste of time. She did have some half-baked tale about Garrett Rollins and a rumored affair with a student."

"There were lots of rumors about Garrett and students. That's one of the reasons he was nudged out of teaching and into the archives."

"Any proven?"

"No, and I'd guess it was more like flirtation. Garrett liked the adoration. He's kind of a 'look at me type,' if you know what I mean."

"I wonder how he'd like a 'look at me behind bars' scenario?"

"He went to school with Darrell Rosen so I suspect he has protection there."

"Not according to Joan. She wants me to expose him and a host of other tasks she'll explain at our 'next meeting.' How can I avoid her, please, I need help."

Bess laughed, opening her car door, turning back to him. "Poor Harry. Just part of a detective's life, I guess."

"Hmm, don't suppose you feel sorry enough to kiss me goodnight, do you?"

"No, I do not. Not here, not now. Goodnight. See you tomorrow for lunch." She squeezed his outstretched hand, then hopped into her car.

CHAPTER 52

When Bess arrived home, she kicked off her shoes, changed into sweats and lit a fire in the study fireplace. Then, she made a quick omelet and toast and brought her plate to eat by the fire. She had just taken the last bite of toast when the phone rang.

It was Roger. "Bess, hi, got a minute?"

"You're not backing out of dinner tomorrow, are you?"

"No, just wondered if you'd learned anything new, from either LeBlanc or Predo."

"Not too much, but it's clear that what Louie found in that knapsack is Mac's knife. He remembered it from years ago. He was always fascinated by Mac's scrimshaw collection."

"Who'd have put it there, do you think?"

"I haven't a clue, but if I had to guess, I'd say someone stashed it there in a hurry and picked it up on the way to see Milt."

"Anyone, in other words. Figures. How're you and your boyfriend getting on?"

"Roger, I'm getting very tired of this. Harry is a friend, not a boyfriend."

"Does he know that?"

"Yes, so please, stop the comments and let's end this silly turf war at dinner tomorrow, okay?"

"I just want you to be careful."

"Roger, I'm forty-two-years old. I've been taking care of myself for decades."

"He's not who you think he is."

"What's that supposed to mean?"

"It means he's dangerous. Killed his girlfriend in a car accident. He was DWI. She died instantly. Don't suppose he's shared that story with you?"

Bess' stomach turned over and she nearly dropped the phone. "Not that it's any of your business, but no, he hasn't, but why would he?"

"Because you'd been driving all over creation with the guy, that's why!"

"Not when he's been drinking. In fact, he barely drinks, as far as I can tell."

"Only takes one time. But, look, you're right. It's none of my business except that I do care what happens to you. So, just be careful, okay? Maybe the guy's learned his lesson, reformed, whatever. Would've been in prison if Daddy's millions hadn't gotten him off and out of the country."

"Roger, I'm really tired. I'll see you tomorrow, okay? You're coming to the Forum, right?"

"Yup, see you then. Night, Bess. Take care."

Bess set down the phone, unsure what or whom to believe about almost everything. There were murderers and adulterers running all over campus, now Harry and this latest revelation. What had happened to her quiet, ordered world?

CHAPTER 53

As planned, Harry was waiting in the parking lot at precisely 12:30 with picnic stowed in the backseat. He waved, watching her approach, surprised to see her solemn expression. Had something happened?

As Bess neared him, her expression brightened and she smiled. "Where will we go? Can't be too far as I need to be back by quarter of two to meet my advisees."

"I have just the place," he said, holding her door open.

Both were quiet on the short drive to Osprey Point, a narrow strip of headland jutting out into the ocean about five miles south of campus. Bess hadn't been to the Point in years. It was a cragged, beautiful place, but too exposed, cold and windy for walks except in summer. Harry drove the car to the edge of the small parking lot. From this vantage point, the entire coastline to the north lay before them, the church spire in Old Harbor visible as well as the school's farmland, barn and silos, ringed with stone walls that reached to the sea.

Bess leaned back, sighing as she gazed out to sea. "I'd forgotten how lovely it is here. Thank you for thinking of this."

"What would you like? Molly has made chicken salad sandwiches. Hope that's okay. There are also cookies, fruit, chips, potato salad and assorted drinks. What can I get you?"

Bess peered into the picnic basket. "A sandwich and bottle of water would be great. Might eat a few chips, too, if you opened a bag."

They ate the delicious sandwiches brimming with chicken, herbs and a hint of curry, in silence for several minutes before he asked, "How was your day?"

"So far so good." She set down her sandwich, placed her drink in the car's cup holder, and turned away from the ocean to look at Harry. "How about yours?"

"Uneventful. Took Dad into town on errands. No sleuthing yet."

"You said there was something you wanted to speak with me about? Is it about Milt's death or questions about school?"

Harry set his lunch down, and stared in front of him for several minutes. "No, it's not about the murder. It's about me. I want to tell you something before you hear it from someone else."

Too late, Bess thought, saddened to glimpse the pain in his eyes and demeanor. "Oh?" She reached out, placing her hand on his arm.

"It happened six, almost seven years ago. I was engaged, to a woman named Stella. We hadn't set a wedding date and, in fact, had been engaged for less than a week when it happened. We'd been at a party with good friends. My college roommate and his wife were celebrating their tenth anniversary.

"I'd, we'd had a lot to drink and had considered spending the night in Marblehead. Bill and Lenore had urged us to stay, but Stella wanted to go home. We were living in Boston then, not far from my parents, in fact.

"I thought I was okay to drive. I felt strong, and steady, just a little light-headed, but no means staggering around or slurring my words. Stella was much drunker than I was, and I'd had to carry her to the car.

"As soon as we started out, Stella passed out and I put on some music to keep me awake. Lenore had sent me with a pot of coffee, but it was only a 45 minute drive so I hadn't bothered with it. We were only about 8 miles from Bill and Lenore's when Stella stirred and began vomiting, in my lap mostly. At the same time, she grabbed me round the neck.

"I tried to push her off so I could find a place to pull over and help her. We were on a dark, poorly lit winding back road and were coming to the crest of a hill when she grabbed at me again and her hand covered my eyes for no more than 5 seconds, I think. It may have been more, I don't remember all of it.

"The truck hit us then, head on and the car rolled and flipped, pinning us."

"Oh, Harry, how horrible it must have been."

"We were both conscious for a short time. Stella was screaming. Then, she was silent. I never saw her again."

Bess reached over, arm across his shoulder in a half hug. "I'm so sorry. I can't imagine how terrible that must have been for you."

"I was charged, Bess. They tested me in the hospital. I was legally drunk. Today, I'd have been sent to jail, I'm sure of it. Dad's lawyers worked overtime and got me thousands of hours of community service, a suspended license and three years probation. So, now you see who you've been spending time with."

"It was an accident."

"I was drunk. Maybe if I'd been sober, I could have reacted more quickly and decisively, gotten us off the road, avoided the truck, who knows. But I live every day knowing I was responsible for Stella's death."

"Maybe it's time to forgive yourself?"

"Maybe."

"I'm sure if she loved you, Stella would want you to forgive yourself, don't you think?"

Bess placed her hand on his cheek and he grasped hold of it. "Now, my dear Bess, you're probably thinking, now the guy has to drive me back to campus."

"I'm thinking no such thing."

"I don't drink more than a half a glass of wine on occasion. Oh, there were the usual beer bashes in college, but I'm not nor ever have been an alcoholic. I would never put any human being in danger again, least of all you."

"I know," she said, quietly. "I'm not worried. I trust you, remember?"

He smiled for the first time since they had arrived at the Point. "And, I promise never to do anything to betray that trust. It's, you are very precious to me." Tears rimmed his eyes as he spoke, drawing her close to him, kissing her softly.

Bess returned his kiss, her lips parting in a longing she had never expected to feel again. As she pulled away, she glanced at the car's clock and saw the time. "Oh, Harry, we have to go. I'll, we'll be late."

"Are we okay? Are you okay?"

She nodded solemnly before sitting back, buckling her seat belt. "Thank you for telling me. I know it must be agony to retell."

As they drove away, she reached out her hand and he took it, bringing her fingers to his lips. "Thank you, dear Bess."

Chapter 54

After all the kerfuffle, the monthly Forum proceeded smoothly with students discussing a number of topics including a few brief mentions of the murder. The monthly Forum idea had originated several years earlier when weekly Meeting for Worship turned into "popcorn sessions" with students hopping up speaking about, simply to hear themselves talk. The Overseers, faculty and administrators devised the Forum to create a space for students' more mundane talk in order to preserve the sacredness of Weekly Meeting. The plan worked beautifully. Occasionally, a national or international crisis or tragedy would strike and they'd hold a special forum, but as a rule the monthly ritual was sufficient.

Harry sat among the students, cross-legged on the floor, Roger Demaris and Pete Dugan stood by the door and most faculty, staff and board members sat in chairs that ringed the floor. Bess preferred to sit with her advisees as did Jane Fellows. The two friends sat almost side-by-side, students all around them.

Garrett read a short poem he had written, which, in Bess' mind, seemed completely out of context, then sat, ceding the mike to the students who came one by one to speak. As forum proceeded, a line of students formed, waiting to speak and Bess spied Amy Flathers at the end. Slowly, she made her way forward until she stood waiting as a sophomore talked about the disappointing state of the Commons and the need for students to take care of their space or lose it.

Then, it was Amy's turn. Bess held her breath as she shuffled forward, leaning into the mike. "I want to thank someone," she began. "Who saved me when I needed it. I know you're out there listening and I am so grateful. I should have spoken about this last year, when it happened, but well, I couldn't. Now, I can. Thank you." Amy was crying now, and had started to step back when Kevin LeBlanc came from behind, putting an arm over her shoulder, leading her away. Bess turned to find Roger in the crowd and he nodded to her.

Had Kevin been her mysterious savior as well?

CHAPTER 55

"That was great, Bess. Really great." Roger Demaris scooped up the last bit of curried black bean soup, cutting himself another thick slice of crusty Artisan bread. "Haven't had food like this in I don't know when."

Bess couldn't believe she had pulled it off. All three of them sitting amiably around Mac's Grandmother Clarissa's Shaker table. It had been a long time since guests had gathered around the old cherry table. Aside from Jane Fellows, Bess rarely had people for dinner and when Jane came, they ate in the kitchen or in their laps in the study. She had asked Jane to join them, but she had had other plans.

The start of the evening had been awkward, Harry uncharacteristically taciturn. Just about the time Bess resigned herself to having to carry the evening's conversation, Roger turned to Harry and asked him to tell them about his travels. Soon, he was regaling them with stories of his years in Belize in the Peace Corps, and his many experiences teaching English all over the world, most recently in Brazil. He mentioned he did a bit of writing from time to time and this led Roger into a short, colorful account of his own attempts at authorship. "Had one story published a few years back, then kaput — that was it."

"You don't say?" Harry leaned back, regarding the other man.

"Yup, Providence Journal. Was in the now-defunct 'Sunday Magazine'."

Bess nodded, rising to clear the table. "It was quite good, too."

"You read it?" Demaris' look said it all.

"Yes. I liked it, too."

"So, what was it about?" Harry asked, watching the interplay between the two old friends.

"An old fisherman, Otis Black. Friend of my dad's. Passed away last year. Otis had been retired for at least twenty years, but he was a visible presence in the village and along the shoreline. Used to roam the beaches morning to night muttering to himself and the seagulls. They followed him like the Pied Piper, waiting for hand-outs. Some people said he was crazy, but they were wrong. Otis was as sane as you and me."

"Yes, he was." Bess nodded, remembering Mac's long walks with Otis, the two men discussing the tides, impending weather, anything related to the sea, Otis' first and only love.

After supper, the three took coffee to the study where the conversation turned to the investigation. "So," Harry began. "Should we compare notes and help each other, or do we go on keeping everything secret and tripping over one another?"

After giving Harry a hard look, Roger sighed. "What the hell? Why not? There are a few things I can't share just yet, but I guess it'd be okay to run through the rest of it."

Harry slapped his knee. "That's the spirit. Now, let's get started. Who do we like for this murder, and why'd he or she do it?"

Glad to see the two men getting along, at last, Bess leaned forward. "There's still the possibility that it may have been a burglar."

"Or not," Harry said, turning to Demaris.

"No friggin' way. This was an inside job, for sure and it wasn't about robbing Milt. My money's on one of the poor schmucks he was blackmailing. They most likely —"

"Blackmailing?" Bess and Harry cried in unison.

"Oh, ho, ho. So, the bumbling police officer has something you two haven't ferreted out with all your insider snooping. Ha!" He rocked back in his chair, grinning like the Cheshire Cat. "Oh, yeah, Old Miltie was makin' a nice chunk of chain extorting the Richards broad and that less than saintly headmaster of yours."

"Peter? I don't believe it."

"Looks like it. We've checked all their bank accounts, even yours, Bess. Don't go getting' all pissy — it's routine. Milt was making regular deposits each month and they match Thurberts and Richards' cash withdrawals on particular dates to the penny. So unless we've got one of the biggest coincidences in banking history, Milt was on the take."

"But why?" Bess shook her head, unwilling to believe that Peter could be involved in any wrongdoing.

"In Miz Richards' case, we suspect she's been dipping into the till, big time."

"I knew it." Harry slapped his knee again.

"Oh, yeah, she's loaded. Friggin' rollin' in it."

"But she lives for free in the dorm," Bess said. "Couldn't she have save up? I mean, she wears expensive clothes and all, but otherwise she seems to live quite frugally."

"Unless you count the brownstone in Boston, real swishy neighborhood, and the big country house on the Cape. Both places are filled with antiques and shit. We're working on warrants for both places. Seems like a few of the school's valuable antiques may have disappeared over the years and we're wondering if they may have ended up in one of Miz Richards' less frugal domiciles."

"I can't believe it." Bess rose to pour more coffee, shaking her head. "Carol comes from very modest means. Her parents both worked in the mills. Skrimped and saved to send her to business school. She told me once that she spent most of her childhood hungry. How could she possibly have afforded all that? I don't know her salary, but it can't be that much higher than faculty members, can it?"

"'Bout double, actually. You didn't hear that from me. Parmenter'd have a coronary over his friggin' confidentiality. But, it's beside the point. Her salary could be triple what it is and it wouldn't pay for all that broad's got stashed away. No, she's got a pretty lucrative, alternative source of income. From the look of things, she's been rakin' it in for years."

"But how?"

"Shoddy bookkeeping, skimming off the top of the last three capital campaigns. Separate accounts for each annual fund. Double and triple billing, contractor pay-offs, bribes, you name it. She's made out like a bandit on kickbacks alone."

"Can you prove it?" Harry asked.

"Not yet, but we're workin' on it. We want to be sure, so we're lookin' into things very quietly, keeping her in the dark while we poke around. Don't want her disappearing on us. Even if she abandoned the houses, she's got considerable cash reserves somewhere."

"I've made some inquiries, too," Harry said. "My sources paint a similar picture. Her books just don't add up. What about Thurbert? Think he was dippin' in, too?"

Bess gasped.

"No, at least we haven't found any evidence to suggest that he was. But, he was payin' up. Much as admitted it when I questioned him yesterday. Won't give me a clue as to why, but I thought you might have an idea."

Roger's dark eyes turned to Bess, waiting, watchful.

CHAPTER 56

"Well, I don't," Bess said, rising and moving across the room to the French doors, peering out into the darkness.

"Bess, if you know something and you're not saying —" Harry left the sentence unfinished.

"You think it has something to do with me, don't you?" She spun around to face him, angry tears rimming her eyes.

Before Harry could answer, Roger stood and moved to her side. "Now, hold on, Bess. Non one's saying anything. We know he's a friend of yours, that's all. If you don't know, you don't know."

"Well, I don't."

"Fine," he said, stepping back, surprised at the sudden tension in the room.

"Bess, I'm sorry."

"She knows you are, man. Now forget about Thurbert, okay? Can we do that?"

"If he's a suspect, of course, I'll help and see what I can find out."

"I donno, Bess. Pete and I have gone at him three times. He's not gonna crack."

"Maybe not with you, but he trusts me. Perhaps he'll confide in me."

"Go for it, then, if you think you can get something outta him. Who else we got?"

"The LeBlancs," Harry said, still eyeing her as he spoke to Demaris. "I'd say they both had motives and their alibis are pretty flimsy. She had a ninety-minute class that she regularly steps in and out of, leaving students to lead. She could've sneaked out of the gym, zipped over, stabbed Milt and been back in time for the cool-down. At least, she didn't have any trouble leaving the class when we wanted to speak with her."

"Me neither. She's somethin', isn't she?"

"She did say that that night it was her advanced class and she couldn't leave them," Bess added.

"A bullshit answer, if I've ever heard one. Gave me the same crap. What about her hubby?"

"Ex-husband," Bess said. "He told us he was an hour away at a soccer game."

"Told Pete and me that he takes his own car to the game in case one of his players is injured."

Harry sat up. "And, someone got hurt that day?"

"Yes and no. Apparently, one of their key players, Paul Corcoran, took an elbow to the ribs in the first half. Said he was fine, all the kids thought he was fine, but LeBlanc insisted on taking him outta the game and drivin' him back to campus at halftime. Raised quite a ruckus on the team, 'cause it was a close game and they needed Corcoran.

"LeBlanc left his assistant coach behind. Wouldn't you think he'd have sent him back with the kid? It was an important game, which they lost. Kids are still griping about it."

Bess tried to remember if she had seen Paul Corcoran that evening or the following day. "Was he really injured?"

"Bruise is all."

"So?" Harry sat back, running his fingers through his hair.

"So, I donno. Could've been a legitimate call. Hell, what do I know about preppy soccer etiquette. All I know is, LeBlanc was back on campus with plenty of time to kill Wickie. Left the Corcoran kid with the trainer and disappeared for over an hour, according to the trainer. I asked your athletic director, too, that Stark woman. She was a bit more evasive, but she did confirm that LeBlanc came back with Corcoran."

"Have you asked Kevin about this?"

"Yes, says he was phoning the boy's parents, calling over to the Abbey, checkin' on the game, runnin' around the locker room, shit like that. Some of it checks out, some's a little fuzzy. Did he have time to sneak over and off Milt? Absolutely. Did he? Who the hell knows."

"What about Milt's other girlfriends, present company excluded?" Harry asked, smiling at Bess. She did not return his smile.

"Bigalow broad was outta town. There is the Nettleman dame. She's a piece of work and a busybody, but murder? What'dya think, Bess?"

"I don't believe Joan is capable of murder. She despised Milt, but I don't think she'd kill him. In fact, I think she rather enjoyed playing the role of the spurned lover. She's always had a flare for the dramatic. And, Milt gave her something to do. She watched him day and night.

"In fact, I'm surprised she didn't see his killer because she could usually identify whom he was with at any given time, where he went, what he ate. That is when she wasn't teaching. It was kind of a hobby for her. I think she'd relaxed her vigilance a little lately because she's been busy planning gallery events, but maybe she noticed something or someone the day he died. Did you ask her?"

"She's got a million theories about the case," Harry said, leaning back in his chair. He looks tired, Bess thought, watching him. Tired and defeated.

Roger laughed. "That's for damn sure. The woman's insatiable."

"Calls me daily with new developments. Every day it's someone new she's pointing the finger at."

"Lady's got the hots for you. She's been after poor Pete, too. Joanie says she was in town after classes that day, but unfortunately she chose that evening to relax her vigilance. And, speaking of vigilance, gotta go. I'm on duty in half an hour."

They walked him to the door and Demaris waited, assuming the other man would accompany him out. Then, sensing that his dinner companions had unfinished business, he bowed out.

Bess closed the door behind him and returned to the study, gathering up the cups and coffee things. He followed her, making ineffectual attempts to help.

Once in the kitchen, she busied herself at the sink, ignoring him. Harry watched her quietly for several minutes before coming to stand beside her. "Bess, can you stop, please? Can we talk for a few minutes?"

"I'm really tired." She stared straight ahead. "So, if you don't mind, I'd like to clean up and —"

"As a matter of fact, I do mind. You won't stop what you're doing? Okay, I'll just talk. I was not accusing you. I have no desire to pry into your private affairs. Your relationship with Peter Thurbert is your business, not mine. I'm really sorry if I stepped out of line."

"Well, you did."

"Fine, I'm a jerk. There, are you satisfied? I know it makes you uncomfortable, but I want to be your friend, more than your friend, if you'll let me. I care about you, and there's not a damn thing you can do about it. I know you and I —"

"You don't know me," she said, turning to face him. "You who has lived all over the world, doing all kinds of things! What could you possibly know about a small town schoolteacher who's never been anywhere? You don't have the slightest idea how I feel or think about anything — not my friends, not my job, not anything."

"Is this about what I told you at lunch? Are you pushing me away because of that?"

"Of course not," she said, her voice softening. "That was a horrible accident, a terrible tragedy for you and your beloved fiancée. I wouldn't dream of, well, let me say that your revelations have nothing to do with this conversation. I am just sick and tired of everyone, yourself included, thinking they know me and know what's best for me. I'm just saying —you couldn't possibly know me and maybe it's best left that way."

"Maybe it is." He grabbed his coat from the peg near the back door. "But, you know, I could say the same to you, about the assumptions you've made about me. You don't know me either, and what's becoming obvious is that you really don't care to know me, do you?

"Goodnight, Mrs. Dore. Thanks for dinner. It was delicious." He slammed the back door as he left, rounding the house in the dark on his way to the front drive.

Stunned, Bess sat at the kitchen table, tears stinging her eyes. He was right. He knew her better than she was willing to acknowledge, and yet, she knew next to nothing about him. He had tried to let her in, relating the tragic accident and Stella's death, but she had not made the slightest attempt, really, to learn more about Harry Winthrop. Even Roger had been more solicitous of Harry, inquiring with what appeared to be genuine interest, about his travels and career.

Did she care? Of course, she did. Since the first time she had laid eyes on Harry Winthrop, she had cared very much, but she was also terrified. Terrified of the unknown and even more terrified of caring for someone and risking the terrible grief of loss all over again. One thing was certain, Harry Winthrop was not Peter Thurbert. He would not be so easily put off, nor did Bess want to push him away as she had Peter.

CHAPTER 57

A small crowd gathered for Milt's memorial, about a dozen faculty and a few students. Susan LeBlanc attended as did Carrie Thurbert who sat next to her workout partner, dry-eyed throughout. Carol Richards was not in attendance, Bess noted, nor was Kevin LeBlanc or Roger. Harry, too, was absent. Peter spoke briefly and one student rose to recall a time that Mr. Wickie had helped him with a job application. Other than those contributions, the hour-long meeting was held in silence.

Bess and Jane walked out of the Meeting House arm in arm, running into Carrie and Peter on the steps. "Carrie," Jane nodded, stiffly.

Bess came forward, hugging first Carrie, then Peter. "Well, at least that's over," Carrie muttered to no one in particular. "What a nightmare." She was dressed in high heels and a black silk suit that fit her like a second skin, white silk blouse open in the front revealing her skeletal chest and minimal cleavage. Ash blonde hair, perfectly coifed, held back with silver combs.

Peter looked stricken, but managed to give them a wan smile. "A sad business. Too bad his family could not have attended."

"If he really had any."

"Carrie, that's enough. Let's go. Bess, Jane, we'll see you later."

"What a bitch," Jane whispered as they watched the Thurberts retreat. Bess remained silent, but she had to admit. In this case, Jane was right on target. Milt might have been a miserable human being, but he was dead. What did Carrie have against him? Did she know about the blackmail and the reasons behind it?

CHAPTER 58

Hard Lumps of earth pressed against the soles of Bess' thin flats as she made her way along the woodland path to campus. Why had she not worn her hiking boots and changed in her classroom?

After a few rainy, warmer days, the temperature had dropped during the night, freezing the soggy earth. Grooves and furrows made by bicycle tires and feet were now frozen, treacherous peaks and valleys along the well-used path. It was the Friday before Thanksgiving. The school's holiday break would begin at noon, giving the students the entire next week as vacation.

As she neared the campus, Bess' thoughts turned to her early morning conversation with Peter Thurbert. From six to seven each morning, the headmaster sat at his desk and fielded calls from parents, students, faculty, and staff. Bess had phoned at six-thirty this morning and asked to see him. His early morning office hours were known by all and appreciated by those who would otherwise find it impossible to reach him. Since Bess regularly availed herself of this time to catch up or consult with him, Peter had not been surprised to hear from her. He offered to take her to lunch and she had accepted, saying, "Perfect. I'll walk to campus and you can drop me off later, if that's okay?" He had, of course, agreed, and they rang off, Bess feeling guilty at her deceit.

Lost in thought, she failed to notice the branch frozen in the mud in the middle of the path. Hard, jagged tentacles grabbed the toe of her shoe and she lost her balance, crashing to the ground, her scream echoing through the silent woods.

"Damn," she muttered, rolling over. Her ankle twisted painfully as she struggled to extract her shoe from the branch's grasp. Groaning, she slipped her foot out of the shoe and freed the ankle, then pulled and tugged to free the blue flat, now bent and scratched. Reasonably certain that her ankle would not bear her weight, she struggled to stand, tears stinging her eyes. She was still a quarter mile from school.

"Mrs. Dore, is that you?" Billy's voice came from the woods in front of her and Bess realized that she lay in a heap, unrecognizable, her jacket covering her face.

She sat back down, smoothing her skirt. "Yes, Billy, it's me. I'm afraid I may need your help."

"Coming, hang on!" It sounded as if he dropped and armload of wood, then his footsteps drew nearer and he appeared at the edge of the clearing.

Gently, he reached down, grasping her under the arms, helping her to stand. "Your ankle, huh?"

"Yes, I don't think it's broken, just a nasty twist. Perhaps if I walk a little, I can stretch it out. Oooh!" She winced, leaning against him.

"I don't know, Mrs. D. Maybe I'd better carry you back?"

"Don't be silly. I'll be fine. I just need to walk it off. Let's get started, ooh." She faltered again, nearly tumbling to the ground.

"That's it. If you won't let me carry you, at least give me your bag. Now, hand it over."

Meekly, Bess handed him the canvas rucksack, which he slung over his right shoulder. "Now, come on, lean on me, hard. I won't bite. Just till you walk it off."

Smiling, Bess slung her arm over his shoulder, and they started off. A quarter mile had never seemed as long, as she hobbled along, recognizing with every step that Billy could have carried her in half the time. Her stubborn pride was not only keeping him from his work, but making her very late. As they hobbled onward, she thought about the previous evening and what a mess she had made of things with Harry. Her pride again, she thought, when will I ever learn? And, then she was crying.

"Hey, if it's hurting that much, why don't you let me carry you the rest of the way, okay?" His dark eyes regarded her, full of concern and confusion.

"It's not the ankle, Billy," she sniffed, embarrassed, but unable to stem the flood of tears. "It's my life. It's a wreck, a complete wreck and it's all of my own doing. Here I've been for the past ten years, blaming the world for Mac's death, for my being alone, when I could have changed things anytime I chose."

"Aren't you being a little hard on yourself? It isn't easy to lose someone you love."

She stopped and turned to him, "Lizzie was very dear to you, wasn't she?"

He stared down at her for a few second before saying, "Wow, where'd that come from?"

"I'm sorry," she said, instantly regretting her words. "I didn't mean to pry."

"It's okay. Just no one's mentioned her for a long time. Yeah, I loved her. Would've married her if she hadn't, you know."

Bess nodded. "She was a sweet girl. So full of joy and promise."

"Before he —" Billy spit out the words, eyes blazing with hatred, then shook his head and said no more.

"Who? Mr. Mederois, Lizzie's father?"

"The bastard," he muttered, speaking more to himself than her. "Never cared about anyone but himself and getting ahead, no matter who got hurt."

As they hobbled towards the Infirmary, Bess thought back to Lizzie's funeral and her father, Joe Mederois, prostrate with grief, throwing himself on her coffin, refusing to allow it to be lowered into the ground. He'd lost a daughter and with her, all his hopes and dreams. With nothing to live for, he had died of a heart attack less than a year after his daughter.

"Here we are," he said. "You're in luck. Looks like Nurse's in."

Gloria Moniz, the school nurse greeted them at the door, immediately taking charge. "Billy, run over to the classroom building. Let them know about Mrs. Dore. Then, we'll —"

"Gloria," Bess interrupted. "That's not necessary. Billy, please go back to your work. I'll call over and let Mags know. They'll find someone to cover my first class, or maybe Gloria could phone for me?" She smiled at the gray haired nurse, giving Billy a sly wink.

"Well, I'd better call right away," Gloria sputtered, disappearing into the office next to the examination room.

Bess reached over, squeezing his forearm. "Thank you, Billy." He flushed crimson and she withdrew her hand. "I mean that. I don't know what I would have done if you hadn't come along. I'm grateful for your strong shoulder to lean on, and to cry on. Sorry my emotions got the better of me. Must have been the shock of the fall."

"Who's been crying around here?" Gloria said, stepping back into the room.

Bess shrugged and Billy left without a word.

"Mags has arranged coverage, my dear. Now let's see about that ankle, shall we?"

CHAPTER 59

An hour later, Bess sat in class, ankle taped, listening to her students critique one another's drawings. At present, Cathy Petry was discussing her abstract painting, "Unrequited Love," her fellow students giving her their rapt attention. For the first time in many years, Bess identified with her students. Since the arrival of Harry Winthrop, she felt as if she had been thrust into a second adolescence. Forty-two-years old and she felt as unsure and confused as the fifteen and sixteen year olds sitting before her.

By twelve-thirty the campus was nearly deserted, the classroom building enveloped in a kind of hushed silence. She gathered her things, enjoying the quiet. She had arranged to meet Peter Thurbert at one, but was surprised to find him knocking at her classroom door a half hour early. "Peter, hi." She had planned to spend the ten minutes it would take to hobble to his office, preparing what she would say. Now, she felt ill-prepared to bring up what would certainly be unsettling for both of them.

"I frightened you. I'm sorry, my dear. I heard about your accident and thought I'd save you the trip to my office, no pun intended. If you're not ready, I can wait outside."

Bess smiled, relaxing now in the company of her dear friend. "Not a bit of it. I'm just moving a little slower, that's all."

"Then, please. May I have the honor of carrying your books, m'lady?" Without waiting for an answer, he grabbed her rucksack and the stack of papers on top of it. "Can you make it okay, without help?"

"Yes, thanks. All set."

She hopped on one foot down the stairs, gripping the banister tightly.

"I thought Pop's might be best," he said. "Kitchen's stopped serving and the Coop's closed. Pop's okay with you?"

"Oh, Peter, I didn't mean for this to be such a bother. I'm sure you have a million things to do. The last thing you need is me dragging you into town for lunch."

"Nonsense. Nothing I'd rather do than spend time with a dear friend. I've been looking forward to it since you called. You know I'd spend more time with you, if you'd let me. Besides, Carrie's family arrives tomorrow and after that I'll be a lost cause until they depart next Friday. Better to catch me now while I'm still sane."

"That's nice that you'll all be together for the holiday." She had no plans as yet. Her brother, Ron and sister, Molly had both asked her to come to them for Thanksgiving, but she had declined. She wasn't up to listening to Ron's wife, Margot complain about the kids and her husband, nor was she eager to hear one of Molly's partner, Judith's patronizing lectures about how "it's okay to be alone" and how "women don't realize their inner strength." Her one regret was missing time with her niece, Daisy and nephew, Will, Ron's children.

Daisy and Will spent two weeks every summer with Aunt Bess, and the occasional weekend when Ron and Margot's last minute plans failed to include securing an overnight babysitter. Bess enjoyed their visits, but after being caught one too many times, dead-tired with an empty refrigerator on a Friday afternoon, she had spoken to Ron and established a few rules about last minute drop-offs.

Pop's Diner was quiet when they arrived. "How's the detecting going?" he asked as they settled in a corner booth.

"Fine, I guess." Bess suddenly wished she were miles away, anywhere would do.

"That's not really what I mean," he said, when Pop interrupted to take their orders. Each ordered a bowl of chowder and agreed to share a club sandwich. As soon as Pop disappeared, he said, "What I meant was — how are you and Harry Winthrop getting along?"

"Fine," she said, a bit too curtly, irritated at this unexpected turn in the conversation.

"He's a nice guy. I'm glad you two are hitting it off."

"Why is it that everyone's trying to marry me off to Harry Winthrop?"

"Don't be ridiculous. No one's trying to marry you off to anyone. We're just happy you've found a friend."

"Am I really that pathetic?"

"Bess, you're overreacting."

"I'm sorry, you're right, of course." She was acting ridiculous. "You know, I was sitting with my ninth graders this morning, thinking that my emotions are as out of control as theirs. I feel like a frightened, confused teenager."

"Must be love." He smiled, not a trace of sarcasm in his tone. "You're entitled. Can't say I don't wish it had been sooner with a different guy."

"Peter, please."

"Sorry, couldn't resist. Don't worry. I'm not going to fall down on my knees again. I'm through begging."

"You're also married, remember?"

"Yes, there's that, too." He gave her a rueful smile. "Carrie and I have actually had a bit of thaw in our relations of late. We'll manage to stick it out for the long haul, I expect."

"I'm glad. I never wanted to be the cause of pain to either of you."

Pop set down their food, asked if they wanted anything else and disappeared before Peter said, "Bess, you weren't the cause of anything. It was all me. I took advantage of you at a time in your life when you were most vulnerable. It was wrong of me."

"Can we please change the subject?"

"Of course, but I am interested in your Mr. Winthrop."

CHAPTER 60

Pop's chowder was the best in the village, brimming with clams, creamy and perfectly seasoned with a hint of fresh dill. Bess and Peter savored their soup and club sandwich in silence for several minutes before she said, "He's not my Mr. Winthrop, especially after last night."

"You quarreled? That's a good sign."

"Of what?"

"Means you care about each other. Means you're comfortable enough with each other to be honest."

"I don't know about that," she said, remembering Harry's revelations about the accident and knowing Peter was right.

"For what it's worth, I believe Mac would approve."

"Peter, how can you say such a thing? Harry Winthrop represents everything that Mac despised. Everything he spent his life trying to —"

"Bess, whoa, slow down, now. I'm talking about Harry, the human being, not his name or family."

He was right again and she knew it. "But do you see us together, really? We're so different. What kind of foundation do we have for a relationship?"

"Well, for starters, the man's in love with you. And, I believe you are in love with him. Now, hold on, hold on," he said, raising his hand as she started to protest. "You asked me a question and I'm trying to give you a complete answer.

"He's a good man, Bess. Got a couple of degrees, in biology, marine studies or something like that. Ph.D., too, I believe. And, no, he didn't buy it. He's also done more for his fellow human beings than both you and I will do in a lifetime. All kinds of volunteer work, teaching, helping to build communities, you name it. And, he hasn't spent the last decade in a cushy, protected little enclave like Old Harbor Friends either. He's been working in the ghettos of South and Central America teaching kids on whom society had long since given up."

"How do you know all this?"

"His father talks about him all the time. Been regaling me with the adventures of young Harry as long as I've known him. They are all the family that remains. Younger brother was killed in an automobile accident his senior year in college. Harry's fiancée died in an accident as well. He was driving, poor man. For a week, doctors didn't know if he'd survive either."

"Do you know anything about her, the fiancée, I mean?"

"Let's see, Harry Senior has spoke of her. Iris, Frances, no, I think her name was Stella. Yes, that was it, Stella. Society girl from Boston. Was beautiful, accomplished, what have you. Terrible tragedy."

Bess thought again about Harry's handkerchief with "S & H" embroidered in delicate, fine stitches.

"Then, of course, Harry's mother and sister died in an airplane crash a number of years ago. Too much to bear, really, when you think about all that family's suffered. I imagine father and son have tried to fill the void, but it can't be easy. Despite it all, they are two of the most generous, kind-hearted souls I know. Share the same great sense of humor, too, but I expect you've seen some of that. I heard you had dinner with them."

"Yes," she replied, not trusting herself to say more.

"He's a writer," Peter went on. "Pretty successful one, I gather. Published a number of books — nature writing, novels, all kinds of stuff. Carrie's looked him up on the Internet since she's smitten like all you other women. She's found, and ordered, a couple of his nonfiction books, but can't seem to locate the novels.

Apparently, he uses a pen name. His father's given me some of his shorter essays to read. Mostly about the natural world. Well written, quite beautiful actually."

At this moment, Pop appeared and began clearing the table. "Anything else, folks?"

"No, unless you want tea, Bess?" She shook her head. "Just the check then, Pop, thanks. We'll be out of your hair in a few minutes."

"No need to hurry. Take all the time you need."

Pop disappeared with their plates. Bess waited until he was out of earshot, before saying, "Oh, Peter, I've been such an ass. All my snap judgments."

"Don't be too hard on yourself, my dear. This hasn't been the easiest of times. And, I expect Harry can take it. What was it you wanted to talk with me about, anyway? Mustn't neglect school matters completely."

CHAPTER 61

Bess blanched, swallowing hard, staring at Peter Thurbert across the table.

"Uh, oh, that bad, huh?" Peter's warm smile only served to heighten the guilt she felt at blindsiding him in this way.

"Not exactly," she stammered, folding and refolding her napkin until it lay fanlike across her lap.

"Come on, Bess, out with it. You can tell me." His eyes teased, as he reached across the table to squeeze her hand.

"It's about Milt." Bess looked away, afraid to find betrayal in her friend's eyes.

"What about Milt?"

"Roger, Sergeant Demaris knows about the blackmail, Peter."

His face drained of color. "What blackmail?" He leaned forward, whispering now. "Bess, whatever are you talking about?"

"He's checked, Peter. He knows Milt was blackmailing you," she whispered, watching her friend reel back as if she had slapped him.

"It's not what you think."

"I don't think anything, Peter. Really, I don't. I don't know why I even agreed to talk to you about this. You're my dear friend and I have no right. It's none of my business."

"No, I want to tell you. Let's go. We can talk in the car." He threw money on the table, at least three times what the check would be, grabbed their coats and hustled her out the door.

Once they were seated side by side, he began. "It's about Jane."

Bess gasped, certain now what was to follow. She shook her head. "No, you don't have to tell me, really. I should never have asked."

"No, I want to. It will be a relief to tell someone. Where to start? There's no easy way, I guess so here's the thing. Jane and I are lovers. Have been for many years. There was a time when I thought you knew, since you're such good friends, but I can see from your expression that I was incorrect. Jane assured me she would never tell you, but I know how women friends are. No secrets and whatnot. I never wanted her to tell you, of course. I couldn't stand that you would think less of me because of it, because of how weak I've been.

"Milt found out of course, and demanded payment or he threatened to go to the Board, to Carrie, to everyone, really. So, I paid, and paid, and paid. Jane didn't want me to, but what choice did I have?

"I haven't seen her, we haven't been together, since Milt's death. I feel like such a heel, to both women. Nothing I do will ever make things right." He started the car and pulled out of the lot. "Have an appointment in fifteen minutes, I'm 'fraid."

Bess thought about Kevin's revelation about Carrie Thurbert and Will McGuire and wondered if Peter knew. She certainly would not tell him. "Does Carrie know?"

"No, I hurt her so much with you. How could I confess my weakness again? Jane and I started up almost immediately after you made it clear you weren't interested."

And, after you'd confessed all to Carrie and made me the 'other woman,' Bess thought ruefully.

"Jane knew I cared deeply for you, but she still took me in. Oh, Bess what a mess I've made. How much hurt have I caused? I care deeply for Jane, I really do, but Carrie and I, we've been through so much together. How can I leave her now?"

"Oh, Peter."

"Yes, I know, pretty awful, huh? Your illustrious head no better than Milt Wickie. Perhaps, I'm worse since at least Milt carried on his affairs in the open."

"Poor Jane."

"Yes, she doesn't deserve any of this. Milt was the reason for my early retirement, by the way. After a while, the money wasn't enough. He wanted me out. Had designs on the job himself, if you can believe it."

"Yes, I can. He was a horrible man. Why, he deserved to be —" She stopped short, staring at Peter, her unspoken suspicion hanging in the air between them.

"I didn't kill him, Bess. Though, God knows I wanted to sometimes. But I didn't. I was ready to move on. It wasn't losing the job that bothered me. I love Old Harbor Friends and the people here, you know that." His eyes filled with tears.

"I know, Peter. I know. Don't let's speak of it anymore."

"I'll talk to Demaris today."

"I'm sure he'll keep your relationship with Jane confidential."

"And you?"

"Don't think another thing about it. I won't say a word, not even to Jane," she said, wondering how she would ever face her friend.

Peter pulled the car into her driveway and stopped. "Thank you, my dear. You are a dear friend. Do you need help getting inside?"

"No, thanks, I can make it just fine." Sliding out of the seat, she stood and braced herself before turning back to say goodbye. "Thanks for lunch. Take care of yourself, Peter."

As she watched his car pull away, Bess wondered what other secrets still lay in the shadows of the world she had thought she knew so well.

Chapter 62

After puttering around the house, fussing over laundry that didn't need doing and dusting that could easily have waited, Bess finally gave in to her throbbing ankle. A steaming pot of orange-almond tea and a new Anne Greyson novel in hand, she headed for the study where she settled into her favorite easy chair, propping the ankle on a footstool piled high with cushions. Before stepping into the world of Helen Brown and her newest adventure, she picked up the phone.

Her first call was to Roger. He answered himself, on the second ring. His deep, steady voice was soothing after the day's turmoil. She found herself remembering their long ago friendship and wishing there was a way to revive it without all the hurt. "Roger, it's me, Bess."

"How're ya doin'? Better mood today?"

She chose to ignore his reference to her quarrel with Harry. "I've talked with Peter."

"And?"

"Has he phoned you yet?"

"Nope."

"Well, he's going to. He told me he would be in touch today."

"Confessing, is he?"

"No. Roger, I hope you'll listen to his story with an open mind. I believe it's the truth."

"Give him a lie detector test, did you?"

"No, but I know him and I —"

"What did he tell you anyway?"

"I'd rather he tell you. I'd like not to be involved, if that's okay."

"Well, if he doesn't call today, I'm gonna call back and shake it out of you."

"Roger, please, I'm not in the mood for this today."

"Look, Bess, I'm sorry you're having a bad day, but I've had two weeks of friggin' bad days and I'm sick of this case and all these people. Unless your Mr. Thurbert has an airtight alibi, besides the word of his ditz of a wife, or unless he solves the case for me, I'm gonna continue to regard him as a prime suspect."

"I know him, Roger." What was she thinking? The man was impossible. How could she have imagined they'd ever be friends? "Peter could no more kill someone than I could. The reason he was being blackmailed is hardly a cause for murder."

"Look, I'm givin' him the benefit of the doubt, okay? I won't send the paddy wagon out to pick him up yet. He has till tomorrow morning to fess up."

"How magnanimous of you."

"Relax, will you?"

"Roger, about last night."

"Hold on a minute, Bess." He covered the receiver and she heard muffled voices before he came back. "Thurbert's on the other line. Talk to you later, okay?"

Hanging up, she sighed, then dialed the number for Winthrop Hall. Molly answered. "Sorry, Miss. Young Mr. Harry is away for the night. You might just catch him at the accountant's before he leaves. He's on an errand for his father."

Bess thanked her and dialed the accountant's number, finding a crisp voice on the other end. "Barnes and Hawkins."

"Yes, hello. I'm trying to reach Harry Winthrop and they told me at his home that I might catch him at your office. Might he be available?"

"He was here. Could you hold, please, Miss —?"

"Oh, of course, so sorry. Dore, Bess Dore."

Thirty seconds later, she heard his voice. "Bess, is that you?" He sounded hurried, anxious.

"Harry, yes, it's me. I'm so sorry to bother you. I, I just wanted to say something. About last night and I —" Her voice broke and she paused, unable to speak.

"Bess, look, I'm here at the reception desk. I can't talk now, but —"

"But, I can," she said, finding her voice. "I've been incredibly foolish. You've been nothing but kind and caring to me since you arrived and I've responded with snobbishness, cruelty and arrogance."

"Maybe I'll see if Sally here can transfer me to a private line."

"No, please. I don't want to hold you up. I just wanted to say. I mean, I wanted to ask if you might give me another chance? A chance to show you that I'm not the heartless, superficial little fool you've seen the past few weeks."

"You're none of those things. Look, let me ask Sally to transfer me or she'll have to listen to me —"

"Would you have dinner with me? If I promise not to go into another tirade?"

"I'd love to. When?"

"I was going to ask you tonight, but Molly says you're going away?"

"Yes, a quick trip to the city. I have a few things I want to check like a certain person's brownstone and another lead."

"Oh?"

"I'll tell you when I see you, okay?"

"Then, tomorrow night, here, for dinner? Seven o'clock?"

"I'll be there. Take care of yourself and that ankle."

"How did you —" He hang up before she could ask how he knew about her fall.

Chapter 63

Restless, with no wish to be alone, Bess called Jane and invited her to dinner. She then spent the remainder of the afternoon hobbling around the kitchen, cooking and preparing supper, activities that never failed to relax her. Rummaging in her stores, she found the ingredients for a creamy seafood chowder, using haddock and shrimp from the freezer, and cornbread. She then assembled a simple field greens salad and decided individual floating islands would be nice for dessert. Jane loved desserts and floating island was one of her favorites.

At five thirty, she changed into faded jeans, a thick gray turtleneck and blue lambswool cardigan, the latter knitted by one of her students several Christmases ago. Miles too big, Bess loved it. When she wore it, she remembered Laurie, a gifted artist, albeit beginner knitter.

After checking things in the kitchen, she poured a glass of white wine, taking it to the study where she built and lit a fire. She then sat back, propping her foot until Jane arrived.

As always, the evening was lively, full of animated conversation about life, school, literature and their mutual angst about the ongoing investigation. Jane refrained from asking about Harry and Bess volunteered nothing until they sat in the study after dinner with mugs of chamomile tea. Somehow, the discussion turned to Peter.

In the year following Mac's death, Bess had confided to Jane about Peter's advances. It had been Jane who had encouraged her to put a halt to the headmaster's evening visits to the cottage to "check in and see how she was doing." It had been Jane who insisted Bess see a therapist, Jane who buoyed her spirits, Jane who refused to allow her to blame herself for Peter's unsolicited attentions." He's taking advantage of you," she had told her grieving friend. "And, you've got to stop it or I will."

Bess had stopped it. She would never have gotten through the mess without Jane, so numb and lost had she been without Mac. Now, it appeared that almost immediately after she had given Peter her ultimatum, he had taken up with her dearest friend. She could barely look Jane in the eye as they talked.

Jane stretched out on the sofa, mug of tea perched precariously in her lap. "Let's not talk about Mr. T. anymore. You know how he bores me silly. For what it's worth, I agree with you though. Casper Milquetoast wouldn't kill a fly if his life depended upon it. My money's on Kevin."

"You think so?"

"He certainly has the temperament, and the best motive."

"I feel a little sorry for Kevin."

"Well, don't. And, don't look at me as if I'm the wicked witch. Sometimes you can be so naïve. Kevin's been screwing around on Susan for years. Milt was probably revenge on her part. You know, I'm surprised Kevin never hit on you."

"You're kidding."

"No, I'm not. You are hopeless, you know it, not to mention forgetful. Remember I told you about eight years ago, he practically raped me after the Harvest Ball? You know, the big bash they had to kick off the Capital Campaign? I know I told you about that. We were both drunk, but still, he was way out of line."

Bess nodded. She did remember. "Sorry, of course, that was terrible."

"You were still in heavy grieving mode," Jane added, speaking more to herself than Bess. "But Kevin has always been inappropriate with students, just like Garrett Rollins. And, don't forget poor little Nanny Pollart, the choir director. She left after one year. Couldn't take Kevin's constant harassment."

"I did hear gossip about his womanizing, but I can't believe Kevin would carry on with students. Why he's one of the most popular teachers."

"Exactly. That's how he lures them in. He falls all over them, they fall in love, then he takes full advantage of their adoration. Not saying he still does, but he did. It was disgusting."

Bess thought back to the first time she met Kevin LeBlanc shortly after he came to the school. He and Susan had come to dinner with the Thurberts and Mac and Kevin had spent hours talking about teaching and their mutual interest in local environmental issues. She also recalled Kevin's keen interest in Mac's scrimshaw collection. She could still see them hunched over the display case, its glass top thrown open as Mac removed each piece, recounting its history. If she closed her eyes, she could almost see the whalebone knife in Kevin's hands.

CHAPTER 64

Harry's experience breaking and entering had been limited to several break-ins at his own house and forty-five minutes practice on the streets of Trinidad with Carlos Parente. On a scorching hot day, Carlos had helped him select the set of polished steel lock picks and then given him a quick tutorial on their use. As he wiggled and teased one of the three locks on the ornate front door of Carol Richards' brownstone, he wished he had paid more attention to his tutor.

It was dark, the street deserted as the first lock yielded and he moved on to the second, which gave way with only a few wiggles. As he began working on the third lock, he heard the sound of heels clicking on the pavement and turned to spy a woman approaching. "Hi, there," she called, as if it were perfectly natural to find a strange man on her neighbor's steps in the middle of the night. "No one's home."

"Thanks, I know," he said, palming the picks, and turning to face her. "I expect Carol any minute. You a friend of hers?"

"Hardly know her. Never here. Comes for the occasional weekend, that's it. Waste of a great location, if you ask me."

"Well, she's coming for Thanksgiving because we're spending it together. I'm Reggie, Reggie Richards, her brother." What a stupid name, he thought, descending the stairs to shake her hand.

She beamed, holding out a gloved hand. "Dottie Bingham, pleased to meet you." Her green eyes were thick with mascara, and she smoothed back platinum strands. Except for these errant few, her hair sat like a helmet on her head. "You have a key, I see."

What was she thinking, Harry wondered, watching her. He could have been Ted Bundy and here she is flirting on the sidewalk in the dark. "Yes." He pulled his own keys out of his pocket, waving them. "Well, nice to meet you, Ms. Bingham. I don't want to keep you."

"It's Miss," she purred, leaning closer until he could smell the bourbon on her breath. "Shall I wait to make sure you get in okay? I'm very good at opening things, if you get my drift?"

He did and the image evoked was not pleasant. He forced a smile. "You're too kind, Dottie, but it's me that should be seeing you safely home. Let me walk you to your door."

"So gallant. No, no, not necessary. I only live two doors down. Number 518. Do drop by to say 'hello' over the holidays. I'll be out Thanksgiving Day, but otherwise, I'll be in waiting for your knock. Unless you'd like to come in for a nightcap?"

"Thanks, but I promised Carol I'd start dinner." He walked her along the sidewalk until they reached her front steps. For an awful moment, he feared she might try to kiss him, but after a coquettish wink, she sashayed up the steps. Her door opened with a turn of the knob and he waved, hurrying back to his work. Obviously, Dottie Bingham had been peeking out her window and spying on her neighbors. What a strange occupation for so late at night.

The third lock was a snap and he pushed open Richards' door, stepped into the darkened hallway wondering what kind of an alarm system she had. A silent alarm light was already blinking on the wall to his left. Five minutes, he figured, before the police arrived. Flicking on lights, he ran from room to room, snapping photos of the furnishings. As the first sirens sounded in the distance, he had completed his circuit and was on the last bedroom. Opulent and overdone was his assessment.

"Time's up, Harry, m'boy." He made his way down the steps and ran to his car parked on the next block. "Bye, bye, Dottie," he called into the night, blowing a kiss as the lights of the first squad car turned onto the street. A crowd was assembling.

CHAPTER 65

Before heading back to his hotel, Harry had one more stop in the south end of the city. Shortly after leaving Richards' tony environs, he parked near an apartment complex in a humbler neighborhood. A small fenced in park with swings, slide and freshly painted wrought iron benches lay across the street, the sidewalks swept and well-tended.

After five minutes of ringing the doorbell, he realized it was broken and knocked. The door clicked open and he climbed the stairs to the third floor. The door to 3C was opened by a burly man in his twenties dressed in graying, wife beater undershirt, two sizes too small, and a pair of soiled, baggy canvas cargo pants. "Yeah? Whatcha want?"

"Hello. I'm looking for Paula Rapoza. Is she in?"

"Who the hell wants her?"

"Harry Winthrop. I'm from Old Harbor, from the school. Are you Mr. Rapoza?"

"So what if I am?"

"Look, sir, I don't mean to intrude, but it's very important that I speak to Paula. Is she here?"

Before the man could reply, a voice within called, "Jimmy, who is it? Your mother?"

"Naw," he yelled over his shoulder. "Some guy for you. Come out here, will ya."

A slight woman, dressed in a white uniform with 'North Shore Retirement Community' embroidered over the left breast pocket, appeared in the doorway. Instantly, the man's face softened. "Who is it, honey?" She smiled, looking from her husband to Harry.

Harry was smitten. Anyone who could love Jimmy, must have a heart of gold. "Harry Winthrop, Mrs. Rapoza. I've come from Old Harbor, from the school."

"Cabral," she said, eyes lowered. "I'm married now." Patting her husband's arm, she stepped aside. "Come in, won't you? Jimmy, honey, go on back to the kitchen and eat, or you'll be late. My husband works nights, Mr. Winthrop." Fond eyes followed Jimmy until he disappeared into the next room. "I work days, so supper is our only time together."

"I am really sorry. I promise not to be long." He took the seat she offered, settling into a worn recliner, one of only three pieces of furniture in the sparse, lonely living room. Paula sat in a director's chair opposite him. Between them, a metal steamer trunk served as a coffee table. "This can wait, Mrs. Cabral. If you'd like to eat together, I can come back in fifteen minutes."

"It's alright, really. Would you like coffee? It's instant. Jimmy's promised me a Mr. Coffee for Christmas. He's been putting money away every week for it," she whispered. "He doesn't think I know. I wish he wouldn't do it. We need so many other important things."

Harry smiled. "Thank you, Mrs. Cabral, but I'm fine."

"Paula, please. Now what can I do for you?

"I'm curious about your roommate, Lizzie Mederois."

"Lizzie, whatever for after all this time?"

"Call it a hunch, or call me crazy, I don't know. Have you heard about Milt Wickie, from the school?"

She nodded. "My mum called me."

"Do you remember Louie Predo, the gardener?"

"Crazy Louie, you mean? Of course. Is he still as crazy as ever?"

"Yes, and no. We believe he may be confused about the two deaths — Lizzie's and Milt Wickie's. His mind seems to have them all jumbled up. I don't see a link and thought maybe you might?"

"I can't imagine any. Of course, I hardly knew Mr. Wickie." She fell silent, studying her hands resting in her lap. "Unless, did Louie find Mr. Wickie? I mean, did he find the body? You do know, he was the one who found Liz."

"Yes, I knew he'd found her. No, he didn't find Mr. Wickie, but he did find a bag that we believe held the murder weapon and perhaps other possessions that may have belonged to the killer."

"How awful."

"If you would, please tell me about Lizzie."

"Not much to tell. Very smart, pretty, in a plain, simple way. Her family put a lot of pressure on her, especially her dad. She had to relieve the pressure somewhere and she did, with men."

"You mean Billy Blackburn?"

"They were friends. Maybe sometimes more, but she wasn't in love with him like he was with her."

"Oh?"

"I mean, she cared for Billy, who wouldn't? He was gorgeous. He was certainly her closest friend. Probably told him things she didn't tell me, but love? Billy worshipped the ground Lizzie walked on and she didn't even know the meaning of love. Was beaten out of her when she was really young."

"Physical abuse?" She nodded. "You said 'men'."

"I probably spoke out of turn. Never knew for sure, because she was kind of secretive, but I think there were a few guys she was seeing regularly. One was a teacher. She called him 'Paul,' but that wasn't his real name. I heard her talking to him one night, on the phone. They were talking about her exam and she was giggling, asking if he was going to give her a good grade. When I came in, she hung up fast."

"Did you know she was pregnant when she died?"

"Yup. She'd just told me two days before she did it, killed herself, I mean. She was trying to figure out if she wanted to keep it."

"Billy the father, do you think? Or, maybe the teacher or one of the others?"

"After her funeral, Billy and I had a long talk. He didn't say the baby was his, but he was so broken up about the baby's death and Lizzie's, I was afraid he might kill himself. I even told my advisor, Mr. McGuire. Grief does strange things to people, doesn't it?"

Harry nodded, watching her slender fingers, as she rubbed her hands back and forth, up and down her thighs. Her dark eyes were framed by an oval face and coal black hair, pulled back and tied loosely at the nape of her neck. She reminded him of Raphael's Madonna. Paula Cabral seemed so young, and fragile, her alabaster skin luminous in the soft light of the room's one lamp.

"I remember poor Mrs. Dore's grief. Is she still at the school?" He nodded. "Total personality change. She had always been so friendly and outgoing. She and her husband always had students to their house for dinners, holidays, picnics, even sleepovers. She was always mothering someone. After he died though, forget it. Grief just shriveled her up till it seemed like she died right along with him, you know? I heard she got better after a few years. I hope so. She was a nice person. Have you met her?"

"Yes, and I'm happy to report that she's much better these days."

"That's good to hear."

"Now, I'll get out of your hair and let you get back to your husband." Harry rose and she followed him to the door. "Paula, thank you for your time. Please apologize to Jimmy for taking your family time. He's right to guard it."

She blushed. "Oh, go on." She opened the door and Harry gave her a slight bow and departed.

Back on the street, he went to the trunk of his car. After several minutes of rummaging, he unearthed an empty envelope, slightly dirty, but serviceable. Once again he entered the apartment building, climbing to the third floor. Reaching the door of 3C, he extracted all the cash in his wallet, three hundred and sixty dollars, stuffed it into the envelope and scrawled "Merry Christmas, Paula and Jimmy." After slipping it under the door, he beat a hasty retreat.

As he drove away, he hoped Jimmy would not take offense at the small offering, or his use of their surnames. Perhaps he should have addressed it to 'Mr. and Mrs. Cabral,' but it was too late now.

CHAPTER 66

"Earth to Bess. Are you still with me?"

Bess shook herself, standing. "Oh, Jane, this is all so awful. All these horrible suspicions about our friends and colleagues. These are people we care about. I just hate it."

"You're right, love. Here. Jane patted the seat beside her. "Come sit by me. We won't talk about the wretched murder anymore. Besides, I'm dying to hear how things are going with Harry."

"Another mess, I'm afraid." Bess flopped beside her on the sofa, nearly spilling Jane's tea. "I don't know where to begin. I've made such a colossal mess of things there."

"What happened?"

"Nothing really, I've just been on such an emotional rollercoaster since Milt's death. I don't seem to be able get a grip on how I'm feeling or thinking from one minute to the next."

"Must be love."

"Peter's words exactly. You two must think alike."

"Mmm, don't know about that, but some things are so obvious that one can draw only a single conclusion. What gives? Tell me what's going on with you two?"

"Nothing." She rose to clear the tea things. "And, you can wipe that lascivious grin off your face."

"You listen to me, Bess Dore. After ten years, you're entitled. You must be horny as hell."

"Stop it. You're very wicked, Jane Fellows. I think I need something stronger than this lukewarm tea if we're going to discuss my sex life. Want a brandy?"

"No, thanks, but I'll take some Amaretto, if you have it. Hey, let's do a Tarot reading and see what it tells us." Jane leaped up to assist with the aperitifs.

Years earlier, the two friends had read a number of books on the Tarot and had consulted several readers in the city. They then began experimenting with readings on each other, always with a bottle of Amaretto at their side. They had spent many happy evenings reading each other's cards and speculating on the future. They never took their prognostications very seriously, but had had a lot of fun.

Bess brought their glasses back to the sofa and set them on the coffee table. "Not tonight. I'd rather keep my feet planted in the real world right now, if you don't mind. He's coming to dinner tomorrow night."

Jane raised her glass. "Go for it, then! That's my advice."

"First, I have to apologize, to ask if we can start again. I've been so wrong in so many of my assumptions about him. I've been such a blind, snob. Had him pegged as a complete gadabout, useless playboy, whatever, everything that Mac and I despised. And, he's none of those things. He's younger than me, you know."

"Perfect. Three years is nothing. If men can carry on with babes twenty and thirty years younger, so can we. And, honey, I say this with love and affection — you've got to ditch this 'Mac and I' stuff. It's been ten years. You've got to let him go. He would want you to let him go."

"I know, I know. Let me finish, okay? It's just, he's not. He's not the person I thought he was."

"Who ever is?"

"Jane, I think I'm in love with him, but I'm not sure I can trust my emotions."

Jane set her glass down and grasped Bess' shoulders. "You've got to get a grip. Do you hear yourself? You're babbling. Martyrdom and self-flagellation went out centuries ago. Take a big gulp of your Amaretto and listen to me."

Jane held her knees now, eyes pleading. "I loved Mac, you know that. He was a great guy and you two had a wonderful marriage, but he's not the only guy in the world. He's gone and Harry's here. A flesh and blood hunk, to boot. You can't go on living your life, worrying about what Mac would think or want. You'll drive yourself crazy and squelch any chance at happiness."

To Jane's surprise, she answered. "I know."

"You do?"

"Yes, I do. I need to let him go. When the term is over and I have some free time, I'm going to go right through the house and clear everything out. I'll have a big jumble sale and sell it all, or give it away. All his clothes, all the papers in the attic that should have been pitched long ago. They're all going.

"I can only imagine what people must think of me. Batty old Bess wearing her dead husband's clothes, never changing a thing in the house, in my life or routines, acting as if he is still alive and will walk in the door any minute. It's a wonder I haven't been committed, or fired for being just this side of a lunatic. No matter what happens with Harry, I will always be grateful that his coming into my life forced me to take a long, hard look at it. Not a pretty sight."

Jane smiled, squeezing her hand. "You're a gorgeous sight, my friend. Always have been. And, you deserve happiness whether it comes in the company of Harry Winthrop or a rip-roaring jumble sale, which, by the way, I'll be helping with. I have a huge pile of junk in my basement just waiting to be exorcised."

"It was Mac's dying wish, you know."

"A jumble sale?"

Bess laughed, poking her. "No, he wanted me to find someone, after he died."

"Of course, he did. He loved you, silly. He wanted you to be happy and loved. See, here, you've had the green light for ten years and haven't driven full speed ahead? Time to step on the gas, baby."

The phone rang and Bess answered, blushing as she heard his voice. "Hi," she said, softly.

"Sorry to call so late. I just wanted to hear your voice."

"I'm glad you called, and it's not late at all. In fact, I've got Jane with me and we've just had dinner." Jane was making faces, swooning back on the sofa so Bess turned away, not entirely successful in stifling a giggle.

"You sound in fine spirits. I won't keep you."

"Oh, no, Harry, please. You're not keeping me. I'm glad you called." More swooning in the background.

"I am, too. Hearing your voice warms up this sterile hotel room, makes staying here a little more bearable. I wish you were here."

"I do, too." Not trusting herself to say more after wine and the Amaretto, she steered the conversation to safer ground. "So have you discovered anything?"

"Not much." His voice softened. "I'll tell you about it tomorrow night. I'd rather be there, gazing into your beautiful eyes, sitting as close as you'll let me, wondering —"

"Harry —" She stammered, glimpsing Jane behind her.

"Jane's egging you on, isn't she?"

"Little bit."

"Alright, my love, I'll say goodnight. But I won't be as easily put off tomorrow so be prepared. I love you, goodnight." He hung up, leaving Bess weak-kneed and blushing.

Jane clapped her hands. "Oh, my God — it's worse than I thought! You're gone, completely gone!"

Flopping down beside her, Bess wondered whether to laugh or cry. "I don't know how to act around him. Help me, Jane! Mac was never like this."

"There you go, you're doing it again."

"I'm sorry, I know. It's just, it's just, I've never had anyone pursue me like this. I can count on one hand the times someone's told me he loved me. And, Mac — I know, I know — but except at the end, Mac was never demonstrative."

"Well, get ready, my girl. Something tells me your Mr. Winthrop is demonstrative as hell and not afraid to show it."

"Oh, dear, Jane, I think you're right."

Bess laughed, falling into her friend's open arms.

CHAPTER 67

Saturday morning dawned cold and damp, the temperature in the teens. After a fitful night's sleep, Bess awoke with a headache, too much wine and Amaretto, her diagnosis. Feeling listless and unsettled, she picked at her poached egg and toast, forcing herself to take a few bites before dumping it in the garbage.

As she poured a cup of tea, the phone rang. "That you, baby? You sound down in the dumps. Are you sick?"

"Hello, Mother, no, just a slight headache." She suddenly remembered she was supposed to have called her mother about Thanksgiving. "I'm so sorry I haven't gotten back to you."

"Not to worry, my darling. Tim and I have been on the go so you wouldn't have caught us anyway. Now, what's wrong? You sound positively lugubrious."

"Nothing's wrong, just tired. It's been a busy semester and I didn't sleep well last night."

"It's a wonder anyone sleeps around there with this murder business. I wish you'd come stay with us until they find the culprit." Maggie Guildford had called the day after Milt's death, after hearing the news from her friend, and Board member, Babs Chilmark. She had offered to fly to her daughter's side immediately, but Bess had declined with the promise that she would be in touch about coming for Thanksgiving.

"Mother, I have a job, remember?"

"Yes, but some things are more important. It must be simply dreadful for you, especially since Mac's knife was the murder weapon. Tim doesn't think you should be living in the cottage. It's unsafe."

"I'm fine, Mother, really."

"Well, the least we can do is pull together for the holidays, keep our spirits up."

"Mother, I'm not sure I —"

"We are sending you a ticket. Come down to the islands for the week. Rest, get away. Tim and I will spoil you."

"That's sweet of you guys, really, but I think I should stay here. Can I take a rain check till Christmas?"

"Nonsense, mothers know best in these kinds of circumstances, sweetie pie. Didn't I survive the death of your dear father, then Mac? Then, just two years later, my darling Phillip?" She referred to her second husband who had married her and dropped dead of a heart attack three months later. "I am no stranger to adversity, my dear Bessie. And, I know — the best therapy is escape."

Bess felt the walls closing in on her. Truth was, her mother's entire life had been one big escape. First, her father whom her mother barely saw during the last few years of his life, then the endless stream of boyfriends, she had lost count, all who begged Maggie to marry them. Vowing never to marry again, she had been living with Tim for five years, a record for Maggie. "Been there, done that," was Maggie's refrain whenever the subject of marriage arose.

The conversation with her mother was worsening her headache, and Bess wondered how soon she could hang up without causing grievous offense. "Bessie, are you listening to me? I'm calling my travel agent right after I hang up this phone. I need to know your times."

"Mother, I'm sorry, I can't."

"Nonsense and poppycock. You need a vacation and I intend to give you one."

"Mother, no."

"I'm only looking out for you, my dear."

Bess ignored her mother's wounded tone, determined to stand firm. "I'll come soon, I promise. Please thank Tim for me, will you?"

Deep sigh. "We had such a lovely dinner planned in your honor, at the Ritz. Sixteen of our dear friends. We will have to cancel now, I guess." Another sigh. "We'll be on a plane Wednesday. Can't leave you alone in your hour of need."

"Mother, don't be silly." Bess dutifully assumed her role in a now familiar routine. Maggie had no intention of cancelling her plans nor was the Ritz dinner in her honor. For a second, she was tempted to accept Maggie's offer, just to see how she'd wriggle out of it. But then, there was the remote possibility that Maggie would follow through.

"I wouldn't hear of you spoiling your plans." Audible sigh of relief on the other end of the line. "You go ahead with your dinner, and we'll plan something nice for Christmas, okay?"

"Well, my darling, if you're sure?"

"Completely. Now give my love to Tim." Bess' sentiment was genuine. Tim was the first of Maggie's boyfriends she actually liked. "I'll call soon."

"Where will you be for Thanksgiving, sweetie? We'll want to phone."

Bess knew she couldn't tell her mother that she had no plans so she lied. "I'm having people here. I'll be home all day. So try the home phone or my cell."

"How lovely, dearest. I hope it's a shared feast ala the Pilgrims. I hate to think of you slaving away all week and all that dreadful clean-up. Have you hired help?"

"All is well, Mother, never fear. Now, I've got to go. I have an appointment." She failed to mention that it was a doctor's appointment. Apparently, Babs' hotline had not yet picked up the ankle story.

"Ta-ta, angel."

"Bye, Mother." Bess breathed her own sigh of relief as she hung up the phone.

CHAPTER 68

As she dressed, Bess smiled, thinking about the previous evening with Jane, and Harry's unexpected call. "Well, my darling," she said aloud, gazing at Mac's photo on her bureau. "Maybe I'll fulfill my promise to you after all. I think I may be in love again. I hope you approve. He's very different than you in some ways, and in others, very much the same. Don't worry though, dearest, a place in my heart will always remain yours and yours alone."

School nurse, Gloria Moniz had insisted she see Dr. Collins, who ran the only family medicine practice in the village. Collins had office hours Saturdays until two and a very full appointment schedule, but at Gloria's insistence, he had agreed to take Bess during his lunch break. Since she had several errands to run before her appointment time, she decided to head out, cane in hand, to the grocery store, fish market and bakery in preparation for her dinner with Harry. Before departing, she sat, making lists of everything she needed.

All morning something had nagged at her from the previous evening's conversation. As she shrugged into her jacket and grabbed her canvas shopping bags, she remembered what it was — Jane's mention of Kevin LeBlanc's infidelities. Could it be that Kevin had been involved with Lizzie Mederois? From where had that idea arisen? Why did she continue to believe that Lizzie's death was related to Milt's? Roger and Harry had already dismissed the connection, but she couldn't let her intuitions go. She decided to have another talk with Louie.

Maybe she would make Thanksgiving dinner for Billy and Lou and share it with them?

Just as she headed for the door, the phone rang. "Mrs. Dore?"

"Yes?"

"Hi, this is Jackie, from Dr. Collins' office. He's been called to the hospital for an emergency. He'll be gone for most of the morning and has to reschedule."

"Of course."

"If you can come at four-thirty, he'll see you then."

"Today?"

"Yes, he should be back by then."

"Jackie, I don't want to inconvenience him when he's so busy. I can wait until next week, really."

"Oh, no, Mrs. Dore, he was most insistent. Nurse Moniz wants you to be seen today, no ifs, ands or buts."

Bess rolled her eyes, recognizing the futility of further argument. She agreed to be there at four-thirty and rang off, rearranging her plans for the day to accommodate the late afternoon appointment. She would shop and cook earlier so that most of the dinner would be prepared before she went to see Dr. Collins. On a whim, she dialed Kevin LeBlanc's number.

He answered on the first ring.

"Kevin?"

"Yup."

"It's Bess." Silence. "I wondered if you had a few minutes to chat? Could I possibly come by and —"

"Ever the little snooper, aren't you?"

"Excuse me?"

"Can't leave it alone, can you?"

"Kevin, I'm sorry, I just wanted to —"

"Look, Bess, you're a good friend. And, you know how I felt about Mac, but these past few weeks have been hell and I just don't want to talk to you right now, okay?"

"But —"

"Look, I have nothing to say to you, okay? Now, I'm really busy, take care." He hung up.

"What's gotten into him, she wondered, grabbing her things and heading out.

CHAPTER 69

After completing her shopping, Bess bumped into Roger Demaris and Pete Dugan outside the Village Fish Market. They had just said 'hello,' when they spied Carrie Thurbert headed their way. Bess waved. "Carrie, hi. Has your company arrived?"

"Yes, how did you know?" She was dressed in black tights and long sweatshirt, as if she were either coming from or going to the gym.

"Peter told me yesterday. Sounds like you'll be busy this week."

"Look, Bess, I've kept a stiff upper lip all these years, looked the other way, refrained from making a scene. In other words, I've been the good little headmaster's wife, but I don't need to play that role anymore. So, if it's all the same to you, I'm no longer interested in 'playing nice' with my husband's mistress."

"Excuse me?"

"Don't play the coy little schoolmarm. It doesn't suit you, or what you've been up to all these years."

"Carrie, I don't know what you think has been going on, but Peter and I have never been anything more than friends." Bess spied Roger and Pete's expressions out of the corner of her eye and cringed, wondering what they were making out of this confrontation.

"Bullshit." Her eyes flashed fire, Carrie's face a mask of hatred and fury.

"Why do you think I would —"

"Skip it, Bess, would you? I'm not interested in your lies or explanations. Mac died, you were lonely and Peter, ever the obliging friend, moved right in. I'm not blind. I see the way he looks at you whenever you're together. I —"

"Carrie, I'm sorry. I simply will not listen to these ridiculous fantasies. There is and never has been anything going on between Peter and me."

"Stay away from him, Bess. I'm warning you or I'll—"

"That's enough, Ms. Thurbert," Roger said, quietly, stepping between them. "This is neither the time nor place."

"Oh, that's rich, Officer, coming from another one of her boyfriends. Who do you think you're talking to?"

"Someone who's gonna get herself arrested for harassment if she doesn't move along. Now."

"Why, of all the nerve." Carrie pushed past him and stomped off, leaving the three of them standing, mouths agape, watching her retreat.

Shaking so hard she almost dropped her shopping bag, Bess felt tears spilling over. Tears of shame, shock, and anger. Had Carrie really spent the last decade thinking she and Peter were lovers? It seemed so ludicrous, she couldn't get her mind around it.

Pete stepped a few paces away as Roger asked, "You okay?"

She shook her head. "I, I, don't know."

"She's a crazy bitch, Bess. Don't go there. She is probably aware of hubby's infidelity, but has the wrong lady."

"But, I, she, all these years, Roger. It's unthinkable."

"Wanta get a cup of coffee?"

"Thanks, but I can't. I've got a full day and an appointment later. I'll see you. I'm so sorry that you, that both of you, had to hear all that."

"No problem here. Crazy broads rantin' and ravin' are all in a day's work for Pete and me, right, Pete?" Dugan nodded, smiling at Bess.

"Talk soon, then?" she said. "Maybe Harry found something useful in Boston?"

"Let's hope so, we need a break. Take care now. Sure you're okay?"

"Thanks, I'll be fine."

Bess headed home, looking forward to preparing for dinner. Cooking always relaxed her and at this moment, she craved its calming effects.

CHAPTER 70

Bess spent the remainder of the day preparing dinner. She had planned a simple meal of poached, wild salmon with a lemon dill sauce, wild rice and a tossed field greens salad. She baked a thin crusted apple tart for dessert and set it to cool on the counter before departing for her appointment with Dr. Collins.

As usual, the busy physician was running behind so Bess curled up in the waiting room with her Anne Greyson mystery, content to lose herself for a few minutes. It was nearly five when she was finally called in. Don Collins apologized, as he ushered her in to the examining room. Since it was Saturday, he had insisted Jackie go home several hours earlier and was now manning the office. "So, you had a bit of a fall, I understand?"

"Not bad. I've been hobbling around perfectly well all day. Din, I'm so sorry to keep you on the weekend for this, but you know Gloria."

Smiling warmly, he rolled his stool up to where she perched on the table. "Let's have a look, shall we?"

After examining the ankle, he asked several questions before pronouncing it 'a minor sprain.' "Not that minor sprains don't hurt like hell, but it'll probably heal pretty fast. Should feel better in a day or two. Ice it, fifteen to twenty minutes, twice a day. I like to use packs of frozen corn or peas. Aspirin, Tylenol, Advil, whatever you tolerate best, is fine to take for the inflammation." He rewrapped the Ace bandage, much more loosely than Gloria's tourniquet.

Bess was his last patient so when he was finished, they chatted a while, catching up on village news. Bess inquired after his children, all three of whom had graduated from Old Harbor Friends and he asked how teaching was going. Inevitably, the conversation turned to the murder and Collins had many questions. At five-thirty, Bess noticed the time and hopped up. "Oh, Don, I've kept you far too long. So sorry."

"Hey, I'm the one's been giving you the third degree." He walked her through the empty waiting room, pausing at the door. "Go easy on that, Bess. And remember — ice, twice a day."

"Thanks, Don."

"No trouble at all. Pleasure to see you. I miss our parent-teacher conferences."

"Oh, I know what I meant to ask you," she said, stepping back in and closing the outer door. "Remember Lizzie Mederois who committed suicide?"

"Yes, very well. She was in my daughter, Margaret's class. I signed her death certificate. Did the autopsy, too. Never forget it. We had a devil of a time getting the Blackburn boy to let go of her so we could examine her. Had to be forcibly removed, poor guy."

"Yes, first poor Louie, then Billy. I remember hearing about that. Of course, he'd not only lost Lizzie, but his unborn child, poor thing. He must've been devastated."

"Pretty awful, you're right about that. But, Bess, just between you and me. That baby wasn't Billy Blackburn's."

"But everyone assumed and —"

"Yes, they did, but it wasn't true."

"How can you be so certain?"

"Billy Blackburn's was the last case of mumps I treated in the village. He had 'em two years before Lizzie Mederois died. He was sterile, Bess. He couldn't have conceived that child and he knew it. We tested him three or four times. He was worried about it, because he and Lizzie were sexually active, but there was no way he could've impregnated her."

"Oh, my, goodness, we've been looking in all the wrong places," she said speaking more to herself than Collins.

"Say what? Are you one of the investigators, too?"

"No, of course not. Never mind what I said, Don. Thanks again. I've got to run. I'll settle up with Jackie tomorrow."

"No problem. School's footing the bill. Peter called right after Gloria made the appointment. Something about an occupational injury."

Waving, she hobbled to her car. The ankle was still sore, but now that she had been assured that the injury was minor, she saw no reason to baby it. She knew she should head straight home, but she needed to find Louie. To make him tell her what he had seen.

CHAPTER 71

The maintenance barn was cloaked in shadows when she arrived. She pulled her car up alongside the school vans, catching a glimpse of light shining from the apartment above. Grabbing a flashlight from her glove compartment, she headed to the stairway leading up to Lou and Billy's apartment.

When her knocking went unanswered, she opened the door and called, "Lou, are you up there? It's Mrs. D., can you hear me?"

"He's not here."

Billy's voice from behind her, startled her and Bess stepped back, landing hard on the sore ankle. "Oh, Billy, you scared me!"

"Sorry, Mrs. D. How's the ankle?"

"Better, until that move."

"What'd ya want with Lou?"

"Is he around?"

He shook his head. "Gone to his sister's, to help her with something. This is his day off, but he should be back soon. She usually takes him to dinner, then drops him off."

"Oh, well, I'll catch him tomorrow."

"Anything I can help with?"

"No, I really need to talk to Lou. I know he saw something, Billy, but he's afraid to tell us. Has he said anything to you?" He shook his head. "It seems as though he's got Lizzie and Mr. Wickie's deaths all mixed up. There has to be a reason why he's connecting the two, don't you think?"

"He just gets confused. Could be anything with Lou. Probably just the idea of death is enough to set him off. He was this way when Mr. Dore died, too."

"Yes, I 'spose you're right," she said, remembering how hard Louie had taken Mac's passing. "But, what if Mr. Wickie knew something about Lizzie? Someone who shouldn't have been —" She hesitated, unsure of whether she should continue.

Finally, she decided that Billy, like his roommate, might know more than he was telling. "Maybe Mr. Wickie learned the identity of the father of Lizzie's unborn child and he was—"

"But, I —"

"I shouldn't, but I know about you and the mumps, Billy. Dr. Collins said —"

"He had no right to tell you."

"You're right, of course, but listen to me, please. I don't want to cause you any more pain, but if you know who that person is, please tell me, or the police. Mr. Wickie was blackmailing several people. The father of Lizzie's baby might have been one of them. That would be a strong motive for murder, don't you think?"

"I wouldn't know about that," he said, his voice cracking.

What was she thinking, burdening him with her wild suspicions? "Billy, I'm sorry."

"Look, I've got a job to finish."

"I was wondering what you and Lou are doing for Thanksgiving. Would you like to share dinner?"

"Thanks, but his sister's having us both. Look, I've got to get going."

"Of course."

"See you, Mrs. D."

Billy disappeared into the shadows, leaving Bess feeling guilty and sad.

CHAPTER 72

After a trip to the bank and another fruitless runaround with Carol Richards, Roger Demaris spent the afternoon sifting through things. Finally, closing up shop, he headed to Pop's for dinner where he spied Louie Predo and his sister. He knew Karen Predo slightly so decided to say 'hello.' As they chatted, he noticed the gardener was calm, almost rational and he wondered if his sister's presence was the cause.

By the end of their conversation, Demaris was convinced of the killer's identity. It was the same person who had protected Bess and Amy Flathers, the figure in the shadows who had thwarted Milt Wickie's unwelcome sexual advances. How many others had been helped by this unseen benefactor?

Tipping his hat, dinner forgotten, he left brother and sister swearing under his breath as he called Pete Dugan. "I want you out there in five minutes. Got it? Move it now. Tell the rest of 'em to get their fannies over there, too. Jesus Christ, I hope we're not too late."

Bess sensed a presence in the house the moment she stepped out of her car. She shut the door loudly, the sound echoing in the stillness of the woods surrounding her. Her immediate neighbors, the Caseys were away for Thanksgiving week. For once, she missed their nosiness and prying eyes.

As she hobbled up the front walk, she chided herself for not leaving a light on. Climbing the steps, she tripped and fell against the front door, grabbing the brass knocker to steady herself. Safe and Harry would be coming soon. She reached for the key above the cornice, unlocking the door and taking the key inside with her. It was not until she had flicked on the outside floodlight and the front hall lamp, that she realized the presence she had felt in the driveway was someone inside the house. Someone waiting.

He was in the study, she was sure of it, yet she was not frightened. It made sense that he would be there, waiting in the place where it had all started weeks earlier. Setting her purse on the front hall table, she made her way slowly to the door of the study. The room was dark, but in the shaft of light from the hallway, she saw that the display case lay open, glass top thrown back, resting against the bookshelf behind it.

"I know you're there," she said, quietly, standing in the doorway, eyes scanning the darkened room until she found him, his eyes two inky pools of light staring out of the shadows near the French doors.

"Hello, Mrs. D." His voice sounded think and soft.

Until that moment, she had not been sure, but now it made perfect sense. "I'm going to switch on the light," she said, moving towards a floor lamp, watching his eyes as she pulled the light string.

Soft light flooded the room. Bess did not have to look into the display case to know that the other knife was missing. It was in his left hand, blade smooth and icy white, sheath discarded on the chair beside him.

"Billy, my ankle is really hurting so I'm going to come a little closer, so I can sit down, okay?" He stood still, neither responding nor moving to bar her way. "Please sit with me for a few minutes, will you? I won't try to stop your leaving or —"

"Killing you?"

"No, I know you won't hurt me."

"Don't know me very well then."

"Perhaps not, but I'm here. I'm listening."

"There's nothing to tell."

"Billy, I don't know for sure, but I suspect that Mr. Wickie was the father of Lizzie's baby. Is that right?" Silence. "I've thought over and over in my mind about who else it could have been, teachers, students, anyone who she might have been dating. But, I always come back to him. It was him, wasn't it? Am I right?"

"Bastard." His hand gripped the knife as he stepped out of the shadows towards her. "He was a selfish bastard. Used her, then threw her away. Lizzie, who never hurt a living soul. He told her he'd pay for an abortion, but she had to leave school. Said he couldn't have her around to tempt him again. That fucking bastard used her, then tossed her aside like a piece of trash."

Bess nodded. "He was a horrible man. He was everything you said about him and more. But, why didn't you tell anyone? We could have helped."

"Who would've believed a couple of townies?"

"I would have. You know that, don't you?" Out of the corner of her eye, Bess spied movement in the garden beyond the French doors. Forcing her eyes to connect with Billy's, she reached out to him. "And Mr. Dore would have helped, too. You believe that, don't you?"

He shrugged, hanging his head, slumping into the chair beside her. "Doesn't matter anymore."

Bess glanced over his shoulders to the window where Roger and Harry both stood, peering in. She attempted to warn them off with her eyes, reaching out. "Give me the knife, Billy. You know you're not going to use it on me and I'd like to put it away. I'm going to sell all of this stuff. Get rid of it, make a fresh start, get on with my life. What do you think about that?"

He shrugged again, seemingly unaware of her presence, lost in what appeared to be anguish and pain.

"We both need to let go, you and I," she said quietly, inching her chair forward. "We've held on, to Lizzie and Mac, for too long. They would want us to be happy, wouldn't they?"

"Who knows."

"Give me your hand. Please, Billy, I want to help. I'll talk to the police and explain everything."

"I loved her, you know?" Sobbing now, he buried his face in his hands, heaving a sigh as the knife clattered to the floor. Bess moved to put her arms around him, kicking the knife away. "I loved her and couldn't even give her a child. I would have married her and raised the baby as mine. I told her that. I didn't care. The baby was part of Lizzie. That's all that mattered to me as long as we were together."

"Oh, Billy, I'm so sorry." As she held him, Bess gazed up at the pair in the window, now surrounded by several other people, presumably police.

After five minutes, she sat up slowly, resting her hand on his cheek. "Billy, I'm going to open the door. Mr. Winthrop and the police are there, waiting to talk to you. Please don't be frightened. They're here to listen. Can I go and let them in?"

Nodding, he released her and Bess hobbled to the door, ankle stiff and unco-operative. As soon as she released the catch, Roger and Harry burst in, followed by several other officers including Pete Dugan. As Harry embraced her, they heard a groan from behind as Billy's body crashed to the floor.

Bess screamed, trying to reach him, but Demaris held her back. "Leave him be, Bess. He put it right through his heart." Handing her back to Harry, they watched in horror as Billy's blood spread in a widening arc across her Aunt Milly's faded Persian carpet.

Burying her face in Harry's shoulder, Bess thought the same thought she had many times over the past several weeks. Milt Wickie was evil incarnate and had deserved to die.

Hours later, the ambulance departed and the three, Roger, Harry and Bess, sat in her kitchen drinking tea, hers heavily laced with brandy. Fatigue washed over her as she surveyed the kitchen, taking note of the remnants of her forgotten dinner.

Finally, Demaris rose. "That's it for me, folks. I'm calling it a night and I'd suggest you guys do the same."

They nodded and Bess rose, hobbling along to see him out, his arm circling her waist, supporting her.

"Sorry you had such a scare."

"I wasn't scared. Billy would never hurt me."

"The old guy must've tipped him off. I met him at Pop's, havin' dinner with his sister. After that conversation, we tried to pick up Blackburn, but he gave us the slip. Somehow, I figured he'd wind up over here."

"Yes, I suppose it makes sense. What did Louis tell you?"

"It was his usual mumbo jumbo, but he kept going on about the snake. The snake watchin' and on and on. Get it? It wasn't the knife he was talkin' about, it was Blackburn's cobra. The tattoo on his arm, you know?

"He's the one's been watchin' Wickie all these years, lookin' out for you, the Flathers kid and who knows who else. You weren't the only ones, I'm sure. No telling how many girls the bastard tried to take for a ride. After the Mederois girl's death, I guess Blackburn kind of appointed himself campus security guard, assigned to watch Milt the lech. Tried to do what he could to stop him. Finally succeeded, I guess."

"But why now? After all these years, why kill Milt now?"

"According to Karen Predo, Milt was about to terminate her brother's employment and was kicking them out of the apartment. Claimed he needed the apartment for storage, but you know what I bet? Somehow the bastard found out it was Blackburn intervening in his attempted rapes. Taking the apartment back and firing Louie was paybacks."

"Such a horrible man."

"Got that right. Take care now and go to bed."

Closing the door on her friend, Bess found Harry standing behind her. He smiled, lifting her chin, his lips finding hers, suffusing her with warmth. When he released her, she stepped back, slightly dizzy as she gazed up at him.

"Bess, I love you. Please don't throw me out."

In answer, she reached up, arms circling his neck, drawing him to her for another long kiss. "Does this mean I'm staying?" he whispered, voice husky with desire. She answered him with another kiss, leaving no need for further clarification.

CHAPTER 73

Old Harbor Friends welcomed its new head at the close of spring semester. Priscilla Marsden, a Quaker educator, who had been dean of students at a Friends school in Pennsylvania, was the first female head in the school's history. Ms. Marsden, or Pru, as she liked to be called by faculty, staff and students, brought two teenage daughters and a new husband as well as fresh perspectives and thoughts about moving the school in new directions.

Peter and Carrie Thurbert were duly feted and fussed over in their final months before leaving for extended travel, financed by very generous gifts from the Board of Overseers. Eventually, they planned to make their home in Spinnaker Bay, a beachfront community twenty miles up the coast. Pru was already plotting ways to bring him back to assist with the next capital campaign.

Before his departure, Peter had asked to take Bess to dinner and she had accepted. They talked about the tragedy of Billy's death and all the destruction wrought by Milt Wickie, and, of course, Carol Richards, who was being prosecuted for her years of embezzlement. Both her homes and their contents had been seized and her replacement was busy unraveling the years of double bookkeeping and deceit that had covered this thievery.

They also talked about Jane, who had a new love interest, a professor from M.I.T. whom she had met on a trip to Bermuda over spring break. Shortly after Billy's death, Jane had confided to Bess about her longtime relationship with Peter.

The friends were still as close as ever. A far as Bess knew, Carrie was still in the dark and continued to hate her as the 'other woman,' but she had decided to let it be. What was the point of saying anything further?

Lunch over, Bess stepped out of the car, kissing him goodbye. "Good luck to you and Carrie. I hope your travels are relaxing and fun. Come back and see us sometime."

Seizing her arm, he gazed up at her. "I told her about Jane."

"Oh, Peter, was it awful?"

Still holding on to her sleeve, Peter Thurbert laughed. Then, noticing her concerned, quizzical look, he said, "Don't worry, I haven't gone around the bend yet. It's just that when I told Carrie about Jane, that's what she did, laughed. Right in my face. Said she'd known about Jane for years and didn't say anything 'cause she knew it'd blow over. Can you believe it?"

She couldn't, but said nothing, about his revelation or the scene Carrie had caused on the street, accusing her in front of Roger and Pete Dugan.

"Seems Carrie and Milt had been carrying on for a year prior to his death so all the while Milt was blackmailing me, he was two timing on poor Susan LeBlanc with Carrie. Incredible, isn't it?"

"Yes, I hardly know what to say."

"It's a mess, a colossal mess, I know. Don't know if we'll make it, honestly, but we're sticking together for now. We'll get through this transition, try and make a go of it and then, we'll see. We seem to need each other, right now anyway. Thirty-four years of marriage has got to count for something, don't you think?"

She didn't know what to think, but squeezed his hand. "Goodbye, Peter, and good luck."

EPILOGUE

As the months passed, Bess and Harry grew closer. One warm, spring day, Bess headed up the drive to the Winthrop estate. She and Harry were going on a picnic in the fields of the estate. She parked her car, just as the mailman alit from his truck carrying a stack of mail. "Here, I'll take that, Joe," she said, smiling. Joe had been her mailman for years.

"Thanks, Ms. Dore. Nice day, huh?"

It was, indeed, a beautiful day, the hillside surrounding them blanketed with color — daffodils, tulips and thousands of early blooming bulbs and perennials stretching to the woods beyond. Waving goodbye to Joe, she turned back towards the house, idly glancing down at the mail packet in her hand. The name on the topmost envelope arrested her gaze and she looked again, confused. It was addressed to 'Anne Greyson, c/o Harold Winthrop, 5 Meader Lane.' What could it mean, she thought, imagining someone playing a prank at her expense.

Looking up, she spied Harry in the doorway, observing her. "Hello, darling," he called, waving and coming to greet her.

Handsome in open collared blue shirt and jeans, he was grinning, noticing the object of her confusion. "Come in a minute. Molly's just stuffing a few more things in the basket. Weighs about eighty pounds. We'll need a truck to get it to the picnic site and if we eat half of it, we'll be two hippos waddling back home."

"Something the matter, darling? You look like you've seen a ghost."

She handed him the stack of mail, waiting.

He scratched his head, ruffling his hair. "Ah, that, yes. I've been meaning to tell you about that. You like her, don't you? Anne Greyson, I mean?"

"Yes, I do, very much."

"Here's the thing. You know I do a lot of writing, all kinds of things. But, you see, well, the thing is, the books that have been most successful have been. Well, the truth is, Anne, she's not really a she, she's, well, I was going to tell you sooner, but I was afraid you'd be angry. There's no other way to say this, the thing is Anne is, well, Anne is me. There, I've said it — I'm Anne Greyson.

"Close your mouth, darling, or you'll catch flies. It's just a stupid penname. I wanted to write mysteries, but we didn't know if they'd sell or be any good. Dad didn't care, but I didn't want to sully the Winthrop name in case they bombed. Didn't want the Winthrop name to be forever associated with a bunch of dopey mystery novels. Then, they were so successful with women readers, my editor was afraid to reveal the fact that they'd been written by a man. With eight books in the series, editor and publisher won't let me switch from Anne to Harry, I'm 'fraid.

"Are you angry? Disgusted? Disillusioned? Please tell me the happiest five months of my life are not about to come to an end."

Bess laughed then, throwing her arms around him. Harry lifted her up, mail cascading on the ground all around them.

He kissed her lightly on the nose. "So, does this mean you're not mad at me?"

"No wonder I fell in love with you. You're Anne and everything I love about her except —"

"Thanks, darling, I think I can fill in the rest."

Acknowledgements

Thank you to my friend and neighbor, Sgt. Jason Pacheco of the Fall River, Massachusetts Police Department, for talking with me about police procedures. Any missteps in this area are entirely mine as he is always clear and professional.

I would also like to thank my publisher, Larry Anderson at Quicksand Chronicles for his generosity and willingness to take my books "on." To Dona Burke, I am indebted for her formatting wizardry and good humor as we grappled together to bring forth the first version of *Jigsaw* and for the continued wizardry of the Formatting Fairies for continuing the process. If not for Dona, my novels would still be languishing on my computer or in my basement. Most importantly, I would like to thank my dear family and friends, who are always there, no matter where life's travels take me. They make every day a miracle.

About the Author

M. Lee Prescott is the author of numerous works of fiction for adults, young adults and children, among them **Prepped to Kill, Gadfly (Books One and Two in the Ricky Steele series), Jigsaw, A Friend of Silence, and Song of the Spirit.** Her newest contemporary romance series, **Morgan's Run,** debuts in January 2014. Three of her nonfiction titles have been published by Heinemann and she has published numerous articles in the field of literacy education. Lee is a professor of education at a small New England liberal arts college where she teaches reading and writing pedagogy. Her current research focuses on mindfulness and connections to reading and writing. She regularly teaches abroad, most recently in Singapore.

Lee has lived in southern California (loved those Laguna nights), Chapel Hill, North Carolina, and various spots in Massachusetts and Rhode Island. Currently, she resides on the river, where she canoes and swims daily. She is the mother of two grown sons, Ransom and Winward, and spends lots of time with them, their beautiful wives, Alexandra and Stephanie, and her three extraordinary grandchildren, Abigail, Ava and Benjamin. She lost her buddy, Rosie (15-year-old golden retriever) last summer and is still looking for her successor. If anyone knows a dog with the sweet temperament of a golden, but half the size, do let her know. My older son, Ransom recommends a King Charles Cavalier. Time will tell...

When not teaching or writing (both of which she loves), Lee's passions revolve around family, yoga (Kripalu is a second home), swimming, bouncing, and walking.

Lee loves to hear from readers. Visit her website at mleeprescott.com and Facebook page (mleeprescott). Her email is *mleeprescott@gmail.com*.

A Note from the Author

Thank you so much for taking the time to read **A Friend of Silence**. After many years teaching in a Quaker school, this book and its setting are dear to me. I also love writing about village life and hope to follow Roger Demaris in his next investigation. I set this story in a New England village very much like one where I spent a number of years. Although I now live on a river, I return to the ocean often. Was fun to drop in a few local details, as I do in all my novels, even if actual persons and places are figments of my imagination!

A Friend of Silence is the first mystery featuring Bess Dore, Roger Demaris, and Harry Winthrop. A second in this series is in the works, probably within the next year or two. There is excitement and, I fear, some tragedy ahead for these characters and the peaceful village where they reside. Many authors have a favorite character, and, I must confess, Ricky Steele (of the Ricky Steele series) is mine, however, in Roger Demaris I have found what may be a second favorite! Look for his character to turn and develop as this series grows.

If you liked **A Friend of Silence** and would be willing to write an Amazon review, I would very much appreciate it! In fact, I will be happy to send my first 25 reviewers a free e- copy of **another of my titles!** If you submit a review, just email me at *mleeprescott@gmail.com* and I will see that you receive your free copy of whichever title you would like!

If you would like to sign up for future book releases and occasional notices about my books, please email me at *mleeprescott@gmail.com* and I will add you to the list. I promise I will not share your address, nor will I flood you with emails. Do visit my website at *www.mleeprescott.com* to read more about my books and to hear what's next. I am really excited by my upcoming **Morgan's Run** series, set in the incredible United States southwest, another special place I visit often. First Morgan's Run title is scheduled for release in January of 2014!

Finally, this book has been revised, proofed and edited many, many times, but I, and my intrepid assistants, are human so if you spot a typo, please email me at *mleeprescott@gmail.com* and I will fix it. If you'd like to know more about my other books, please scroll ahead to the next section that is followed by sample chapters of **Jigsaw!**

Warm wishes,

M. Lee Prescott

Contemporary romances and mysteries by M. Lee Prescott include:

Mysteries

The Ricky Steele series
Book 1: Prepped to Kill
Book 2: Gadfly
Book 3: Lost in Spindle City (coming soon!)

Also featuring Ricky Steele:
Jigsaw

Single titles

Romantic Suspense
A Friend of Silence

Contemporary Romance
Swoon (coming soon!)
Glass Walls (coming soon!)

Young Adult Romance
Song of the Spirit (coming soon!)

PROLOGUE

The gloves snapped as he slipped them off, disposing of them as he always did after an outing. A deeply satisfying sound, the snapping of latex, powdery dust feathering up into the air. Brother loved it. Just as he had loved Rosie in those final moments as she begged for her life. "Oh sweet Rosie," he crooned lying back on the musty cot in the darkened room, his lair. "You made me soooo happy."

Already the euphoria was ebbing away, sucked into the insatiable maw of time, eroding his pleasure, washing away his joy. Try as he might, Brother was powerless to stem the flow, the precarious happiness seeping away only hours after the outing until all that remained were powdery smudges dotting his furrowed brow.

CHAPTER 1

July 27, Thursday

"Alright ladies, take the field!"

Bobby Gagnon, coach of the Flint Flames of the greater Fall River Women's Softball League, frowned watching 'his girls' take their positions. In his forties, a twice-divorced, recovering alcoholic Gagnon still looked like the triple A ballplayer he had once been. While his hair was thinning on top, his wiry, muscular frame looked much as it had in his twenties thanks to years as a brick layer.

"Jesus Christ Peters! Put something into your throw-- anything! I haven't seen a rag like that since--

"Souza! The catcher, Souza, the catcher, for Christ sakes! Her mitt's where it always is, at the end of her goddamn arm!

"That's the way Gladys-- stretch for the throw.

"Wilson! Center field's that way! Atta girl!"

As Gagnon continued yelling, coaxing and browbeating, the occasional compliment thrown in, his eyes scanned the street. Finally the person he'd been waiting for hopped out of a dark green pick-up, J & T Limited lettered in black and gold on the cab's door. The pick-up took off and Bobby turned back to the field, feigning indifference as the latecomer jogged onto the field.

The explosion came as she reached the bench, stooping to tie the laces of her cleats. "Whitman, it's about goddamn time you showed up! I wanta talk to you!"

"Hi Bobby, nice to see you too." Julia "Juls" Whitman smiled, straightening to her full height, gray blue eyes regarding him without a hint of consternation. She stood at least six inches taller.

"Where the hell's Mikawski?" Bobby resisted the urge to hop up on the bench to continue his harangue. He didn't much care for women looking down at him.

"Isn't she here?"

"No, and if she doesn't show in five minutes, you're pitching."

'But I--"

"Put a sock in it and start throwin'. I gotta a date tonight and we're starting on time for a change. Belles have been warming up for forty-five goddamn minutes."

"Rosie'll be here. She'd never miss a game," Juls called over her shoulder trotting out to the mound.

Fifteen minutes later the game was underway with Juls pitching-- still no sign of Rosie Mikawski.

By the third inning, Juls, agitated and distracted, allowed three runs to score, two of them on errors.

Gagnon blew up. "What the hell are you doin' out there, Whitman? Jesus Christ!"

"Watch your language Bob, there are kids watching," called Dan Powers, husband of Ruby, the Flames second baseman.

Powers' words had little effect. After the next pitch yielded a triple, Bobby charged out to the mound, arms flailing, eyes bulging, curses punctuating the night air.

Juls endured his screaming for several minutes before exploding herself.

"Stop it Bobby! I didn't want to pitch and you knew it! How do you expect me to concentrate when I'm worried about Rosie? This isn't like her, I talked to her this morning and she was psyched for this game. Something's wrong."

"You got that right, and you're it!" Gagnon snarled, worried himself, but unwilling to show it.

"Look, you've had it," he continued, turning towards the outfield. "Mendoza- get your fanny in here, now! And you, get out there where you belong."

"Fine," she mumbled, turning towards left field.

"Juls," he called after her, his voice softer. "She's fine. Forget about it and play ball. We'll go over to her place right after the game, okay?"

He watched Juls' retreat, her long straight back knit with tension. Even in league issue orlon, she was just short of gorgeous with those long, thin legs and slender hips. Juls Whitman had commanded his secret admiration since the day he'd volunteered to coach the Flames. Her hair had been long then, tied back in an unruly braid that reached her waist. Shoulder length now, the auburn hair was tied back in a ponytail that stuck out above the strap adjuster on her cap. A smile to die for and lips that begged to be kissed, the woman had no idea of her effect on men, least of all, middle-aged Bobby Gagnon.

Tuck Potter, Juls' partner in a suburban caretaking business was a boyhood friend of Bobby's younger brothers. Tuck had coached the Flames for five years, but the business had grown to the point where it was impossible for both partners to be unavailable three or four nights a week during the summer. Tuck had described the team as a "great bunch of ladies" and he had been right. Coaching the Flames had been Bobby's salvation.

Years earlier, the J and T partners had had a brief affair, but nowadays, Tuck described Juls as "one of the guys." It was bullshit, of course, since Bobby knew damn well that Tuck still harbored more than friendly feelings for his partner. Juls had prevailed, and she now kept Tuck, and most men for that matter, at arm's length.

Gagnon hadn't failed to notice the tears rimming his pitcher's eyes and she was right, it wasn't like Mikawski. The Bedford Belles were their biggest rivals and Rosie would never have missed this particular game voluntarily. All the punch knocked out of him, Bobby withdrew to the bench, glumly taking his place alongside his players.

The game dragged on, Juls' dread mounting with each inning. The Belles finally put them out of their misery, burying the Flames under a merciless barrage of hitting. The ump called the game in the seventh, Belles-12, Flames-1 as darkness descended over the Globe Corners field, the headlights of passing cars a distraction the Flames would no longer have to endure.

Juls gathered her things scanning the crowd. "Where's Tuck?" she asked to no one in particular. "He was supposed to pick me up! He should have been here hours ago. The one night I really need him!" She waved at her teammates who were heading for a beer at Archie's across the street.

"Go in and call Mikawski," Gagnon yelled, tossing the equipment bag into his trunk. "If there's no answer and Tucker isn't here by the time you're back, I'll run you over."

"You sure?" Juls asked, dropping her bag at his feet. "What about your date?"

"Screw that, now get goin'. Give her hell so we can go in and get a goddamn beer to drown our sorrows after this fuckin' game from hell."

"Thanks Bobby, watch my stuff okay? Be right back."

Gagnon threw her bag into the car, starting the engine and pulling the Impala up in front of Archie's. Knowing Rosie Mikawski as well as he did, there was no way he'd be havin' a beer in the foreseeable future.

Two minutes later Juls appeared, "No answer," she said, hopping in. "Let's go."

"You know she's probably all fucked up, three sheets to the wind at the Bluebird right now doncha?"

"No way."

Gagnon didn't believe it anymore than she did. Softball and her teammates were Rosie's whole life.

Bobby had spent many evenings with Juls, Tuck and Rosie drinking, playing cards, enjoying cookouts on the beach, going to concerts, out to dinner. Just last weekend they had all sailed to Nantucket on a friend's boat, camping on the beach, all the men in one tent and Rosie, Juls and two other women in a tent up the beach, giggling all night long.

Mutt and Jeff he called them. When the two friends walked into a room one was first struck by the contrasts-- Juls' tall, slender beauty, alongside the handsome, but shorter, stockier Rosie. The latter's coal black curls wild and unkempt, her dark eyes dancing with light mirrored her personality. Rosie was gregarious, loud and physical in her affections, whereas Juls, although friendly, was quieter, more reserved. Beneath the facades, however, dwelt two kindred spirits and together, they created a whole, distinct from their individual selves, a palpable warmth radiating from the pair that enveloped all around them in its warm, comforting embrace.

Their easy camaraderie was nearly impossible to resist and people were drawn into their circle of friendship. For Bobby Gagnon-- to whom women had always been strange, elusive creatures-- the friendship with Juls and Rosie had been a revelation.

The "girls" as Tuck called them, had known each other since grade school, remaining close friends through high school and college despite long periods of separation. Bobby never tired of listening to the stories of their growing up years. The Whitmans had never approved of Rosie Mikawski from the Flint, but that hadn't mattered a wit to their daughter. During her high school years, Juls was sent away to a boarding school in the Berkshires, while Rosie stayed at home, but the friends wrote, sometimes five or six letters a week, calling as often as they could. Weekends, if Rosie could get away, she'd coerce a friend into driving her up to visit Juls, sneaking her out of the dorm.

As he started down Willett, Bobby began praying. "God make everything be okay," he thought, as he pulled the Impala up to park across the street from Rosie's building.

"What?" Juls asked, looking over at him.

Not realizing he'd spoken aloud, he mumbled, "Nothing," adding hoarsely, "Come on let's go give her hell."

CHAPTER 2

Dan "Tuck" Potter walked into Archie's Tavern not three minutes after Bobby's Impala rounded the Globe Corner rotary, disappearing from sight. Spying the Flames clustered at their usual tables by the jukebox, he waved, grabbing a beer on his way to join them.

"How'd ya do?"

"We stunk up the field," Karen Ramos replied, her leg slowly extending, pushing an empty chair towards him. A come hither move if he'd ever seen one and he'd seen most of 'em.

"No?"

"Yup. Lost twelve to one," Ann Greeley said, rising to fetch another round. "It's okay. We have two more shots at 'em. Besides, we were missing players. We'll get 'em next time, you wait."

"Gagnon must be a happy camper. Where is the lad anyhow and for that matter, where's my partner?"

"They've gone to Rosie's. She didn't show for the game, Bobby's pissed and Juls is a basket case."

As Ann prattled on, Karen leaned back in her chair eyeing Potter, her eyes leaving little doubt as to her intentions. The team uniform-- baggy on most of the women-- fit Karen like a second skin. The top was stretched tight across her ample bosom, nipples clearly visible under the thin, white orlon. Reddish blonde curls-- frisky even after three hours shoved under a baseball cap-- ringed her heart-shaped face and her dark eyes danced with mischief. Karen was pretty and she knew it.

She had always had the hots for Tuck, but her interest had never been returned. He barely knew she was alive except when he needed to locate one of his buddies, Juls, Rosie or Bobby. Fuck him, she thought, not my type anyway, too preppy with all that tousled, sandy hair and sea blue eyes. His tan canvas slacks were worn and ripped, but she had to admit, they looked gorgeous on his trim athletic body. A faded blue work shirt fell loosely over the broad shoulders and although Karen had never seen what lay beneath the shirt, she could imagine.

"Well, ladies, gotta go. See you at the next game."

He had barely sat down and now he was rushing off, as usual, trailing after Juls. It was always Juls, more like a marriage than a partnership, Karen mused, grabbing his untouched Pabst, calling "thanks" as she turned back to her teammates.

"Phew," Tuck mused as he headed towards the North end, driving at least twenty miles over the speed limit. "Cat's on the prowl tonight," he said aloud, thinking that Karen Ramos was trouble with a capital T. He'd just broken up with one bitch and he sure as hell didn't need another.

After Gracie had packed up and left a year and a half ago, Tuck's lady luck had taken a decidedly sour turn until Marcia came into his life. In the beginning, their relationship had been sweet indeed. A friend of a friend, they'd hit it off from day one and Marcia had fit right into the gang. Then, she moved into the beach house he shared with J and T's office and things had gone downhill fast. Juls didn't like Marcia, but hell, Juls hadn't liked any of his girlfriends except for crazy Annie from Boston. Juls claimed he only dated bitches, but she and Annie had hit it off from the start until Annie had fallen in love with big Jim and run off to Colorado to run a saloon. They still sent Christmas cards.

He had to admit, Juls was right, he did attract bitches, no doubt about it. As soon as Marcia moved in she started screaming, a continual screech that never let up except when Juls was in the office, which wasn't often. During Marcia's residence, Juls had avoided the office as much as possible. Too much of an effort to be pleasant.

When the whole gang got together, it was easier for his partner to keep her distance, but in the office it was impossible. From day one Marcia insinuated herself into every facet of the business and once she grabbed hold of a project, there was no wresting it away from her. Tuck had initially encouraged his live-in's involvement, but things had quickly gotten out of hand. He smiled, remembering Juls' long overdue explosion after a particularly trying day with Marcia.

"That's it Tuck! Either she goes or I do! No... that's not right. I'm not going, Marcia is and you're telling her as soon as she gets back!"

"Telling me what?" Marcia purred, voice smooth as silk as she sauntered in from the kitchen.

Taking in the saucy stroll, the self-satisfied grim-- Marcia had a wicked smile-- and the haughty flip of her silky blond hair, Juls took a deep breath and let her have it.

"Marcia, I started this business with Tuck almost twelve years ago. It's a good business, we make a decent living, we get along and our customers are happy."

"So what'dya want, a medal?"

Tuck cringed, fearing he was about to witness a murder.

Juls ignored the sarcasm, "Then you come along and suddenly Mr. Longfield's calling saying you've insulted his wife. We've got dirty units that you were supposed to have had cleaned and we've got a phone bill that's three times what it usually is. The there's the--"

"Can I get a word in?" Marcia interrupted, her voice squeakier than usual.

"I'm not finished."

"You're just jealous, that's it isn't it? You can't stand it that Tuck and I are partners now and doing a great job without you!"

Tuck intervened at this juncture. "That's enough Marcia. Juls is right, it's our business, hers and mine and you've been screwing up. It's my fault, I take the blame for encouraging you to become involved in the first place. Stupid move on my part. Sorry hon, you're gonna hafta bow out. It's not working and if Juls hadn't spoken up, I would have. The Longfields are two of our oldest customers; they've been with us since the beginning. There was no reason for you to treat Janet like that, calling her dog---"

"A fucking guinea pig! I can't believe what I'm hearing! The little rodent bit me, for crying out loud, and all you care about is the old bat and that decrepit husband of hers! What's the matter with you people?"

"What's the matter with us is that J and T is built on good will and friendly service neither of which you seem able to deliver," Juls replied. Her voice had lost its fire, but her cheeks were flushed and blotchy, betraying the anger still smoldering beneath the surface. "And we don't have the money for all these hour long phone calls to California, New York and wherever else you're always calling."

Jaw set, her face flushed and angry, Marcia glared at the partners standing side by side behind the desk. "Fine, I'm outta here. Screw the both of you and your cozy little partnership. No one could step between you two and live to tell about it anyway! I've been offered a job in New York starting next week so good riddance!"

"What the--?" Tuck stared at her.

"That's right. I'm leaving Sunday so you can go back to your pathetically chummy existence."

So, Marcia had departed and Tuck had heard nothing from her and didn't expect to. Something told him that Karen Ramos would make Marcia look like Pollyanna. Best keep his distance from that one. Besides, it wasn't as if he needed lady friends. A coed working for J and T this summer had already caught his eye and if he and Kerry hit it off, the last thing he needed was Karen breathing down his neck.

Marcia had been right about one thing, he and Juls did lead a chummy existence. However, he doubted that Juls had ever been jealous of Marcia or any of his girlfriends, she just didn't have it in her. He had known his partner for nearly fourteen years. She was warm, funny, stubborn, practical in business matters, athletic, compassionate, opinionated, a fiercely loyal friend, a forgiving opponent, a hard worker, a loving daughter and sister, but jealous? Not Juls.

They'd met in Laguna Beach, California where they were both attending an advanced workshop on the craft of leaded glass construction. Amazed to find fellow Fall Riverites so far from home, they had sought each other out during the workshop, spending their free time together during the six week course. At the workshop's conclusion, they extended their stay for four weeks, traveling up the coast to Northern California, Washington and Oregon. A brief romantic fling during that trip had ended the day they stepped off the plane in Providence.

While a fierce attraction lingered, by the time they arrived at home, they had decided to go into business together and Juls had insisted romance give way to friendship if they were to work together. By his own admission, Tuck had already dated and discarded more women than he could remember and she wasn't about to start a business only to have it fall prey to his romantic whims. Tuck reluctantly acceded to her wishes, but more than once over the years he had regretted the promise made in the parking lot of Green Airport. He was still very much in love with Juls Whitman.

The past twelve years had been prosperous ones. They'd started with the glass shop, making windows and lamp shades on commission as well as restoring old windows in local churches and the turn of the century Victorian homes of Fall River, Newport and surrounding areas. While the business grew steadily, stained glass was not the booming business on the East coast that it had been out West. After three years, J and T branched out in another direction, becoming J and T Limited in the process.

Most of their business now was caretaking the summer homes, condominiums and multi-million dollar beach houses of Windy Harbor, a wealthy summer enclave fifteen minutes southeast of Fall River. The tiny coastal town had grown by leaps and bounds over the last twelve years as farmers sold out for millions to the affluent New Yorkers and Bostonians voraciously gobbling up the last stretches of virgin coastline. A sleepy little fishing and farming village for many generations, Windy

Harbor had finally been discovered. Like it or not, the locals had had to adapt and many did not do so graciously.

The hostility of Windy Harbor's natives had in fact been largely responsible for the initial success of J and T. Snubbed and shunned by their neighbors, the Harbor's newest residents had had no where to turn for help and services until Juls and Tuck appeared on the scene. With open arms and friendly smiles, the partners catered to their clients every whim with efficiency and discretion. J and T looked after clients' properties in winter and summer, handling all rental agreements and arranging to have services-- water, phone, electricity, trash collection and so forth-- resumed or terminated with the changing seasons.

Having spent the better part of his adult life in the Harbor Tuck knew the plumbers, electricians, carpenters, painters and various other service oriented people. One room in his weathered shingled beach house served as J and T's office. Thad Potter, Tuck's father had been left the house by a maiden aunt. Since the elder Potter refused to leave the Fall River home where Tuck and his brothers had grown up, when Tuck had approached him about starting the business, he had been only to happy to deed it over. Juls' house was ten miles away in Tiverton, R.I. just outside the Fall River city limits.

The partners took excellent care of their clients, running errands, searching for missing pets, investigating petty thefts-- trash barrels and mail boxes were the most frequent targets-- arranging for cleaning services, planning parties-- or hiring caterers -- and helping to arrange for clients' memberships in the area's yacht , golf and beach clubs and Windy Harbor's Ladies Literary Society, the most exclusive and selective of the all the 'clubs.' While not always successful in wheedling memberships for the newcomers into the Harbor's closed societies, the partners endeavored, if unsuccessful, to sooth bruised egos by suggesting alternative activities for their wealthy clients, many of whom had never heard the word "no" until they moved to Windy Harbor.

Business had grown so much that J and T now had a waiting list and while there were two rival companies proffering the same type of service, J and T was still the "agency of choice" for those lucky enough to "get on the list". Not a bad way to make a living if you liked people and both partners did. Marcia had not and it showed.

As he turned onto Rosie's street, Tuck spied the Impala and pulled up, parking behind it. Brushing thoughts of Marcia and Karen aside, he wondered what had been important enough to keep Rosie from the game, she lived and died for softball for Christ sake. Slamming the door, he cursed under his breath, angry at himself for missing Juls at the field, "damn the Willises and their fucked up lawn sprinkler!"

His heart-- already in his throat after taking the front steps two at a time-- nearly stopped as the first of Juls' screams pierced the stillness of the night.

CHAPTER 3

Racing up the stairs, Bobby puffing along in her wake, Juls reached the third floor in seconds. Rosie's unit was at the end of the hall, number sixteen.

The building was over eighty years old, but Gladys Kenney, the owner kept it in immaculate condition. The plaster walls had recently been white-washed and at the far end of each hallway, window seats had been built in, green and white awning striped cushions inviting passersby to linger. Despite its pristine appearance, the building was still in the heart of the roughest part of the city. In an effort to thwart thieves who continually absconded with her framed prints, Gladys had decoupaged fine arts posters along the corridor's walls. Wall scones bolted to the walls bathed the passageway in soft light, the overall effect one of peaceful serenity.

After several minutes with her finger pressed to the buzzer, Juls went to the window seat, rummaging under the seat cushion to find the key Rosie kept hidden there. "Shit! Why won't this work?" she cried, jabbing the key in, turning to the left and right. The lock refused to budge.

Hand on her shoulder, Bobby reached from behind. "Here, let me try babe."

"I'll get it," she said, shrugging his hand off. "It just... takes a minute to... there, finally!"

She flipped the light switch by the door as they stepped into the living room, into the warm inviting space where they had spent so many evenings drinking, watching movies, playing cards, talking and laughing together. Tonight the room smelled musty, the air close and still and she wondered why all the windows were closed on such a warm summer night.

Rosie collected Native American and Mexican textiles and favored the stark lines of the mission style in her furnishings. All of her pieces were reproductions of Gustaf Stickley designs, well-made, handsome and sturdy like the woman herself. Hanging from the cream colored walls were three Navaho rugs in bold patterns of red, gray and black. The floor was covered in gray wall to wall carpeting, clean and new like the rest of the building, another large Navaho rug lay across its center the same reds and grays slashed through it in a chevron pattern.

The large, comfortable sofa was flanked by two matching armchairs, all three pieces covered in off-white cotton duck; a number bright woven throw pillows echoing the colors of the rugs. Rosie's pride and joy stood in front of the sofa-- a massive oak coffee table, also in the mission style, built by Rosie herself in a woodworking class at the local community college.

The morning papers were scattered across the table's polished surface and Rosie's body lay at its far end. She was dead, no question about that. The body sprawled half in the living room, half in the bedroom, legs twisted back at unnatural angles, naked except for gray athletic socks which Juls recognized as her own, loaned to her friend several weeks earlier. Black curls obscured the face and aside from a few scratches here and there, her body appeared untouched, white and smooth in its deathly pallor.

Her good arm lay at her side; the scarred left arm-- burned in a childhood accident-- tucked beneath her. There was quite a lot of blood pooled beside the body that appeared to have come from her underside and pieces of a jigsaw puzzle were scattered around the floor, some floating in the blood like tiny amoebae.

Juls screamed, rushing to her friend's side. As she began to claw at the smooth white rope still wrapped around Rosie's neck, Bobby roused himself, leaping forward to yank her back. "Juls, stop it. We can't touch her!"

He pulled her back and Juls let go, the movement causing the body to roll towards them leaving the severed left arm on the floor behind her. Her arm had been amputated at the shoulder.

"Jesus," he whispered. Juls screamed again, beginning to shake violently.

"Oh my God, oh my God," she mumbled over and over as he dragged her towards the kitchen phone.

As she struggled, lunging towards her friend, he tightened his grip. "Cut it out, Juls, come on now for God's sake, we can't touch her. We've gotta call the police, they need to see her just as she is. You can't help her, babe, she's gone, now come on."

He reached the phone just as Tuck burst through the door. Juls crumpled into her partner's arms and Bobby turned away as the police dispatcher answered at the other end of the line.

The next few hours a blur. The three sat huddled on the sofa as the police went over the apartment, occasionally pausing to ask questions. Cameras flashing, their voices hushed and somber, a small army of men collected samples, searched through drawers and closets going over every inch of the three rooms. Occasionally neighbors peeked their heads in and were led to the window seat in the hall where an officer waited to take their statements.

"Make them stop," Juls moaned, almost incoherent as the hour approached midnight. "Rosie hated having her picture taken. Please, Tuck, please make them stop." In her Flames uniform covered with grass stains, blood and dirt, she looked like a small child inconsolable after falling off of her bike and skinning her knee.

"Juls, it's okay," Tuck said, drawing her to him. "Hush now, Rosie's past caring. How much longer officer?" he called to Jack Mederois, the homicide detective in charge.

"They'll be taking her out in about five minutes. I have just a couple of questions for Ms. Whitman, then you folks can take off."

True to his word, not five minutes later the photographers packed up their gear and Rosie's draped body was carried out on a stretcher. As his officers began sealing the crime scene, Mederois came to sit beside them.

"Where will they take her?" Juls asked.

"City morgue first. We'll have to keep her a few days, then we'll contact the family and see about the funeral home and all."

"There is no family, just me."

"Well then Ms. Whitman, we'll let you know when you can have her collected and--"

"Oh God, who would do this?"

"We were kinda a hopin' you might give us a hint. Some one with a grudge? Ex-boyfriends, disgruntled co-workers, whatever? Or someone new, that she just recently met?"

"There's no one like that. Everyone loved Rosie. No one who knew her would hurt her."

"How 'bout someone she might've met recently? A new boyfriend maybe?"

"None that I know of."

"Do you guys know what Ms. Mikawski was doing today, someone she might've been seeing? Mr. Gagnon says you unlocked the door and there are no signs of forced entry. No broken windows, jimmied locks, what have you. Seems like she must've known the guy. Had to have let him in."

"I don't know what she was doing today except for the game. Softball. We play on a team and we had a game tonight."

"So I see. What time was that?"

"Five."

"She was long gone by then, I'm 'fraid. Preliminary exam puts time of death around one, two somethin' like that."

"Oh, God, the whole time we were playing, Rosie was lying here." Juls crumpled against Tuck, fresh sobs wracking her slender frame.

"Sh, okay now," Tuck whispered, holding her tighter as if his grip might somehow stop the trembling

"I know this is tough, Ms. Whitman. Just a couple more questions, please. What can you tell me about her arm? Was she able to use it, the scarred one I mean?"

"Yes," she sniffled, regarding him. "Sometimes it stiffened up in the cold, got tingly at unexpected times, things like that, but it was only a scar. It happened when she was four. A kettle of hot water spilled on her. Her family always called it an accident, but her father was a drunk. Rosie had no memory of it, why?"

"Just curious. She's a big woman, strong, I mean. Seems like the type who'd put up a fight, but there's no sign of a struggle and I just wondered if maybe one arm was weaker than--"

"How did she die? I mean, was she--"

"Strangled. That white rope around her neck, guy brought it with him."

"And her arm?" Tuck asked.

"Happened after she was dead. Thank God for that at least." Mederois studied Juls, aware that she was fading fast, withdrawing into herself, unaware of her surroundings. He turned to Tuck. "How 'bout the apartment? Was your friend in the habit of leaving the door unlocked?"

"Never," Juls answered for him. "I'm sorry, but I have to know. Was she? I mean she was naked so was she--"

"Raped? Doesn't look like it, but we won't know for certain until forensics gets through with her."

Juls moaned.

Tuck gripped her tighter. "Look Detective, we're gonna split, okay? She needs to get outta here."

"Sure thing, I'm sorry Ms. Whitman, about your friend and all, and about keepin' you so late. Let's leave it for now and we'll talk in the morning."

He rose, joining his men a few of whom were still collecting their gear. "Oh," he called back over his shoulder. "One more thing-- did Ms. Mikawski like jigsaw puzzles? I mean, would she have been working on one do you 'spose?"

"Not that I'm aware of. I didn't even know she owned any jigsaw puzzles," Juls said, looking to Tuck for confirmation. He nodded at Mederois.

"I thought not."

"How's that?" Tuck asked.

"Can't be sure till we check a little further, but, well, we've seen this type of thing before."

"Jesus, a serial killer!" Bobby cried, instantly regretting his words.

Juls' face, red and blotchy from crying, froze in horror.

"We don't know that Mr. Gagnon. There are similarities to other cases, but we'll have to look further. Let's not go spreadin stuff like that around, okay?"

"Oh God," Juls moaned, as the two men half-carried, half-dragged her from of the apartment, driving her home.

Several shots of brandy and two sleeping pills borrowed from a neighbor and Juls settled down on tear-soaked pillow, a drugged, fretful sleep finally overtaking her. Tuck slept beside her bed in the chaise, Bobby on the living room sofa.

28366214R00199

Made in the USA
Charleston, SC
10 April 2014